A horrific explosion kills hundreds of people in the tunnel under the English Channel. At first it appears to be just another Islamic terrorist attack but slowly, as the threads of the plot are pulled, something even more terrible emerges.

One cold, foggy night, a EuroStar train, loaded with more than four hundred holiday passengers enters the English Channel Tunnel for a routine trek between Paris and London. On board, Andrew Bolling, Special Council to the British Prime Minister, is making his way home from a disappointing weekend in Paris. As the train careens through the underwater tunnel, a horrifying explosion rips the train apart.

Jeffrey Hunter, Chief of Staff to the British Prime Minister, is charged with spearheading the investigation into the attack. While he fights to protect his country and unravel his friend's involvement, he discovers that the true motive for the attack is something no one has yet suspected.

Praise for The Cornmarket Conspiracy

"...a powerful saga that provides more than a conspiracy story, but a social examination that will keep readers engaged and thinking long past the tale's conclusion." – *D. Donovan, Senior Reviewer, Midwest Book Review*

"Five Stars: *The Cornmarket Conspiracy* is a fast-paced tale of greed, corruption, and abuse of power that grabbed me from page one and refused to let go. Author Sharon Hoisager maneuvers an intricate plot using multiple POVs that instantly hooks you in and keeps you engaged with its twists and turns. The narrative switches POVs with each chapter to provide easy access into the headspace of the antagonists. The characters feel flawed and realistic, making them compelling to read. . .To cap off, *The Cornmarket Conspiracy* was a joy to read. Highly recommended." – *Reader's Favorite Book Reviews*

"Hoisager delivers a page-turning story laced with a mix of treason, conspiracy, and international intrigue as she weaves her characters through London and Paris, making *The Cornmarket Conspiracy* a very exciting read that begs for a sequel." – *L.L. Abbott, author, The Blackwater Operative*

"...a gripping and compelling thriller from Sharon Hoisager, where you're kept hooked to the very end to find out what exactly happened." – *Alex Telander, Manhattan Book Review*

"In *The Cornmarket Conspiracy,* no one can be trusted. Hoisager's sophisticated writing style makes this book a serious drama that will keep readers on edge as they unravel the intricate web of motives behind a heinous terror attack. Striking the perfect balance of intense and contained, The *Cornmarket Conspiracy* has all the qualities to make a gripping political thriller." – *The Book Review Directory*

The Cornmarket Conspiracy

Sharon Hoisager

To Sally! Hope you enjoy!

Moonshine Cove Publishing, LLC

Abbeville, South Carolina U.S.A.

First Moonshine Cove edition
May 2021

ISBN: 9781952439087

Library of Congress LCCN: 2021907761

This book is a work of fiction. Names, characters, places and incidents are products of the author's imagination or are used fictitiously. Any resemblance to actual events, locales or persons, living or dead, is entirely coincidental.

Cover design by Peter O'Connor, BespokeBookCovers.com; Interior Design by Moonshine Cove staff

For my mother, Patsy Crossley, who sparked my imagination by taking me to the library often and to every historical site within driving distance; and to my dad, Buddy Crossley, who worked hard to make everything possible for all of us.

Acknowledgments

To my publisher Gene Robinson, thank you for giving me the opportunity to accomplish a lifelong dream. Thank you also to Peter O'Connor, your talent is world class. To Daryl, thank you for always loving me, and being unconditionally supportive of every dream and crazy idea I have. To Alexa, Laurel, Colton, and son-in-law Hayden, thank you for being so extraordinary, and making my job as mom so easy. Thank you to Susan Halbert and Shelly Wooldridge, my multi-gifted sisters who patiently read my manuscript with an eagle eye and discerning mind, and still acted like this book was the best thing they'd ever read. Your loving support is unwavering. And thank you to Susan Metzger, for your constant encouragement.

About the Author

Sharon Hoisager has been a professional writer for more than thirty years. As a writer and marketing consultant, Sharon has been published in *Christian Retailing* magazine with

articles on promoting adult and children's books. Sharon has also been a prolific ghostwriter for several nationally recognized authors, published in numerous financial, economic and political publications. She has also written and produced promotional packages and marketing materials for a myriad of investment, financial, and health publications. Sharon holds a BBA in Finance from the University of Texas at Austin. She has three adult children and lives in Arlington, Texas with her husband and golden retriever Tucker. *The Cornmarket Conspiracy* is her first novel.

www.SharonHoisager.com

CHAPTER ONE

A heavy fog settled over Coquelles as the sleek yellow and white EuroStar screamed past the twelfth century village and continued across the French countryside. Careening at 267 kilometers per hour, the high-speed train cut across the northern coastal plains of France, headed for London's St. Pancras station. Aboard the train, 397 tired travelers, exhausted from a weekend of Christmas shopping and holiday partying slept, read, and stared out the black windows at the distant lights of quaint little farms bordering the tracks.

Nearing the French coastline, the tracks joined a converging network of parallel tracks and a thick overhead grid of electrical power lines that appeared to run headlong and disappear into a concrete wall cutting into a French hillside. The concrete wall, with two gaping black holes, seemed ready to swallow trains whole as they passed through the mouth of the channel tunnel. The tracks then began a steady descent, sloping down 112 feet below the sea floor on its journey from Paris' Gare du Nord station to the heart of Britain's largest city.

At exactly 10:03 p.m., the EuroStar, now traveling at the tunnel's speed limit of 160 km/hour, entered the tunnel to begin its 31 mile trek to the British aisle. Travelers on board were lulled by the gentle rocking of the train as it sped along the tracks, through the dark tunnel. The weary travelers, most well accustomed to the underwater leg of their journey, knew that in just 35 minutes they would emerge on English soil, and would soon be pulling into London's busy St. Pancras station.

In car 703, Andrew Bolling folded his half-read copy of the Sunday *London Times* in his lap and propped his head against the window for a few minutes of sleep. Even after arriving in London, he still faced another twenty- minute car ride out to his flat in Notting Hill, where he would only get a few short hours of sleep before he would be expected back at his office in Downing Street.

Maybe the weekend in Paris with his university buddies hadn't been such a good idea after all, he thought. He had initially been happy to have the opportunity to see his old friends, but this trip had turned out to be nothing like he'd thought it would be. Two of the three that he'd expected to see hadn't even bothered to show up, which was OK with him. But that had left just him and Raz, his old college roommate, whom he had not seen in quite a while. The Raz that Andrew remembered had always been happy, carefree, perpetually up for a good time. But now Raz had seemed serious and distant, which was totally out of character for him. He was distracted, even irritable. The whole trip had been a disappointment and a waste, he thought to himself.

Andrew glanced down at this watch: 10:06. By his calculations, they'd be pulling into London at 11:30, and with a little luck, he would be home by midnight. He could squeeze in six hours or so of sleep before he'd have to be back in the car, headed to #10 Downing, where he needed to be ready for his weekly 8 a.m. with the Prime Minister. He hated these weekly appointments. The P.M. was always in a bad mood after hearing the Sunday morning talk shows and Monday morning political polls, replete with disgruntled talking heads whose favorite past time is critiquing the government and criticizing administration policies. After four years in the P.M.'s office, Andrew was growing weary of the political merry-go-round.

With a final glance at this watch, Andrew noticed the time: 10:14. He closed his eyes, and laid his head against the window.

At precisely 10:15 p.m., the farmers of Coquelles heard an ominous rumbling from under the earth, like a deep earthquake. The china cups rattled in the cupboards, and the wind chimes in the garden could be heard tinkling. Dogs barked in the distance. As sleepy farmers rose to look out their windows, they were astounded as the rumbling sound turned into a thunderous explosion, and then a flash of light from the northwest that briefly lit up the night sky.

Minutes later, sirens interrupted the cool calm of the winter night, and only then did the French farmers understand that the world was now forever changed.

CHAPTER TWO

Jeffrey Hunter fumbled for his glasses, knocking them off the nightstand and onto the carpet under his bed. He grabbed his vibrating cellphone off the night table, squinting at the name lit up on the little screen – Annelise Craig, his long-time assistant.

Why in the heck would Annie be calling him at 12:10 a.m.? Bad news no doubt. As Chief of Staff to Britain's Prime Minister Trevor Wellington, he knew that any call after 10 p.m. would entail some sort of emergency that demanded his immediate attention. Damn, there went his 6 a.m. run yet again.

"Yeah . . . Hello . . . Hello?" Jeffrey was trying to sound alert, as the P.M.'s Chief of Staff was always expected to be.

"Jeffrey . . . Hey, it's Annie. Listen, something terrible has happened. You're going to need to get dressed and get in to the office." Before she finished her sentence, Jeffrey was sitting bolt upright in his bed. As she began detailing what she knew, Jeffrey instinctively started fumbling around among the items on his nightstand for the television remote. His worst nightmare, the one he had known was coming for quite some time, had just begun.

There in the pitch dark of his bedroom, Jeffrey listened in horror as Annie outlined in detail what she'd just seen in a late-breaking news report online. She'd been up late cruising the Internet, and suddenly splashed across the screen was the story that had seized her attention: there had been an explosion and a horrific fire in the English Channel Tunnel, and it was believed that a train full of travelers had been trapped in the tunnel at the time. Hundreds of lives had likely been lost. The television across the room glowed in silence with live pictures from outside the tunnel. Other than a few emergency vehicles around the entrance, there was not a lot to see. After listening to Annie's description for a few seconds, Jeffrey bolted from the bed, threw on the faded navy sweatpants and hooded jacket that were lying on his bedroom chair, and was out the door in minutes.

Jeffrey burst into the Prime Minister's office just twenty- five minutes later – Alexander Trawick, Britain's National Security Advisor; Fletcher LaForge, the Deputy National Security Advisor; and Rex Smythe, Britain's Home Secretary, were already gathered around the Prime Minister's desk. The Prime Minister was nowhere in sight. Dressed in a disjointed array of sweat pants, jogging shorts, and faded t-shirts, it was obvious each had been yanked from their beds with the shocking news as well.

"Gentlemen, where are we at?" Rushing into the room, Jeffrey could tell from the stunned looks on their faces that the ramifications from the catastrophe would be staggering.

"It's bad, Hunter. Almost four hundred passengers were on board, plus the crew. It looks like there are going to be very few survivors, if any. That's about all we know right now," Trawick said.

"Where is Wellington?" Jeffrey said, although he already knew the answer.

"He's at COBRA," Trawick shot back, giving the acronym for the Cabinet Office Briefing Room A, the designated government office where the Prime Minister and other top military, police, and intelligence agencies could monitor emergency situations in Britain. The last time the room had been utilized were the few times in recent months when several incidents of vehicle-related terrorism had swept London. Tonight, the emergency headquarters had once again been completely brought up to full speed operation with secure video and audio links to the police and military onsite, all accomplished within ninety minutes of the tragedy.

"OK, Trawick, why don't you get over there and stick close to the P.M. We need to make sure this office is kept in the loop on all the incoming information and every decision being made. LaForge, Smythe, and I will stay here and start mapping out the administration's response going forward." As the P.M.'s Chief of Staff, Jeffrey started making the assignments as he knew Wellington would want them.

The men spent the next hour beginning the mammoth tasks of coordinating the rescue and recovery and mapping out a plan for the government's response. The emergency personnel over at COBRA would handle the immediate logistics, but Jeffrey knew that the administration would be responsible for mapping out a plan moving forward. Jeffrey pushed his slim government-issued laptop aside and pulled a fresh yellow legal pad from the bottom drawer. This was no time for official reports or formal government documents. Hunter needed space to think.

Down the left margin of the crisp top page, Hunter and the men started their own short list of likely suspects, including every terrorist organization known to be operating in Western Europe. Given the size and scope of the disaster, they immediately decided to operate on the assumption it was a terrorist attack until someone uncovered evidence that it wasn't.

Launching a response to a catastrophe of this magnitude would require an extraordinary rescue, recovery, and law enforcement response as well as having enormous implications for National Security. And of course, everything would have to be coordinated with other leaders in the European Union, the United States, and the UK's other allies. While the country had certainly planned and prepared for an array of potential terrorist hits on their own soil, this was a worst-case scenario. Very few of their drills or strategic exercises had prepared them for a terrorist hit on this scale.

Jeffrey Hunter and the rest of the P.M.'s crisis team had plenty of experience dealing with emergency scenarios: random bombings, assassination attempts, and the occasional rogue terrorist attack. It was a reality of the modern world, and the UK had dealt with their fair share of terrorist threats and attacks in the last two decades. But there had never before been anything on this level – never anything close to this extent of death and devastation. This was a global-level terroristic attack, and would require an unprecedented level of response from the Prime Minister. Hell, the Queen and Parliament would be involved ...

along with the United States and half the countries in the civilized world.

Staring down at his crisply lettered list, Jeffrey assessed the potential terrorist organizations. ISIS, of course, was at the top of the list of obvious suspects, followed by al Qaeda, the IRA, Boko Haram, and every radical Islamic extremist fringe group in the Middle East. London – or Londonistan – as *Time Magazine* had aptly dubbed it in a recent cover story about the global terror threat, was a known hotbed of radical Islamic activity, and a major train bombing should not surprise anyone.

The fact that the explosion had all but destroyed access to one of the major engineering feats of the last century was a devastating blow. It would take an enormous amount of time, money, and manpower to fully repair and secure the Channel Tunnel. Nicknamed the Chunnel by a generation of Western Europeans who now used it as casually as any other regional train, it had been providing fast and easy commutes between Paris, London and Amsterdam for more than a quarter century.

Jeffrey had traveled through the Chunnel hundreds of times, especially since his old buddy Wellington had been elected Prime Minister, and he had been appointed to lead the P.M.'s staff after his election. Like most other Britons, he took the tunnel for granted, never thinking much about its vulnerability. Thinking back to an article he read about the Channel Tunnel years ago, he remembered that the passageway is actually comprised of three tunnels, two tracks dedicated to carrying trains in each direction, from London to Paris and Brussels nonstop, and a third utility tunnel that ran between them used for maintenance and repairs. Realizing the massive number of people and commercial goods that utilized the tunnel every single day, Jeffrey knew that this single act of terrorism would set Great Britain back many months – potentially years – disturbing its flow of imports and exports, as well as disrupting commerce and damaging Britain's critical tourist economy. The shock on Britain's economy would be severe, especially given the already heavy economic blow from the controversial Brexit vote. The full economic impact — not to mention the lives that were lost — would be a devastating blow.

By 4 a.m., Wellington was back at #10 Downing, leaving the COBRA offices for the time being to the military leaders. When he walked in the door at the warren of offices that make up the P.M.'s central London office, Jeffrey almost didn't recognize his eternally affable old friend. His normally handsome and well-trimmed face was now lined with deep creases running across his forehead and white puffs billowed under his eyes. With Wellington's disheveled hair and unshaven jawline, Jeffrey realized that he had not seen him like this since their late nights of drinking back at University — and that was a lifetime ago.

After pausing to exchange some updates with his top staff, Wellington disappeared into his private office. Behind closed doors, Wellington telephoned the Queen, speaking with her for exactly ninety seconds. These conversations were always short, direct, and for all practical purposes, simply a formality. The Queen had her own news sources, her own advisers, and for that matter, her own agenda. She would no doubt want to address the British people who would look to her for empathy and leadership. But in reality, her response was of no consequence to the reality of dealing with the situation. This was no time for figureheads or ceremonial heads of state. The country had a global-scale catastrophe on its hands.

Next, Wellington phoned his good friend Peter Duddridge, current Leader of the House of Commons. He would need to speak to Parliament today as quick action would be required. Duddridge scrambled and was able to set up a joint emergency meeting of the House of Commons and the House of Lords for 11 a.m.

The Prime Minister spent the next couple of hours methodically working the phones with the leaders of Parliament, various heads of government, and other world leaders. After speaking with Duddridge, his next call went to Angus Burnett, the former Arizona Governor and now newly-elected President of the United States. Burnett had only been in office a few months, but so far Wellington had forged a friendly, if not entirely trusted relationship with the former rancher and real estate magnate. Politically and personally, they were about as far apart as they could be, but making and maintaining these kinds of relationships was where Wellington excelled. He instinctively knew that as with any terrorist attack on this level, his country was left momentarily vulnerable. The attack had the potential to invite other attacks and adverse complications – both domestic and abroad – and had to be handled with great sensitivity. With four years sitting at the helm of British leadership under his belt, Wellington was a master at the political maneuvering and diplomatic balancing act that was required.

While Wellington worked the phones and shored up support from the international community, Jeffrey, as the P.M.'s Chief of Staff, was thrown into emergency mode managing the details. After delegating a long list of responsibilities off to LaForge and Smythe, he spent the next few hours working through a preplanned checklist that had been formulated years ago to be enacted on a day just like today, laying out the framework for the government's immediate response. Jeffrey spent two hours on the phone with the heads of the various military, police, and disaster response teams, which had been immediately deployed and had already been on-site for hours. Communication channels with the country's first responders were confirmed to be up and running. Just before dawn, he spent twenty minutes on a conference call with his counterparts at MI6, Britain's foreign intelligence division, discussing the details of the agency's immediate terrorism response plans and what the next twenty-four hours would look like.

All major rail stations across England, Scotland, and Wales were closed for at least twelve hours until they could be searched and secured. Buckingham Palace and both Houses of Parliament were put under tight security and closed for all visitors. National monuments and landmarks were sealed shut. Across Europe and the United States, the terror threat levels were raised to the highest level, and security at airports around the world were put on high alert.

Jeffrey organized a press conference for 9 a.m. for the Prime Minister to address the nation and dispatched Wellington's top speech writer, Mariel Duckworth, to produce a first draft by 7 a.m. Wellington might be the face of Britain's government, but right now, Jeffrey Hunter, his oldest friend in the world, was its hands and feet.

By 6 a.m., Jeffrey was satisfied that he had done as much as he could at the moment to launch the rescue and recovery, and that the initial stages of the investigation were in action. Still running on pure adrenaline, and realizing he'd have to soon face the pack of media already gathering outside their offices, he dashed back to his townhouse for a quick shower and change of clothes. He knew he would be facing the world's press corps within a few hours along with a host of other demands on him that day, and he couldn't very well do that wearing an old t-shirt and tattered navy sweatpants.

Once he was back home and in the shower, for a few brief minutes while the warm water hit his face and washed over his body, Hunter was able to breathe and let his mind wrap around the tragedy that had just struck his country. He let his mind wander to the people on the train – fathers and mothers returning to work in London . . . families traveling to visit grandparents for the holidays . . . students returning home from university. The magnitude of the death of these innocent people was almost too much to comprehend. When did the world get so scary and dangerous? How did people get so entrenched in evil that they could exact this kind of terror on each other? It was more than Jeffrey could fathom at the moment.

A wave of despair crept up over his thoughts and threatened to crash down over his whole body. The situation he faced was devastating, but in that moment, Hunter did what he always did when his job became overwhelming: He set his emotions aside and locked them away – he'd deal with them later. As was his usual practice while grappling with the enormous task of helping to run one of the most important countries in the world, he began to organize his thoughts, running over the herculean list of things he would need to accomplish today. After a few final moments of hot steam and quiet solitude, he turned off the water and reached for a towel.

As he stepped out of the shower, his phone began buzzing on the bathroom counter. No name popped up in the little caller ID window, just a local London number, which was odd. Spam calls were automatically blocked on this line, and no one had this number, other than a couple dozen aides and top government officials, and they would've shown up on Caller ID. He reached for his phone, wondering who might be calling the Chief of Staff to the British Prime Minister on his private cell phone before dawn on this catastrophic day.

CHAPTER THREE

At thirty-seven years old, Jeffrey Hunter had spent his life on the British fast track. Born and raised just outside London among the centuries-old buildings and quaint cobble-stoned streets of Windsor, his boyhood home was literally in the shadow of the Queen's country palace. His father, a Solicitor and Member of Parliament, had made certain his oldest son checked off all the items on the to-do list of life for a young man headed for success and power. At thirteen, he was shipped off to neighboring Eton for boarding school where he studied hard, played cricket on the school's varsity team, and rubbed shoulders with the sons of Britain's political and economic elite. Jeffrey was a skilled athlete and a top-ranking student. But it was his burgeoning friendship with fellow classmate Trevor Wellington that had set the course for his life.

Wellington had been a popular student, studious, and obviously highly intelligent, even in a school where every student showed a high proficiency for academics. Easy going and friendly, with dark brown hair that he always wore swept back from his forehead and fixed in place with a fair amount of hair gel, he was the epitome of an accomplished politician even from a young age. He had a natural gift with people, always looking each person in the eye and making them feel like they were the only person in the room. He excelled in every area except one: his overly-trusting and affable demeanor often led him into trouble when street smarts and shrewdness were called for. He was naïve and often too trusting of others which invariably allowed others to take advantage of him. He and Jeffrey Hunter had established a fast friendship based on the fact that each brought valuable advantages to the partnership: Wellington was outgoing, whip-smart, and a natural born leader. Jeffrey Hunter was a loyal and steadfast friend, but had an innate discernment for people and ideas that proved to be imperative in the rough and tumble world of British politics. Their rare partnership helped guide the two to the top of the social and academic heap at Eton and on to the University of Oxford. Through the years, their friendship and unwritten alliance grew stronger and had ultimately worked to deliver Wellington to the top rung of political power in Britain, with Hunter always one close step behind. Twenty-four years in the making, their friendship was the backbone of their success. And now, it served as the backbone of the Wellington administration's leadership in the United Kingdom.

Hunter stepped out of the shower to grab his phone, his usually carefully combed dark blonde hair falling in a damp tousle across his forehead. His aquamarine blue eyes, once his calling card with any member of the opposite sex now divulged a series of tiny wrinkles, revealing the pressures of working so close to the top echelon of British government power. His once athletic body was still in reasonably good shape, especially for a politician who spent way too many hours behind a desk or in restaurants schmoozing with other politicians and lobbyists.

Jeffrey used to love politics, the game of shaping policy, changing lives, and having a front row seat to history. In fact, that's why he got into the political world in the first place. At university, he and his old buddy Trevor had forged a grand and ambitious plan that together they could help reconstruct Great Britain back into the kind of world power it once was, leading it once again into a position of world prominence. Oh sure, when people list the great nations of the world, Great Britain is always on the list. But in reality, Hunter and his buddy — who now held the title of Prime Minister — had known for a long time that Great Britain's position on the world stage had faded greatly in recent years. The small island nation that had once ruled half of the civilized world was in reality a modern-day figurehead. Its economy was dwarfed by the real global powerhouses, the United States, China, Japan, and the European Union, which as of two years ago, no longer included England. Without a resurgence of political power and an economic transformation, England would sink into oblivion like other former world powers — Italy, Spain, Greece, and others — who had also faded into the backwater of world prominence.

But those days were largely over. Hunter was tired now. He and Wellington had enjoyed some moderate success at the helm of Her Majesty's government: together they'd pushed through a fair number of reforms that were slowly but surely breaking down some of the antiquated social traditions that still held England in a quaint but outmoded social hierarchy. In many ways, young people in England were still granted opportunity based on their name or who their grandparents were, rather than talent, skill, brains, or hard work. But that was changing – slowly. They had also had some marginal success in reenergizing Britain's economy and expanding the country's economic base to help it compete in the twenty-first century.

But the world was changing too, and Hunter wondered if he could keep up anymore. The world's global power base was increasingly hanging in constant instability. World peace was not controlled by strong and compassionate leaders, but instead was constantly threatened by ruthless and dangerous tyrants who had no trouble ordering the genocide of an entire race, let alone the murder of innocent men, women, and children on a Christmas-time train. The world had become a dangerous place, and Hunter didn't know if he had the stomach for fighting the good fight anymore.

Dripping with water, Hunter reached for his black iPhone and touched the green icon to accept the call. For a moment he stood motionless on the bathroom tile, trying to make sense out of what he was hearing. The person on the other end of the line spoke with a heavy accent, and it took Hunter a moment to wrap his mind around what it was he was hearing, taking the almost indistinguishable phrases and breaking them into words, and then deciphering it into English. Once his mind had translated the speaker's accent into the King's English, he stood stunned, staring at the evaporating fog on the bathroom mirror, revealing his own ice-blue eyes staring back at him. As the caller's words sunk in, a hollow hole opened up inside his gut.

CHAPTER FOUR

Annelise Craig slid her phone onto the bedside table and sat down on the edge of the bed giving herself a moment to regain her composure. After calling and alerting her boss about the biggest tragedy to hit their country on his watch, she needed to take a moment to take it all in.

Sitting there in the dark, her eyes once again fell on the iPad screen, filling with updated news reports about the unfolding tragedy. Annelise's long strawberry blonde hair fell down around her shoulders, making soft curls against her ivory skin. Her slender fingers massaged her forehead as she struggled to organize her thoughts. She could hear the measured breathing of her husband Richard, still sound asleep on the other side of the bed. That man was a bear and could sleep through anything, she thought.

Annelise Craig – Annie to her friends – was smart, but more than that, at just thirty-two years old, she was tough and could manage any crisis without breaking a sweat which made her invaluable to her boss Jeffrey Hunter. His job required a Herculean amount of discernment and finesse, and Annie Craig was exactly the person to help him do it well. For the eighteen months she had worked in the Prime Minister's office, she had already proven herself invaluable at working alongside Jeffrey Hunter as he managed the day to day operations of Wellington's administration. Although she carried the non-descript title of Assistant to the Chief of Staff, she handled the delicate dance of high stakes political drama with delicacy and diplomacy. Jeffrey Hunter was already highly dependent on her professionally, as well as being his loyal friend.

Annie's head was spinning with thoughts of who should be called and what she should do first. The press would be swarming the office when she arrived, so she had to clear her head and be ready. She should call Andrew right away before Richard woke up, she thought to herself, and let him know what was going on. He would need to know.

She slipped into the small office adjoining their bedroom and decided against turning on the lights. Dialing Andrew's number in the dark, her call went straight to voice mail. Odd, Andrew always kept his phone charging right next to his bed at night and the ringer turned on, ready for the occasional call that was a necessary part of his job as Special Advisor to the Prime Minister. She would have to call him later; it was too risky to call now, as she could hear her husband began to stir in the adjoining room.

Well before daylight, Annie had showered and thrown on the navy blue dress that was her go-to when she needed to look professional but didn't have time to fuss. She whisked her hair back in a low ponytail and dabbed on a quick coat of mascara. She realized she needed to wake her husband and fill him in on the awful news before she darted out the door.

"Richard, honey, wake up . . . something's happened."

"Wha? What? What's happened?" Richard slowly turned over, opening his eyes, just enough to sleepily peer at his young wife, perched on the edge of the bed.

"I've got to go into the office. There was an explosion, on the Chunnel train. It's bad. I think there are going to be an enormous number of casualties, and the tunnel is damaged... maybe destroyed. I've got to leave. It's going to be a terrible day for a lot of people. You probably need to get up too."

Her husband of four years blinked at her, taking it all in. So here it was, the deadly blow for which London had been bracing for years. Since New York's 9/11, London knew its day would come. Certainly, there had been terrorist hits before . . . July 2005 when Islamic terrorists hit three London train stations and a bus depot in one day. But even with that terrible devastation, the English knew that it was only a matter of time before London would suffer something on the scale of the Twin Towers. Certainly Paris, Brussels, and other European cities had seen terroristic tragedies, but only the UK, with its close ties to the United States, would give the terrorists satisfaction in their thirst for the blood of Westerners. And today was the day.

"No . . . no. There's no way . . . I can't believe it. When? How many dead? Turn on the television." Richard stumbled out of bed and grabbed the remote off of his side table. The flat screen on the wall blinked on, and all that was visible was a night shot of ambulances with lights flashing, stationed at the mouth of tunnel. The queue of emergency vehicles was waiting for victims to be pulled from the rubble and brought up out of the tunnel on a service car that was running down to the wreckage. Talking heads sat dumbfounded at a news anchor desk, fumbling for information that was trickling in from the scene.

"I've got to go. I'll call you later and let you know what's going on. Not sure when I'll be home." Annie was out the door before Richard could respond, and she rushed off into the night. Richard could hear the tires of her Volvo squeal as she sped out of the driveway and onto the small lane that connected their flat to Kings Road in Chelsea. She would be at the office in fifteen minutes.

CHAPTER FIVE

"As Salam Alaykum wa Rahmatullahi wa Barakatuhu."

Rasul Aziz turned his head to the left, as was customary as he murmured the last words of his morning prayer. Rolling up his prayer rug, he hurried out of the mosque into the glistening dawn. It was unusually cold in Paris for a December morning.

Moving down the street at a quick clip, he couldn't help but notice the headlines screaming from the news stalls as he dodged the foot traffic on Avenue de Flandre. "Channel Tunnel Massacre, Hundreds Dead," . . . "Explosion Rips Through Chunnel, Scores Feared Dead," . . . "Terror Strike Unleashed on EuroStar Train." Rasul averted his eyes and crossed the street, avoiding a contingent of French policemen who were loitering near the corner. They were there, no doubt, in a show of force on this tragedy-soaked morning.

Although Rasul had made his home in this part of Paris for more than a decade, he hated this neighborhood. Avenue de Flandre flanked what is known as a "No-Go" zone for French citizens and other mainstream Westerners. Thousands of hard-working immigrants eager to live productive lives make their home within its borders, yet the notorious neighborhood has become a slum for a large swath of Muslims who are living on the fringes of French society. It is a dangerous place largely ruled by a mixture of drug lords and Muslim Imams who command more respect and authority from the neighborhood inhabitants than the French police.

It is a rough neighborhood for most, but not for Rasul. Though he is a French citizen by birthright, his parents emigrated from Yemen before he was born and still speak their native Arabic at home. He blends in with the people of this Muslim neighborhood effortlessly and moves easily between his Western persona, and the identity of his childhood and native culture. He is not fully Yemeni, nor is he fully

French. Raised by Yemeni parents in the French Capital, and educated at the finest university in England, Rasul can never shake the feeling that he is a man with no real home and no real nationality.

As Rasul hurried down the street with his prayer rug tucked under his arm, he thought about his old friend Andy Bolling – or Andrew as he was now called. No doubt dead, his body must be blown into a thousand fragments and lost forever deep under the English Channel. Images whip through his mind of the four years he and Andy had melded a friendship that had now spanned almost two decades. He could still see Andy's boyish face that first morning in September, now almost twenty years ago, as his friend burst into his 1st year dorm room at Oxford. "Hey, I'm Andy Bolling," he blurted out, thrusting out his right hand. Rasul, quiet and intense, had never had an English friend, at least not really. But they became fast friends, real mates, from the first day.

Andy, always the jokester, insisted on calling him "Raz," and the name had stuck. All over the small medieval college town of Oxford, he was simply Raz. For four glorious years, he wasn't the Muslim boy, unwelcome in so many French shops and bistros. He wasn't the immigrants' son, the kid from the Muslim slum. The brilliant, yet shy, kid who excelled in school didn't truly fit in in either world. He wasn't French, and yet he wasn't completely a Yemini Muslim either. He was Raz, a young man with no place to truly call home.

But Andy had been his real friend. Roommates all four years of their Oxford career, he had opened up Raz's eyes to everything the world could be. They studied Latin, physics, and philosophy by day, and hung out in all of the pubs that line the cobblestone streets of Oxford by night. Raz viewed it as his four-year vacation from Islam. For four years he lived life as almost any other western college guy. Four years of intense study, marinated in alcohol, and seasoned with women.

His third year at Oxford, he, Andy, and two American foreign-exchange students Charlie Turner and Jorge Morales had shared a flat a few blocks from campus. Charlie and Jorge were Americans, both from Dallas, and both studying abroad for their junior year. For almost ten glorious months, the four of them had a blast. Late on weeknights, after studying all afternoon, they'd hang out in the dark little bars of Oxford. On the weekends more often than not, they'd catch a train into London and hit the bars and dance clubs in SoHo and Mayfair. Raz had never been around Americans too much, and he found them fascinating. Hard working and wildly ambitious, Charlie and Jorge introduced their flat mates to Texas Hold 'em, Tequila, and day trading on the London and New York Stock Exchanges. Raz never knew where Charlie and Jorge came by their money, but they always seemed to have a little nest egg to make smallish trades. It was loads of fun and a good way to entertain themselves and make a little pocket change between physics exams and Latin quizzes.

After junior year, their year of studying abroad over, Charlie and Jorge returned to Dallas, and two new flat mates moved in. Jeffrey Hunter and Trevor Wellington were the complete opposite of Charlie and Jorge, but Raz welcomed the change. Too much drinking and partying was threatening his grade point average, and as graduation neared, it was time to get serious about his future.

Jeffrey and Trevor were great guys, very active on campus, studious and serious. Instead of partying the nights away in London's club scene, the four new roommates smoked cigars and argued about the future of Great Britain and its place in the political and economic global landscape. Grand debates about the future of the European Union and the rising political and economic threats of the Middle and the Far East, this was how the four of them finished out their university careers. They were four mates, each one brilliant, hardworking, and idealistic. No one could have foreseen how these seemingly ordinary students' lives would intertwine and converge to affect the world at large, in just a few short years.

But Oxford was a very long time ago. Many of the friendships he made in and among Oxford's seven-hundred-year-old Medieval and Gothic buildings had lasted most of his lifetime – at least he and his old friends stayed in touch with the occasional text or holiday card. But the world was changing. Raz was no more, and Rasul Aziz had taken his place. The world was in a state of political and economic turmoil, and Great Britain, in many ways, was ground zero. As it stood now, Rasul was tired of being a second-class citizen. He was tired of never having enough money or opportunities, and he was tired of the British hierarchy that had kept him out of the social elite, and now in a French slum with little opportunity to move up economically. He wanted position, money, and power, and all the privileges that went with it. And he wanted it now.

Unfortunately, Andrew Bolling's life was just a small part of the price that had to be paid. Rasul Aziz had his instructions, and he had carried them out. But he still had much to accomplish. Rasul brushed aside the thoughts of Andy and his days at Oxford, and focused on his next assignment. He crossed the street again and rounded the corner onto Rue de Crimee', arriving at the front door of his book shop, Paradigm Books.

CHAPTER SIX

Jeffrey Hunter stood staring at his refection in the bathroom mirror. As the fog on the glass slowly started to dissipate, the look on his face reflected back the shock and confusion racing through his mind. For a moment he could not make sense of the words he'd just heard, the implications too complicated and enormous to wrap his mind around. Water dripped down his body and onto the floor forming a small pool on the ceramic tile. Hunter stood motionless, waiting for the fog in his mind, like that on the mirror, to clear.

The words he'd heard, spoken quickly in a thick foreign accent, reverberated through his brain:

"The incident on the train last night was just a warning shot, the consequences for your complicity with the Great Satan. The British people will pay the price for the sins of their government, and we will begin to extract our revenge on the leaders of your government as well. Andrew Bolling had become a problem, so he had to go. He was just the first in line, but many will soon follow. More British blood will soon be running in the streets." Click.

Hunter stared at the black screen. What the hell? He touched two or three buttons, pulling up his list of recent calls. 'Private Caller' was at the top of the list. He punched the redial. Nothing. With his heart pounding in his chest, Jeffrey pulled a fresh shirt out of his closet, ripping the plastic dry cleaner bag off of his newly pressed white shirt. He pulled back on the same suit that he had worn to work on Friday and was still laying discarded on a side chair, grabbed his phone and his work bag, and ran out of the house. Shaken and disoriented, he was in his gray Audi and half way down the street before he realized he'd forgotten to even lock his front door. But it hardly mattered now, he was exposed and he was in danger. Hell, the entire country was in jeopardy.

Could it be true – could Andrew have been on that train last night? In all the chaos and confusion overnight, Jeffrey had hardly realized that Andrew was not among those who showed up at the office last night to handle the disaster. Could the call just be some sort of hoax...a bid for attention by some loser looking for attention? Or was the call a legitimate claim of responsibility – and his friend and colleague was somehow a target of the terrorist hit? If this were true, and Andrew were somehow a target because of his job or his connection to the Prime Minister, then this tragedy wasn't just a random act of terror but a warning shot for the entire British government. Jeffrey's heart raced as he pressed harder on the gas petal, realizing how the need to get back to his office was now more urgent than ever.

His entire life, Jeffrey Hunter had been at the helm and in control of almost every circumstance in his life. Everything had been laid out like a cozy checklist for success. Little had threatened his ascent to power, and he took comfort and security as his birthright. But now he realized for the first time that this situation was completely out of his scope of control. If these people could take out the Chunnel Train – one of the most highly guarded and secure transportation links in the world – they could do whatever they damn well pleased. There was a target on his country, and now there was a target on his back as well.

As he dodged traffic on Brompton Road, he thought about his friend Andrew Bolling, dead in a train tunnel seventy-five meters underground. How could a person who he had worked alongside all these years, a friend who had been a part of his life for two decades, just simply cease to exist – his body disintegrating in a massive underwater grave? Like most of the other four hundred passengers, his body would probably never be recovered. News reports coming in from the rescue site offered little hope. Two survivors had miraculously scrambled from the wreckage before the train was engulfed in flames, but there were no signs of additional survivors.

First reports from investigators on the scene were saying that the initial explosion was believed to have been relatively small, probably an IED of some type, probably nothing bigger than a shoebox. After the two survivors from the first car had somehow escaped the wreckage, a second larger explosion and subsequent fire had incinerated almost everything. There was little left except for a tangled mass of iron and steel, much of it melted into one giant tangled pile of molten metal. The heat and smoke from the explosion and fire in the west bound to London tunnel had emanated through the connecting tunnel, causing additional damage in both the eastbound to Paris tunnel, as well as the smaller maintenance tunnel that ran between the two main tunnels. The death toll was going to be just over four hundred, including passengers and the thirteen-member crew.

Britain had a long history of fighting to defend itself over its more than ten centuries. It had endured two World Wars, Civil Wars, uprisings, bombings, battles, and no small amount of bloodshed in its storied history, but no single act of terrorism had ever waged anywhere near this level of death and destruction. The bombing of Pan Am 103 over Lockerbie took 270 lives, but this would be so much worse, not to mention causing the destruction of one of the world's most important transportation routes. It would take years to reopen the tunnel. The damage to Britain's financial and economic sectors would be enormous.

Turning again onto Downing Street, Jeffrey Hunter pulled into his reserved parking spot, and surveyed the crush of television trucks, cameras, lights, and their respective journalists all lined up like bobble heads in a carnival midway. He grabbed a baseball cap from the back seat and pulled it low over his eyes, and pulled a rumpled gray wool coat from a bag in the backseat that had been destined for a charity collection. Flipping the collar up on the well-worn coat, he dodged a couple of reporters milling on the end of the line, and circled his way around the back of #10 Downing, heading for the back door that was used just for these kinds of emergencies. He usually detested the media, and this morning was no different. His country was under siege and now he had an important phone message to deliver.

CHAPTER SEVEN

Annelise arrived in the back alley behind #10 Downing, and squeezed into a small spot between two news vans. The place was crawling with reporters, and she figured no one would be leaving anytime soon. Darting into the building, she tried ringing Andrew's cell again for the third time. No answer. *Where in the hell was he?*

Annelise wasn't used to being out of touch with Andrew. The last eighteen months had been a whirlwind since she went to work at the Prime Minister's Central London office. Being Jeffrey Hunter's assistant was a dream job come true. What she had not bargained for was falling in love with Andrew Bolling, Special Assistant to the P.M.

She had only been married four years, and was very much in love with her husband Richard. Or so she had thought. She would have been the last one she or anyone else ever suspected of having an affair. But that changed the day she first caught a glimpse of Andrew Bolling in the hall on her first day of work. Medium build with dark wavy hair, he wasn't even her type. But something about the way he glanced into the room she was sitting in as he passed by, caught her attention. When he walked in and introduced himself, she remembered thinking he was the best-looking man she'd ever met. He was smart, intuitive, creative, idealistic, and worst of all, a real ladies' man. After two or three office conversations, she was thinking about him constantly. Soon, she had fallen hopelessly and completely in love with Andrew Bolling.

But right now, he wasn't answering his phone, or even responding to text messages. She knew that he had caught a puddle jumper plane to Paris over the weekend to hang out with some college buddies, but he should have been back early last evening. With the train attack last night, he was probably holed up in an office somewhere with the P.M., trying to lay out a course of action. That's problem #501 with having an extra-marital affair, she thought... in an emergency, you often can't contact each other, and even worse, you can't express excessive concern for the other person. You've got to be a top-notch actor, with impeccable skills of deception and self-control. But she was sick and tired of acting. She was tired of these games. But for now, she would just have to wait until he contacted her.

Once inside the building, she made a beeline for her desk, up front near the Prime Minister's Suite, and just outside her boss's office. As she rounded the corner at the end of the first hall, she came face to face with her boss, Jeffrey Hunter. He didn't look good.

"Annie, come in to my office. We've got to figure some things out."

Annelise Craig – Annie to almost everyone in the office – dropped her purse and her leather tote bag on her desk, pulled out her lap top and rushed into his office. Taking the first seat in front of Jeffrey's desk, she noticed that Fletcher LaForge, the Deputy National Security Advisor was already there, as was George Stanthrope, the press secretary. But no Andrew.

"Annie, glad you're here. We've already been going over some things we need to accomplish, and we've got to get you up to speed."

"But first, I'm sorry to tell you, I've got some terrible news...."

Annelise braced for more bad news.... *What the hell else could be wrong now?* flitted through her mind.

" . . . Andrew Bolling was on that train last night. We're assuming, of course, that he didn't make it. I'm sorry to have to tell you this. I know you and he were good friends . . . ."

For a moment, Annelise stopped breathing. Her heart seemed to stop beating. A wave of nausea washed over her. The words coming out of Hunter's mouth became unintelligible, and then as if time were going in reverse, the room started to spin. Everything went dark.

When Annelise came to thirty seconds later, she was laying across Jeffrey Hunter's brown leather couch, with Hunter, LaForge, and Stanthrope peering down at her with concerned looks all around. After gathering her composure, she was horrified at the emotional and physical vulnerability she'd just exhibited. This was the Prime Minister's office, damn it. She couldn't be passing out in a crisis situation. She mumbled a quick apology, offered a lame excuse blaming exhaustion and dehydration, and regained her position in the chair opposite Hunter.

Only when everyone's attention was focused back on Jeffrey Hunter's stoic face did she allow herself to once again let the realization of Hunter's words sink in. The thoughts began to race around her brain: *What the hell? Andrew?? Dead? There's no way . . . There must be a mistake.* He wasn't on that train last night . . . He'd told her that he was flying back around 7:30 p.m. on BritAir. He must be at home still or stuck in the traffic gridlock outside. She just needed to get back to her desk and try again to get him on the phone.

Hunter was still talking. She reassured herself that Andrew Bolling, the man she had fallen desperately in love with over the last year and half, was somewhere en route to the office right now. There was just a misunderstanding about his itinerary last night, and it would all be cleared up as soon as he got to the office.

In the meantime, Annelise forced herself to focus on the matters at hand. The P.M.'s office had an enormous task ahead to handle this crisis, including a brief speech by the Prime Minister at 9 a.m. and then another Press Conference at 6 p.m. to address the British people. They would also be coordinating the rescue and recovery operation with their counterparts in Paris, coordinating communication with other heads of state, and most importantly, working with the British police and national security agencies to find out who committed this horrific crime. She forced herself not to think about Andrew or where he might be. She would deal with that later.

CHAPTER EIGHT

Jeffrey looked down at his watch...12:30 p.m., and thought again that he was ready for this meeting to break up. Even though it was a meeting with the P.M. and his National Security Council, Jeffrey was desperate to get back to his desk and get some real work accomplished. But right now, he was stuck listening to a bunch of blowhards and paper pushers eager to be in on the action. The real work being accomplished was taking place deep below the English Channel at the explosion site, and across town at the Secret Intelligence Service headquarters where the nation's top investigators and intelligence operatives were doing the tough work of trying to decipher who actually committed this heinous act and figuring out how in the hell a bunch of vile terrorists were able to blow up one of Britain's most important assets.

As the meeting droned on, Jeffrey began to review in his mind the meeting he'd already had with MI5 – Britain's domestic counter-intelligence agency – a couple of hours ago. Immediately upon returning to the office this morning, Jeffrey had already met with the country's top investigators to brief them on the cryptic phone call he had received this morning, and to turn over his phone for analysis. Although the call had shaken him up a bit, Jeffrey didn't really give it much credence. There were crackpots all over London. Hell, there were loonies all over Great Britain, eager to jump on the opportunity for notoriety that a terrorist attack offered. The London police would no doubt have at least one or two crazies show up today and claim responsibility. Real terrorists do not call up the office of the Prime Minister and announce themselves. He was sure it was a hoax. The biggest pain was that he would now be without his phone for a few days. They had given him a temporary, but without his private phone with all of his personalized apps and contact list, he would have to limp along on one of the most critical days of his tenure in office.

The meeting mercifully was brought to a full stop when Wellington announced he needed to leave and handle critical phone conversations with some other European heads of state. Calls had been coming in all morning from Asia, Germany, and Japan, even Russian President Putin had made a courtesy phone call. This wasn't just Britain's problem... it was a full out global crisis, and somebody had to start work on coordinating the global support.

As soon as the meeting ended, Hunter bolted out of the room and down the hall toward his office. Fletcher LaForge, the Deputy National Security Advisor, was trailing him, calling out to him as Hunter disappeared down the hall.

"Hunter . . . Let me know anything that comes across your desk about the investigation . . . it's important that we coordinate any new information you're receiving with our office. . . ."

Jeffrey grunted a response without bothering to turn around. LaForge was a nice enough guy, and it was obvious to everyone on the staff that he had a brilliant mind, but Jeffrey privately found him to be annoying and more than a little unexceptional in his job performance. What's more, Hunter had known LaForge for more than twenty years, going all the way back to his days at Oxford, so their shared history provided a foundation for a true friendship, albeit often requiring more patience than Hunter could afford at the moment.

LaForge persisted down the hall behind Jeffrey, calling out behind him...

"Hunter, I'd like to meet with you to discuss the investigation at your earliest convenience . . . ."

Before Hunter even entered his office, he could tell there were people waiting for him.

"What the hell is it now?" he called out as he entered the room.

Standing directly in front of his desk, Hunter immediately recognized John O'Leary, one of the top investigators with MI6, the Secret Intelligence Service's Foreign Intelligence division. He'd brought along several members of his entourage, half a dozen other investigators whose principle job it was obviously to do whatever he told them.

O'Leary was a big man, six foot one, in his late fifties, and easily 250 pounds. He hailed from Glasgow, and with a mop of thick reddish hair and a reddish-gray moustache, he looked like someone straight out of central casting and every bit the part of the Scottish Gentleman. He still wore a hounds tooth jacket that should have made its way into a charity donation bag twenty years ago. His Scottish brogue was gruff and all-business, but legend had it that his investigative instincts were unparalleled, having virtually single-handedly detected and prevented more than a dozen lesser terrorist attacks on London in the past fifteen years. O'Leary was a man who didn't waste time with niceties.

"I've got some questions, Hunter. We've run the source on that phone call you received this morning. Appears to be coming from a laundry business in Marseille."

"What?" Hunter was incredulous. O'Leary stared steadily at him. Fletcher LaForge trailed Hunter into the room, and stopped short when he saw O'Leary and his team in front of the desk.

O'Leary did not appreciate the interruption and glared at LaForge. The two went way back, and their mutual contempt was apparent. They hailed from two different divisions within the Foreign Intelligence wing of the British Government, where they had both worked a dozen years ago. Like quarreling siblings, the two departments were constantly feuding over territory and power. O'Leary turned back toward Jeffrey without acknowledging LaForge. Jeffrey was fully aware of the infighting, but didn't have time to deal with petty political rivalries at the moment.

"Mr. O'Leary, I'm sure you've met Fletcher LaForge, Deputy NSA. He and I and the P.M. go way back. LaForge taught economics and public policy at Oxford while we were all students there."

"Yes, I believe we have." O'Leary's tone indicated his lack of regard for LaForge, and his disdain at having another politician in the room. He continued in his same matter of fact tone: "Let me clarify; the call is clearly not coming from a laundry in Marseille. While the phone number that we traced from the call registers to that address, the caller is obviously using a line encryption device that displays a random number as the source of the call – even cloaking the true origin of the call from the telephone company and from our tracking surveillance programs. Forget Marseille . . . The call could have been coming from anywhere... Paris, Munich, Istanbul, or next door. We're working on it, but it will take more time to more exactly pinpoint the origin of the call. It was probably a burner phone anyway, so at this point, the value of that information is negligible."

"So, what do we do now?"

O'Leary took a seat, leaving everyone else in the room standing, hanging on his next words. "What do you know about Bolling's past? I need to know everything you know about him."

"Andrew? There's not that much to know. He's from Surrey, studied at Oxford with me and the Prime Minister. He was a great guy, a good friend, and an indispensable aid to the P.M. He will be missed."

"Tell me more about his personal life. I want details. Why was he on that train last night? Where exactly was he in Paris, and who exactly was he meeting with? Why was he in Paris in the first place?"

"He was planning to see some old friends of ours from university. Andrew had invited me to go along too, but as usual, I was just too tied up with work. Andrew was always good at making time for old friends. I'm not sure who all showed up in Paris for the weekend... just some of our old drinking buddies from Oxford getting together to have some pints, tell stories, and catch up."

"I'll need a list of everyone you know of that might have seen him over the weekend. We've already got contact information for his parents, and will be in contact with them soon enough, although I don't expect to learn a lot from them. And one more thing, did he have a girlfriend... someone he was seeing?"

Jeffrey Hunter flinched at the question. He knew Bolling was seeing someone, he just didn't know who exactly it was. He'd tried to jokingly pry it out of his old pal several times, but Bolling wouldn't budge. He was keeping it discreet for some reason, but why? Maybe she was from the opposition party, or maybe she would be a political liability for someone in his position and he just didn't want to go public. Whatever the reason, Bolling had held his cards very close to his vest on this one, and Jeffrey Hunter didn't have the foggiest idea why. But for now, he was going to stay true to his old friend.

"No. No one that I know of at least, hasn't been anyone for a while." His friend was dead. He wasn't going to stain his reputation right now for no good reason.

CHAPTER NINE

Rasul Aziz unlocked the front door of the book shop and flipped on the lights. The smell of old, dusty books mixed with the faint smell of mold from the pre-war pipes filled the room, just as it did every morning when he entered. He flipped the dangling 'Closed' sign to 'Open,' and threw his black leather jacket on the back of a stool behind the counter.

Moving to the back room, he turned on the radio to 106.7, 'BEUR FM', Paris' Muslim community radio station. A reporter was interviewing the Mayor of London about the Chunnel explosion. Turning the dial to a classical music station, he filled his teapot to the brim with cold water from the small dingy sink in the corner, and turned his hotplate onto high as he waited for the water to boil. Taking out two green teabags, he placed them into his largest mug. It was going to be a long day.

Back on his stool behind the counter, Rasul flipped open his laptop; 47 emails from overnight filled the screen. Skimming the junk emails in quick succession, he deleted all but the last one, from a Gmail account that he didn't recognize, subject line blank.

"Your package is scheduled to arrive today. Please notify us if you fail to receive it." Closing his laptop, he returned to the teapot. Filling his mug, he watched the water turn a light shade of greenish brown. He added one packet of raw sugar and watched it slowly dissolve in the hot water. After letting the tea steep for a few minutes, he raised the cup and took in the musky aroma. Taking a sip, he let the hot liquid glide down his throat. Taking his tea was the best part of his day, he thought.

Raz looked out the front window at the people passing by. Muslim businessmen, some wearing business suits, and a few wearing the traditional thobe tunic, bustled down the sidewalk. There were a large number of students in faded t-shirts, and a few women passed by in their bright colored hijabs. He felt anonymous in this world. Just another shopkeeper. Just another Muslim guy in this backwater neighborhood. The same old feelings that he felt most days rushed over him. He was invisible here, anonymous. Rasul wasn't looking for the limelight. He just wanted out.

Rasul thought about the job he had executed last night. He thought about the look on Andrew's face when he handed him his "gift," all wrapped up in red and green paper with a big fat red bow on top. He'd told Andrew it was a holiday present, a memento for old time's sake. The funny look on Andrew's face was probably guilt that he hadn't bought anything for Rasul. Poor Andy, if only he'd known that the box he carried was no gift at all, but a custom made IED, set with an automatic timer and scheduled to detonate at an exact moment to guarantee maximum damage inside the tunnel. The fact that the initial explosion was designed to set off a chain reaction secondary explosion and fire, causing catastrophic damage to both the east- and west-bound passenger tunnels, as well as the maintenance tunnel would just be icing on the cake. The explosion and fire were calculated to be a terrorist attack of historical proportions, and Rasul smiled to himself at the thought of a job well done.

Maybe that's why he did it. Sure, he had his other ulterior motives, his increasingly considerable off-shore bank account being the main one, but Rasul rather enjoyed the idea that his life was having an impact. He was making a difference, even if it meant others had to pay the price. He thought about it for another moment, and then as he always did, he put the thoughts of Andrew far out of his mind. When he thought of Andrew, it was painful to think he had ended his friend's life. Unfortunately, it had been the only way. And now, it was too painful to dwell on.

At 2 p.m., the little bell over the door jingled lightly and the DHL delivery man dropped a 10-inch square box inside the front door. Rasul gave him a little wave and Arnold, the regular delivery guy, was out the door and already gone. Opening the box, Rasul noticed that it was lighter than usual. Normally he opened it to find cash or handwritten pages with instructions. He briefly wondered if the box might be empty.

Pulling off the packaging tape, he pulled back the flaps of the small box. There taped to the bottom of the box was a simple silver key. Too small to be a door key, it appeared to fit a lock or a box. He turned it over, and very small, etched on the other side were three letters: CMH. Reaching into his pocket he took out a small white handkerchief, the kind he'd carried everyday his entire adult life, a habit he picked up from his British friends at university. Folding the key up in the cloth, he replaced it and patted it to make sure it was securely positioned deep in his pocket.

He went back to his green tea, his third large mug today. Now he would wait.

CHAPTER TEN

High up on the 83rd floor of Hazelwood Tower in Lower Manhattan, Charlie Turner turned on his silver personal phone and carefully typed in his username and password, logging into his account with Merckel & Moss Financial Services, Geneva, Switzerland. After a minute as the information on the screen updated, his eyes widened at the feast of numbers before him. Smiling to himself, he gazed at the glowing numbers, like some ridiculous dream come true: $43,645,081.31. He read the numbers again, studying each digit to confirm they were all there. He checked the deposit details, 8:48 a.m. Source: Cornmarket Holdings, Grand Cayman.

He logged off of his account and sat for a moment staring down Broadway and across Battery Park. As usual, he could barely make out the tourists standing in the almost perpetual line waiting to catch the ferry out to Ellis Island and the Statue of Liberty. In the distance he could make out the grand lady herself, now wearing green stained copper and staring out to sea, as she had every day for the last twelve years he'd worked in this office. It was a gorgeous view, one coveted by just about anybody working in New York City. But he was sick of it. He was tired of the city, tired of the crowds, tired of skyscrapers, and tired of the constant stress of dealing with other people's money. He wanted out, and he was getting closer to his exit by the day.

Today he had made much progress toward that goal. The last twenty-four hours had been very lucrative, but he would have to wait until later to enjoy the thoughts of his windfall. With the terrorism hit in London, it was going to be a rollercoaster day. The markets were diving. Many would lose the shirts off their backs today, but others would make a fortune. Charlie knew the game well. He – and his most valued clients – would not be among the financial casualties today. There was money to be made, even in a tragedy like this. It was unfortunate that hundreds of people had died, but sitting around and moping about it wasn't going to help anyone. He would be among those who profited from this tragic situation, as would his loyal clients. He had work to do.

Charlie took out his personal phone again – this one silver so as never to be confused with the black business phone he also carried – and punched the icon for text messages and typed out a quick text to his buddy Jorge down the hall. *"Lunch – Metro Deli, 12:30."* He punched the lock button on top of his phone and slid it into his pocket. Picking up his work phone, he dialed the number of Jasper Jenkins, CEO and founder of Jenkins Enterprises, the third largest real estate developer in New York State. After four rings, Jasper picked up.

"Good morning, Mr. Jenkins. I hope you are well this morning."

"Well, yes. Good morning. Awful news about that train in London."

"Yes it is, Mr. Jenkins. Just terrible. I pray they will find some survivors."

"Yes, yes. Certainly. I hope so. What can I do for you this morning, Charles?"

"Mr. Jenkins, I'm sorry to be calling you so early on such a terrible morning, but we have some situations that should be considered. As you know, last month we shorted some European currencies, including the British Pound, in view of the country's vulnerable position given its BREXIT vote and the instability of the British economy. This terrorist event, however tragic, has of course had disastrous ramifications on the British pound. It's down by almost 33% this morning on the recognition of the damage that will be sustained by the British economy. I think we should exercise our option immediately and get out of the British market for now. Do you understand my recommendation?"

"Yes, Charlie, I do. Let's do it. I feel like a jerk for making money off of such a terrible situation, but we had no way of knowing. We just need to get out now and let them find a way to fix their own economy in the wake of this horrific situation. We'll take profits now and then revisit a decision to reinvest when they're looking to start rebuilding."

"Excellent decision, Mr. Jenkins. Again, I'm so sorry to bother you this morning. Have a good day."

Charlie clicked the phone off and smiled as he stared back down Broadway again. He loved Mr. Jenkins. Or rather, he loved how easy it was to make money with Jenkins's billions. Charlie thought about the old adage, "It takes money to make money." True, Charlie thought, but better yet, it's so much easier to get rich using other people's money.

CHAPTER ELEVEN

By late morning, Annelise Craig was in a full-blown panic. Andrew Bolling was nowhere to be found. He hadn't responded to a single phone call or text message since she first started trying to reach him at 12:15 a.m.

No, no, no, it's impossible. Her thoughts denying the possibility were on repeat in her brain. *He cannot have been on that train last night!*

She rose from her desk and knocked quietly on Jeffrey Hunter's office door, which had been closed for much of the last hour as he worked the phones, talking to the heads of Britain's various first responders' divisions.

"Come in, come in," came his rushed and curt response from the other side of the closed door.

"Jeffrey, I'm so sorry to bother you. I know you're terribly busy."

"It's OK Annie. What's up?"

"It's Andrew, Jeffrey. I know he wasn't on that train last night. We were working on some projects over the weekend, and he texted me just yesterday afternoon, letting me know that he was catching a 7:30 flight out of Paris on BritAir. He should have been home long before that late Eurostar train even left Paris."

Jeffrey looked up at Annie and recognized that she was taking the news extraordinarily hard. She had worked here for a year and half, working alongside Andrew just as they all had, so Jeffrey reasoned that her obvious case of denial made sense. He tried again to explain it to her again as gently as he could.

"Annie, I don't know exactly what happened, but Andrew didn't fly home last night. He was on the Eurostar. We just received an updated preliminary list of confirmed passengers a few minutes ago. He's on the list."

Annie stood there, blinking at Jeffrey Hunter, stunned. This time she allowed the reality of the news to slowly start to sink in . . . it might really be true, she thought. Andrew might really be dead. Her head started to throb, and her stomach began to churn as though she might throw up right there in the office of the Prime Minister of England's Chief of Staff. She nodded her understanding and then quickly bolted into the hall before she became sick and made another scene. Darting down the hall, she barely got the door to the ladies' private rest room closed before the contents of her stomach came pouring out of her mouth into the toilet. She choked and gasped, the tile room spinning as she grabbed the walls for support.

Sobbing, she grabbed a towel and held it to her mouth to muffle the sound. The grief came in waves, and she held onto the wall to steady herself. His face, his hands, the way his hair curled behind his ear... all these images played on repeat through her mind. How would she ever live without him? How could she conceal the grief that was washing over her like unrelenting waves for one day? Let alone a lifetime?

Annie stood there in the small, dim bathroom, and thoughts flooded back through her mind. She had never wanted to fall in love with Andrew Bolling. Certainly she was not the kind of woman to have an affair, lying and cheating on her husband. Her husband Richard was a good man, everyone liked him. Hell, Annie liked him too. But Andrew Bolling was a bolt out of the blue that she didn't see coming. He was intelligent of course, but it went further than that. He was gentle and caring to everyone, yet he could debate political philosophies and constitutional theories with an intense depth of knowledge and fervor. He was confident, curious, and creative, but also the most loyal friend and confidant. The fact that he was also incredibly handsome was just what had pushed her over the edge into an affair that she did not want or pursue. It just happened, and it had completely transformed every facet of her life. Yet now he was gone forever, just as unexpectedly as he had entered it.

After a few minutes, she heard a soft knock on the door . . . "Hey Annie, you OK?"

It was Rosalind, the pleasant older lady who worked back in the communications office.

"Oh, I'm OK! So sorry! Just feeling a little overwhelmed with all of the bad news today! I'll be out in a minute!"

After a few minutes to compose herself, Annie blotted her face with some rough sheets of paper towel, rinsed out her mouth, smoothed out her hair, and exited the restroom. Thankfully Rosalind was nowhere to be seen. Weaving her way through the office back to her desk to avoid any face to face contact, she managed to make it back to her desk without further scrutiny.

She willed herself to halt all thoughts of Andrew. She simply could not think of him at this moment. People could not know that Andrew's death had devastated her. There were strict rules against dating within the top government office in the country – it was seen as a security threat and left the administration vulnerable to accusations of nepotism and partiality. The fact that one of the parties was married made this situation all the more worse. An affair of this type, even when one of the parties was murdered in an act of terrorism – or especially when one of the parties had been murdered in an act of terrorism – would be a scandal. She would lose her job and quite probably her marriage as well; although right now, that was less of a concern.

CHAPTER TWELVE

By 4 p.m. Monday afternoon, Hunter was relatively certain he'd taken care of all of the emergency agenda items on his list of things to do. For a moment, he could take a breath and let himself take in all that had happened in the last 18 hours. He had been running on adrenaline since midnight last night, and the fatigue was starting to set in.

The recovery teams were still hard at work deep in the tunnel, extracting victims and documenting the tangled, burned mess that comprised the crime scene as best they could. One hundred and thirty one victims had been recovered thus far, with many more trapped in the twisted wreckage. Many would probably never be recovered. Jeffrey was sick just thinking about the thousands of people who represented the families and friends of these poor victims. So much death and destruction, so many lives lost, and so many victims' families' lives forever altered. It was sickening that any person could have so much hate in their heart that they could kill a trainload of innocent victims with so little regard for humanity. Jeffrey hated all of it, and right now, he hated his job very much.

For the first time in eighteen hours, Hunter let himself think about Andrew. First at Oxford, through many years climbing the government ladder, and now in the Prime Minister's office, the two had worked side by side for more than seventeen years. They were good friends, confidants, coworkers, and drinking buddies, in that order. Other than Trevor Wellington, he was Hunter's best friend, and he would miss him terribly.

He knew everything about Andrew and vice versa. When they first met at Oxford, they were assigned to work on a project together for their political theory class and hit it off immediately. Andrew didn't have the same kind of privileged background that had propelled

Hunter and Wellington to Oxford. He had arrived there the old-fashioned way, through sheer hard work and intellect.

Andrew grew up in the Chiswick neighborhood of West London, playing on the streets among middle class homes and working class families. He had attended the local primary and secondary schools, excelling far and above the expectations of his middle class London upbringing. When he blew the top off of his A level exams at the end of secondary school, Oxford came calling with a hefty scholarship offer. It was his ticket out of Chiswick and into the inner sanctum of England's most revered academic circles. His future would be bright indeed.

At University, Jeffrey, Trevor Wellington, and Andrew Bolling had become close friends during their senior year, along with Rasul Aziz, Andrew's wingman all four years at Oxford. Their flat just two blocks west of campus was a constant hubbub of activity with classmates, books, and copious amounts of Guinness and Coors Light. The later beer preference was compliments of Andrew and Raz's previous flat mates Charlie and Jorge, the American exchange students who had roomed with the pair the previous year. Hunter had only met Charlie and Jorge a handful of times at Oxford, but their American beer of choice would forever impact his own taste buds for years to come, by sheer fact of their common friendship with Andrew. Jeffrey's parents always said that the purpose of University was to open one's eyes to the world, and he had laughed at the thought that influencing his choice of beer was probably not what they had in mind.

Jeffrey thought back to his conversation with John O'Leary this morning. What in the hell did Andrew Bolling have to do with this whole mess, other than being in the wrong place at the wrong time, and paying for that mistake with his life? What did that phone call mean this morning? Certainly it was a crank call, but why would anyone be trying to tie Andrew to a terrorist attack? And why would they be threatening anyone based on it? None of it made any sense. Andrew was a high-ranking government official, but there was no way his otherwise ordinary life had anything to do with terrorists and threats against his country. Andrew Bolling wasn't even supposed to be on that train anyway, so the idea that his death could be tied to this random act of terrorism was nonsense. John O'Leary would clear the matter up, certainly.

Jeffrey Hunter picked up his replacement cell phone, needing some answers. Punching the yellow icon for contacts, he pulled out the small business card containing the information John O'Leary had left him with this morning. Adding John's name to his contact list, he punched the phone icon to call the MI6 investigator while formulating his thoughts on how this situation needed to be expedited.

"John? Jeffrey Hunter here, from the P.M.'s office. I wanted to check in and see if you have any updates on the investigation. I know you've only just started, but Wellington is looking for a briefing on where the investigation stands this afternoon. He's got a press conference this evening at six, and he is wanting to get an update. He wants to be prepared."

"Good afternoon, Mr. Hunter. We're chasing a couple of dozen leads right now, everything from a French housewife who thinks she saw someone board the train with suspicious boxes, to a local teacher who thinks one of his students might be involved. Frankly, the phone call you received this morning is the most solid lead we've got. We're just trying to systematically check out each lead, crossing the crackpots off our list, and starting the process of narrowing down the suspects. Has any new information come your way?"

"Oh no, John. Just wanted to check in. Any idea why Andrew Bolling's name was mentioned on the call this morning? That's got me a little shaken up. He was a good man... I don't want his name being needlessly tangled up with this nightmare in the press."

"No clue, Mr. Hunter. We've already talked with his parents, his neighbors, and a couple of other family members. No one seems to know anything. We're in the process of obtaining his cell phone records as we speak, and should have them by later this evening. We'll have a lot better picture of what our Mr. Bolling might have been up to in Paris over the weekend once we have those records. In the meantime, he seems like a good guy; I can't imagine why he would have been targeted. Our working theory right now is that the call was a crackpot who works for some non-Governmental agency in contact with your office. They probably had your number and just wanted to get in on the action. But we'll keep looking into it."

"Thanks, John, please keep me posted."

Jeffrey Hunter put down the cell.

Paris. Who all was it Andrew had told him would be in Paris last weekend? Were Charlie Turner and Jorge Morales, their old American buddies, still going to be there or just Rasul? Raz still lived in Paris, or at least he thought he did. Jeffrey hadn't really talked to any of those guys in years. Andrew had always been the common denominator in the group, the guy everyone else was primarily friends with. Charlie and Jorge had been roommates with Andrew junior year, and then Jeffrey and Wellington had moved in and become his roommates the year after that. Rasul was Andrew's first friend at Oxford, but it was Andrew that served as the glue that connected them all together. Maybe he should make contact with them, Jeffrey thought to himself. Make sure they had all heard the news about Andrew.

Jeffrey buzzed Annie over the interoffice speaker. "Annelise, would you mind chasing down the Paris phone number of a Raz .... No, make that Razim . . . No, it's . . . Rasul Aziz, that's it. He's in Paris I think. Thanks."

CHAPTER THIRTEEN

At 5:30 p.m., a man in a Federal Express uniform pushed open the door of Paradigm Books.

"Signature please," the new man said.

"Oh, sure," Raz said as he grabbed the plastic pencil and scribbled his name, illegibly as usual, across the plastic window. "Thanks . . . You're new, right?"

"Yeah, today's my first day. I'm Tom," he says, jutting out his right hand.

"I'm Rasul. Good to meet you."

With that, the FedEx man was already backing out the door, eager to stay on schedule.

Rasul reached in his top drawer to take out the large knife he kept for dual purposes, to open book boxes, and protection. Not that any size knife would offer much protection in this neighborhood. The weapons around here were much bigger than a four and half inch blade.

Slicing open the packing tape, he folded back the flaps to reveal four copies of Hemingway's *For Whom the Bell Tolls.* Taking each copy out one by one, he slowly opened the front flap of each book and fanned his fingers along the pages, looking for anything that might be tucked among the pages.

Opening the third book and flipping through the pages, he saw the edges of the ivory linen note paper slide out of the book, almost falling to the floor. Unfolding the note, he saw the familiar handwriting in the black ink he now identified as coming from a very expensive ballpoint pen.

The note, as usual, was in all uppercase letters and in letter perfect print, as always.

GEORGE STREET OX1 2AR
TOMORROW NOON

Raz recognized the postal code instantly. He refolded the linen note paper and slid it into his pant's pocket, alongside the silver key. Patting the outside of his pants, he made sure he could feel the folded paper buried deep inside his pants along with the key.

He took the four copies of Hemingway's novel and placed them on the shelf in the Classics section, alongside copies of *The Sun Also Rises, Old Man and the Sea,* and *The Great Gatsby.* As with *For Whom the Bell Tolls,* each of these masterworks had also done their duty as caretakers of an important piece of instruction or vital information. What better camouflage for a book seller than books? Rasul smiled to himself.

Raz gathered up his laptop and slid it into the side compartment of his leather bag. He made sure the hot plate was off and poured out the extra hot water left over from his tea service. Turning on the small light behind the counter, he flicked off the larger overheard light, and taped a small sign to the front door reading "Back in 15 minutes" that he kept handy when he wanted to go for a quick coffee. Grabbing his leather bag, he carefully set the store alarm, and locked the door behind him. The store would be closed tomorrow, but Raz did not give it a second thought. Paradigm bookstore had few customers, and its owner had other important business to attend to tomorrow.

CHAPTER FOURTEEN

Twelve o'clock noon in New York, and Charlie Turner was hungry. He exited his office in Hazelwood Tower and was careful to lock his office door behind him. Twelve years in this office and he had managed to cultivate several friendships with his co-workers, without ever letting them get too close. He kept his personal life on the down low, but made certain to hit the office happy hour a couple of times a month, just to stay part of the crowd, keep an ear to the ground for office gossip that might come in handy, and avoid any unnecessary curiosity about his life. He maintained a careful façade: a solid stable of legitimate clients who earned authentic profits on Charlie's usually above average stock market expertise. He wasn't a high flyer at the firm; he preferred to fly under the radar the majority of the time. But to everyone's amazement – except his – he had managed to make a few calls now and again that earned astounding profits for his very grateful client pool. Most of his co-workers just marveled at his occasional extraordinary luck.

Charlie smiled to himself. Today would be a very lucky day, indeed.

Charlie took the express elevator down from the 83rd floor, and left the building with the usual lunch time throng. Jorge would be just behind him. Charlie exited the building and walked a block down the street to the Metro Broadway Diner on the corner of Broadway and Pine. Run by an old Pakastani immigrant named Bilal and his wife, the place was always overrun with tourists who were perfectly willing to dine and pay inflated prices at any establishment with the word Broadway attached. The regular Wall Street crowd would be nowhere around, and Jorge and Charlie could talk in private.

Charlie ordered a Ham and Swiss on Sourdough bread and a bag of chips at the counter, grabbed a bottle of water, and found a booth in the back corner where they would be left alone. Jorge walked in about the time Charlie was settling into the booth. After ordering his usual bowl of Clam Chowder along with a Diet Coke, he made his way back to the booth and took a seat.

"So, have you checked our position this morning?" Charlie said with a slight smirk.

"I have indeed!" Jorge could not help but break into a large grin.

"That's almost eleven big ones apiece, a nice chunk of change for a day's work." Charlie's smile now matched Jorge's and they grinned at each other, then chuckled as if they were sharing a joke between old friends.

"Yes, I would say so!" Jorge snickered back. He had to take a quick drink of Diet Coke to keep from choking on a chunk of potato in his soup.

Jorge could not believe his luck. Since prep school days at Jesuit High School in Dallas, his friendship with Charlie Turner had been one of his luckiest breaks ever. An unlikely pair, they were from different worlds back in Dallas, but their tight friendship and shared history had brought them both a life of adventure and increasingly, a whole lot of money.

Jorge was from South Dallas and would normally have never stepped foot in the likes of any school remotely similar to Jesuit. His reasonably high IQ had played a small part, but it was his 92-mph fastball had helped pave the way into one of Dallas's most elite private schools. At Jesuit, the sons of some of Dallas' most wealthy citizens jockeyed for grades and sports' accolades among the leafy enclaves of North Dallas.

In late June after Jorge's 8th grade year, a prominent Jesuit alumnus had spotted Jorge at his son's summer league baseball tournament. Knowing Jesuit was always looking for strong pitching on its perennially State-competitive team, the Jesuit alum made a few calls and introduced Jorge's mom to the administration and coaching staff at Jesuit. By the following spring, Jorge was standing on the pitcher's mound at Jesuit's Wright field, mowing down batters from the area rival schools. Jorge helped carry Jesuit to the State baseball finals the next summer, and his name was soon being mentioned all over the state. When colleges came calling two summers later, Jorge had his pick of half a dozen Division 1 schools, eager to bolster their roster with a whip-smart Hispanic boy who could throw a mean curve ball.

While baseball was important to Jorge, he knew better than to bet his entire life on his ability to throw a small round ball. Every pitcher was only as good as his last game, and Jorge had seen his share of "future MLB stars" forgotten overnight as soon as they threw out their shoulder or elbow from overuse. His plan was to use baseball as an entry into the best schools, work his butt off, and then collect his diploma as payment for services rendered. He would let his sharp mind carry him from then on.

Jorge met Charlie Turner in high school algebra his freshman year at Jesuit. Charlie was on the baseball team as well, but other than having a rich dad who supplied a hefty donation to the booster club every year, Charlie contributed little to the team. Charlie was a popular guy, blonde, good looking, and blue eyes that made all the girls at the nearby equally prestigious Hockaday School go crazy. Charlie's house in Highland Park was financed by his father's high flying job at Merrill Lynch in Downtown, where he had ridden Texas's boom economy to a tidy fortune over the last thirty-five years. Charlie and Jorge became fast friends, mostly due to their shared common interests in baseball and girls.

After graduation from Jesuit, Charlie was destined for Texas Christian University in neighboring Fort Worth where he could follow in his dad's footsteps as Fraternity President and overall popular party guy. Coincidentally, TCU's baseball team was one of the most competitive in the country, and Jorge saw the perfect opportunity to continue to develop the twin rails of his road to success: his strong pitching arm and his friendship with Charlie.

So now here they sat twenty-two years later, across the table from each other in a Deli booth in Manhattan, reveling with each other in the realization that they'd each just cleared more than ten million dollars apiece in the biggest gamble of their lives. They both had self-satisfied grins on their faces as the realization of the success of their latest venture sunk in.

"You know we've got to lay low now for a while." Charlie's face grew more serious. "Don't buy anything, not even a new suit, for at least six months. Just business as usual. I shorted Jenkins' position as well, just to keep him happy, keep my numbers up, and to generate a little pocket change."

"How much you going to net off of that one?" Jorge was annoyed that he hadn't thought to get a couple of his own clients in on the action too, just to keep his own performance numbers comfortably above average as well.

"Not much... maybe $40K," Charlie was dismissive.

"When do we make our next move?" Jorge was growing slightly irritated that he had missed out on a nice little profit to tide him over until the big money became available.

"Not for a while, Jorge. British Intelligence is going to be all over this for a while, and the CIA will likely be involved. We've got to go about business as usual and not create any unnecessary attention. We can't touch a penny of this money for months. You'll just have to cool your jets for a while. We both do."

Charlie was finished with lunch and ready to leave. He could tell Jorge was mad that he'd missed out on lining his pockets with a few extra dollars, but Charlie had not given him a head's up on purpose. Two co-workers profiting wildly off of the same seemingly random global tragedy would garner attention. The fact that they were good friends from the same hometown would definitely raise eyebrows. Jorge was smart, but sometimes he missed the big picture. Charlie benefitted from having Jorge around for his little schemes, but he had to keep him a little in the dark most of the time, or things would even get riskier. It's just the way things had to work.

Charlie wiped his mouth with a paper napkin and dropped it on the table. "Let's go."

Before he could stand up, Jorge grabbed him on the forearm, pressing his arm to the table.

"What now?" Charlie gave him an incredulous look.

"Sorry," Jorge released his arm. "Look, I'm short on cash. I was planning to have that money sooner rather than later. If we're not going to touch the money for several months, then you're probably going to have to float me a small loan for the short term."

"How much?"

"At least ten-grand. I've got some expenses I need to cover." Charlie averted his eyes, and looked out the window at the tourists hurriedly making their way up Broadway.

"OK, no problem. We can work something out – for the short term." Charlie rose to leave.

"Then we're good. You take off first, and I'll wait a few minutes before heading back. I'll see you later." Jorge forced a grin and offered his right hand.

Charlie gave a tight smile, and shook Jorge's hand, doing his best to appear casual. He grabbed his black phone off of the table and exited the diner turning back toward Hazelwood Tower. As he walked, he mindlessly clenched his jaw, thinking about Jorge's remarks at the end of their conversation. Wasn't it enough that they were both about to pocket a sizable cache of money that would make both of them filthy rich? Charlie thought about Jorge and his loose cannon ways as he made his way back down Wall Street. And then the light bulb went off, bringing the entire conversation into focus. He clenched his jaw again as he walked, attempting to appear at ease strolling back toward the office.

Great. He thought to himself. *I'm a millionaire co-conspirator to one of the biggest crimes in history, and I've got a drug addict for a partner.*

Charlie knew the signs; he'd known Jorge for far too long. A serious elbow injury in spring of Jorge's sophomore year at TCU had ended his pitching career and had launched his life-long addiction to painkillers. Jorge had fought the addiction for more than twenty years, having been through rehab twice before, the last stint being eight years ago. Since then, he'd been clean for eight perfect years – or so Charlie had thought.

And now they were in the middle of the biggest, most dangerous scheme of their lives, and Jorge was worried about drug money. He probably owed money to some back street opioid dealer punk with a long rap sheet and dangerous friends. He would loan him the money. He really didn't have any choice. If he didn't, he would find Jorge beaten up badly in some back alley, or worse yet, dead.

This was not the kind of problem Charlie needed right now. There was far too much on the line to be worrying about two-bit drug dealers and addicted friends. He would have to forget about the money for the time being, and figure out what to do about his business partner right now.

CHAPTER FIFTEEN

At 5:20 p.m., Jeffrey entered Wellington's office to update the Prime Minister on the current status of the recovery operation deep in the tunnel. Fletcher LaForge was already there, but his boss Trawick was nowhere in sight. Jeffrey rattled off the current facts as he knew them: As of 5 p.m. sharp, Jeffrey had been notified that 225 victims' bodies had now been recovered, and the police would be working throughout the night to identify the dead. The two survivors had been airlifted to London Royal Hospital, and though suffering intense smoke inhalation, they were expected to live.

Echoing Jeffrey's thoughts, Wellington was incredulous that Andrew Bolling could be in any way involved in the attack on the EuroStar train. Jeffrey assured the P.M. of what they both already knew: that Andrew Bolling was far too ordinary and too much of a straight arrow to have had any part in the attack, either as an instigator or even as a target. There was just no way Andrew Bolling would be of any benefit to a terrorist, dead or alive. Certainly, he worked for the Prime Minister of England, but his chief responsibilities were just routine domestic concerns: economic policy, financial research, tracking the British Pound's value against the global markets. It was a dream job for an economics major from Oxford, but nothing that would be of any interest to a foreign terrorist cell or even a homegrown terrorist. After all, Wellington and Jeffrey had both known Andrew Bolling most of their adult lives as well. It was inconceivable he could be a target or a threat. He simply wasn't a factor as far as either of them was concerned.

"Hunter, there's no way Bolling was a target in this attack. There's just no way that makes any sense," Wellington said to Hunter after he shut the office door.

"No, I'm sure it's all just a very tragic coincidence. That phone call was a hoax by some nut who gets his jollies from mucking up the water," Hunter said. "But I still have no idea who would have called me this morning with that ridiculous threat. Dozens of people have my private cell number, but like all of our private cell numbers, it's never been published in any government directory or document."

"I think I have a pretty good idea who would stoop that low Jeffrey, although if it's true, it's pretty disgusting," Fletcher LaForge had been characteristically quiet since Jeffrey entered the office, but suddenly perked up with his new theory.

"Who?" said Hunter, with a look of skepticism on his face.

"Kane, or more likely one of his goons, of course," said LaForge, referencing the current opposition leader of the Labour Party. "They've been trying to bring Wellington down since this administration took office four years ago. They saw their opportunity to smear this office with scandal, and they're doing their damn level-best to connect this administration to the worst terrorist attack in U.K. history. Whether there's any truth to it or not, it will bring suspicion on this office and they'll do all they can to tarnish this administration with innuendo and dubious connections to this horrible disaster."

"Surely not," Hunter shot back. "I can't believe even Kane and his crew would stoop to something so malicious. They're low, but I cannot believe they would try and capitalize on a national tragedy and the death of hundreds of innocent British citizens like that. No one is going to try and draw even the faintest connection between this tragedy and this administration. If they do it, it will be over my dead body," Hunter was jabbing his finger on the Prime Minister's desk as he spoke for emphasis. "Even so," he continued, "I'll mention your thoughts to O'Leary... without mentioning your name of course. We'll let him run down the theory, without linking this administration to the investigation."

"Look, tracking down the bastards that did this – whoever they are – and bringing them to justice are our chief priorities," Wellington was pacing the room now. "We're going to track down and find whoever the asshole is that put that bomb on that train, along with every last member of their wretched terrorist cell, no matter where they are or how long it takes. If it's the last thing I do in this job, we're going to get it done."

"Yes sir," Jeffrey said readily, and LaForge echoed his response.

"Can we trust O'Leary?" Wellington asked.

"Yeah, he's a straight-shooter." Hunter was still tapping his finger on the P.M.'s desk. "He's the best MI6 has got, and I've known him for years. He doesn't care a damn about people's politics or agendas. He's like a dog on the hunt . . . and he won't stop until he tracks down who is behind this. MI6 has put over two hundred agents on this investigation under O'Leary's command. He's not going to be thrown off track by a random name being thrown into the investigation to get us off course. He'll find the bastards who did this. And once he does, we'll put their heads on spikes up at the Tower of London for the world to see."

Wellington clenched his jaw as the stress of the last eighteen hours started to take its toll on him. He had weathered plenty of power struggles in Parliament, an economic recession, half a dozen weather-related catastrophes, a handful of smaller terrorist hits, and a brief insurrection within his own party within the last four years as Prime Minister. This terrorist attack, however, might be what would finally do him in.

For a moment he wondered if he still had it in him to lead the nation through a national emergency of this scale. The job he had set out before him would take up most of his time and attention over the next many months: He'd have to oversee the search and investigation to find the depraved terrorists who killed so many innocent people, manage the political firestorm that would no doubt be unleashed, inform and direct the international response, and most difficult of all, rally the British people to prevail over this national tragedy. There would be plenty of finger pointing all around, with every politician from MP on up trying to put the blame for the tragedy on someone or some group they don't like. There went his list of agenda items he had hoped to get through Parliament. The new course for Britain he had been working on for four years, putting it on track for a seat at the global leadership table for the next century, was now out the window. Certainly, he knew this hour of national disaster would define his administration, but it would take all that was in him to help the country emerge from this national horror. Getting reelected to his position as Prime Minister was now completely uncertain. He turned and looked out the window, and for a brief moment, he just wanted to escape it all.

Turning back to Hunter, he refastened the top button on his white shirt and readjusted his red tie, the one he kept at the office for moments when he needed to look commanding. Outside in the cold December air, ninety-seven news cameras from every top news agency on the planet were trained on the front door of #10 Downing waiting for a news conference with the British Prime Minister. Running his fingers through his dark hair, Wellington grabbed his blue suit jacket and walked steadfastly through the door and down the hall toward the waiting media contingent. Just on his heels, as he had been every step of the last twenty years, Jeffrey Hunter walked lock-step behind the Prime Minister.

These bastards aren't going to succeed in this, Hunter thought to himself as he and Wellington pushed through the front door to face the cameras. We're going to find every last murderer that had anything to do with this. We owe it to the more than four hundred people who died on that train, and I owe it to Andrew.

As Wellington and Hunter stepped in front of the camera, the bright television lights clicked on, and for a brief moment all Hunter could see was the white spots in front of his eyes. Wellington, cool and professional as always, stared directly into the bank of international cameras as he addressed the nation.

"Good evening Citizens of the United Kingdom and to our friends around the world. This morning, a heinous attack was levied not just on the citizens of one country, but against the citizens of all peaceful nations . . . . "

CHAPTER SIXTEEN

Annelise Craig managed to stay in the background as the press conference wound down. The last thing she needed was any extra attention on her this afternoon. She was barely holding it together as it was.

Thankfully, her boss Jeffrey Hunter was too distracted by the weight of responsibilities on his shoulders and managing the crisis to notice her obvious anguish and anxiety. The world was falling apart around her, but Annie was too busy trying to keep herself from collapsing on the floor to deal emotionally with the broader tragedy. She went through the motions of doing everything that was asked of her in her usual professional manner, but inside she was barely keeping her emotions from total meltdown. Now that the press conference was over, she just wanted to finish up anything Jeffrey needed her to do and get the hell out of the office for the evening. She just needed a few minutes to herself to compose her thoughts, deal with the waves of grief, and figure out a way to get through the next few days. Hell, how to get through the rest of her life without him.

Once the television cameras were off and the lights had been loaded back into the trucks, Annie made the rounds through the tenacious newspaper reporters and television correspondents to make sure they had everything they needed, at least for now. Like most members of the political class, Annie had long thought that the press corps was like a pack of dogs. They would chase their prey until you threw them some scraps. They didn't need a lot, just enough to give them something to discuss on their next news clip, to make it look like they were doing their jobs. Once they had their scraps, they would leave you alone, at least for a little while. Annie knew that they were just performing their duties, and that the public had a right to know what was going on, but their tenacity and hunger for details and scraps of news could be exhausting, and she always felt on the defensive with them, as if she'd already done something wrong. The British press were famously intrusive, and Annie did her best to keep them at arm's length.

As soon as the news crews were loaded up and off to update their reports for the wall to wall coverage of the crisis, Annie saw her opportunity to disappear, at least for the night. She looked down at her watch, 8:10 p.m.. She had been at the office for almost fourteen hours straight and had had no sleep for thirty-six hours. Surely, she could leave now. She knocked on Jeffrey's office door and cracked it open. As expected, he was on the phone with the police or one of the other governmental agencies tied up with the investigation, so she gave him a little quizzical look and gesture signaling him that she was planning to leave and wondered if he needed anything else. Jeffrey waved her off, and she was satisfied that it was OK to go.

Gathering up her purse and coat, Annie made her way toward the back of the office suite. The office was still busy with phones ringing and government officials doing their best to help coordinate the recovery operation, but Annie could not function anymore. She had to get out. She would text Jeffrey later and make sure he didn't need her for anything, but for now, she needed to be alone.

Moving down the corridor toward the back exit, she passed Andrew's office door on the left, with the door still shut. With the office in crisis mode, his office had been forgotten for the moment, and no one had probably been in it all day. The investigation was still focused on the rescue and recovery operation, so no one was overly focused on Andrew's death yet. Annie stopped short in front of his door. Turning the handle, she was surprised to find it open.

At this point, all she could think was that she wanted to be with Andrew, the only way she knew how. She opened the door and entered the room quickly, shutting the door quietly behind her. She resisted the urge to lock the door behind her, thinking that would look really bad if someone else tried the door behind her. Her mind always working strategically, she quickly decided that if anyone popped in behind her, she would say that she was looking for any clues to the tragedy that she could turn over to the police. It was a weak but conceivable excuse. In reality, she wanted to be in the only place where she knew she could feel near to him. She wanted to sit in his chair, touch his belongings, look at the framed pictures on his walls and credenza, anything to feel nearer to him right now.

Moving behind his desk, Annie was overwhelmed to see one of his suit jackets lying across the credenza behind his desk. Picking it up, she held it up to her face and breathed in deeply. Oh, so faintly, she could still smell him on the jacket. Musky and sweet, the smell rushed over her and gave her an immediate sense of calm. For a moment, her body told her that he was alive. But her mind and heart knew the truth.

Annie sat down in his chair and laid her hands across the desktop. It was then that the tears started streaming down her face again. Allowing them to fall, she put her head into her hands and let the grief wash over her like a wave. She didn't know how she was going to survive this.

Laying her head on the desk, she sat there for what seemed like an eternity, although it was probably not more than ten minutes or so. When she had composed herself, she methodically started pulling the drawers open, one at a time, and examining their contents. She knew that she probably shouldn't disturb the items in his desk too much -- the police would be in here soon enough and if she was found to have rifled through the desk, it could spark a scandal. But for now, she just wanted to gaze at his belongings. She wanted to see if there was anything left of him in these otherwise innocuous office drawers.

Opening each drawer, she had to smile to herself. Each drawer was meticulously organized, as Andrew was about everything in his life. Files, legal pads, a stapler, old calendars, everything a typical office desk holds. She smiled as she found a tin box of mints in his top drawer, pried it open and popped one into her mouth. He went through these mints like candy, and his breath always smelled like cinnamon as a result. He could be such a kid.

Opening the last drawer, she saw the usual hanging files and fanned her fingers across the tops noticing his perfect print on the labels. *Policy Briefs, Monetary Analysis, Economic Growth Charts* – just the usual boring economic data. She wondered how he found such tedious information so fascinating.

Oddly, she noticed the last file did not have his usual fine lettering on the label. In fact, it was blank. Lifting the file out of the drawer, she noticed it wasn't bulging with data like all the others, it just contained a single sheet of lined paper torn off of one of his legal pads, with his neat handwriting covering one side of the yellow paper.

Across the top line in all caps, were the words *CM TRADES INTO & OUT OF POUND.*

Below was a neat chart, hand drawn with columns across the top, and half a dozen rows of numbers down the page. Across the tops of the columns were the labels: *dates and times, currency valuations into and out of the English Pound and American Dollar markets,* and *percent profits.* And there was a final column that caught her attention: *Events.*

In the events column were six incidents from the last four years that Annie recognized immediately: *Bus bombing at Leicester Square, Assassination attempt on French P.M., Car bomb at Parliament, IED at Piccadilly Circus, Explosion at Stade de France,* and at the bottom, *Train?* The last entry had no date attached.

Annie stared at the list. Each event on the list was an incident she was familiar with and which the Prime Minister's office had been integral in coordinating the investigation. But this wasn't just a simple list of terrorist attacks. Each one was referenced with a value of the British Pound and the Dollar immediately before and after the event – usually not more than a twenty-four or thirty-six hours spread, and an indication of what enormous percent profit had been realized.

What the hell? Annie thought to herself. Andrew was the Prime Minister's chief monetary advisor, but this was something far different than ordinary monetary analysis. This was the value of the British Pound and Dollar in direct correlation with a series of as yet unsolved terrorist attacks here in London, and one in France. The net profits recorded down the page were startling: 47%, 84%, 23%, 104%, 77%.

Annie wasn't a financial expert, but she knew these net profit numbers were astounding.

Yet why was a train incident noted on the list, but without a date, or reference to the value of the pound? Whatever it was, Annie didn't like the looks of it one bit. Why was Andrew tracking the value of two key currencies against a series of random tragedies? Andrew's job was methodical and analytical, but it was also stealthy and highly sensitive. And she instantly knew the Police would be all over this. As she sat staring at the list, her mind trying to make sense of the information, she heard voices in the hall. Instinctively, she closed all the drawers, pushed the chair back into position, and grabbed her coat and purse. Sliding the file into her purse, she waited until the voices had subsided. She waited another moment and then quietly exited the door, noting that no one looked up as she turned down the hall and made her way toward the exit. She just wanted out of there, and fast.

CHAPTER SEVENTEEN

London's Paddington Station was bustling with tourists trying to find their way among the myriad of parallel tracks, students weighted down with backpacks, and British senior citizens shuffling to their trains. Rasul punched the buttons on the ticket machine to purchase his train fare as he had so many times before. His puddle jumper plane from Paris had landed at London's Luton airport early this morning, and he'd called an Uber to deliver him to Paddington Station. Security was tighter than he had ever seen it in the cavernous, drafty train station. London Police were everywhere, posted at the entrance to the station, several along the corridor leading to the trains, and a dozen or more were positioned along the boarding platform along each train. The air was tense, with everyone keeping a close eye on everyone else.

Once his train left the station, in just fifty-six minutes, Rasul would be delivered to the little village that he knew so well. With nothing other than his leather bag, he boarded his train at 9:21 a.m. on Tuesday morning and would be arriving at exactly 10:17. He usually loved this journey – the quaint houses and crumbling storefronts lining the tracks as the train rolled through the outskirts of London, the gentle rocking of the train as it traversed the farms and small villages of Slough and Reading. But today was different. London was different now, and so was Rasul.

Rasul had made this trip at least a hundred times. Back and forth during college: Oxford to London, London back to Oxford. Those trips had been fun and carefree. But not today. Today was all business and Rasul concentrated on the meeting at hand.

As the train pulled into the little station at Oxford, Rasul made his way off the train, through the tangle of students loitering in the station, and out into the brisk cold air and sunshine. He had some time to kill before his meeting, so he strolled down New Road, and onto Queen Street, which transitioned into High Street, with its medieval buildings, churches, and store fronts lining the cobblestone streets. The University was wrapping up its Fall session, so university students and tourists converged on the sidewalks, blocking the path of people like Rasul, who had places to go. He weaved his way down the sidewalk until he found what he was looking for at 131 High Street.

Oxford had always been a magical place for Rasul, just as it was now for all of the thousands of students who lived and studied in its ancient halls and classrooms. Perched on the banks of the Thames, most of its buildings date back to medieval times, and Rasul had always been fascinated by its almost mythical mixture of classic architecture. For centuries, the world's best and brightest had walked the feudal streets of this small village. Future Kings, Queens, Prime Ministers, politicians, actors, poets, scientists, and philosophers had been educated and shaped within the walls of these ancient buildings. As Rasul had felt on his first day at Oxford over twenty years ago, he was still in awe of the history and gravitas of the streets, churches, buildings, classrooms, and even the pubs of this distinguished city.

Rasul had first walked into Chequers Pub as a freshman at Oxford. The pub, housed in a former tenement building dating back to the 1500s, was one of his favorite haunts in college. Its white stone walls and heavy timber rafters were like a haven from the stresses of everyday academic life. He'd spent many an evening at the long wooden tables in the back room, debating political theories and downing pints of the ale and gin. He usually drank so much with his buddies that they typically took turns propping each other up on their way back to their flats at closing time. Most good Muslims would never partake of alcohol. But lucky for Raz, his personal religious practices were a little more flexible, so he ordered a plate of salmon fishcakes and a pint of Pale Ale. It wasn't noon yet, but he had long ago developed a taste for craft beer, regardless of the time of day.

Rasul finished off his fishcakes and drained his pint. He would normally order another, but he needed to keep his head straight today.

He pretended to read the *London Times,* and kept a close eye on the students filing in for an early lunch. Asian, American, European and Indian undergraduates mixed easily with British students who were fortunate enough – or rich enough – to attend the most prestigious university in the world. The elite student body, mixed with the gorgeous architecture combined to produce an almost mythical atmosphere. Oxford is truly a magical place, Rasul thought to himself. But he had changed a lot since he was a student here. Yet he missed the innocence and hope that had inhabited his thoughts when he walked these streets as a student.

At twenty minutes before noon, Raz paid his tab and walked back out onto High Street. Walking briskly back up the street, he turned right onto Cornmarket Street. Cornmarket, once one of the busiest thoroughfares in Oxford, had been converted into a pedestrian walkway just a few years after Rasul and his buddies left this college town. Still lined with six and seven-hundred-year-old buildings, it had been ground zero for so much of his college life, and most of his memories. Raz wound his way along Cornmarket, through the pedestrians and shoppers for three blocks until he reached George Street, passing his old college flat where it still sat perched on the second floor of a 16th Century building. The apartment used to sit positioned above a quaint woolens shop where he would pick up socks and sweaters when the winter snow hit. Today his old flat was situated above a Pret A Manger sandwich shop and a Starbucks. From the looks of things, the building was still offering apartments to let for some fortunate Oxford students.

That apartment held so many memories, Raz thought to himself as he stood below its windows, gazing up at the wavy glass and weathered shutters. Those rooms held happy memories of simpler times and good friends. Raz let his mind wander back for a moment; what had happened to him? He let his mind drift for a moment, and then quickly banished the nostalgia from his mind.

Rasul moved with the crowd down Cornmarket Street, until gradually the shoppers started to thin out. As Raz approached George Street, he could see the back of the building he was looking for at the corner of George and Cornmarket. Circling around the building, he wanted to give it a good once-over before venturing inside. It had been eighteen months since his last visit to this town and this building, and he wanted to scope out the immediate vicinity before going in.

The Oxford Center for Islamic Studies, standing imposingly at the corner of Cornmarket and George streets, was constructed of honey colored stones with gothic spires and pointed arches on the roofline. It wasn't a large building, but had probably been standing alone on this corner for hundreds of years. Circling around to the front, Raz could see that as usual, the building looked dark and quiet. To anyone's glance, they would assume it was closed, devoid of human occupation. Raz made his way to the door, knocked twice, and knowing the routine, stood staring up at the camera that was posted a foot above the door, trained on Raz's face.

After thirty seconds, the door opened, and Raz was greeted by a man dressed head to toe in a white linen tunic and loose fitting pants, his head enshrouded in a white cotton skullcap that fit down around his head. A white beard flowed down across his chest. Raz had never seen this man before, and thought to himself that he might as well have been a ghost. The man said nothing, and Raz quickly realized that his eyes stared blankly toward him. Finally noticing the man's white cane, Rasul quickly realized the obvious. The man was blind.

Following the ghost-like man down the dark, dank hallway, Raz could hear a faint tap, tap, tap, as the man's cane gently hit first the left wall and then the right wall as they moved down the dark corridor. The hallway was very dim, but Raz could see a faint light emanating from a room in the back of the building. He had been in this place before, and he determined that the light was coming from the library at the back of the house. He followed the man in white silently down the corridor, wondering who it was he would be meeting with this time.

Moving into the library, the ghost man waved his cane in the direction of a black leather wing chair in the corner, and Rasul took his seat. The man waited until he heard the sound of the leather creaking as Rasul lowered himself into the chair, and he turned and disappeared back out the door through which they'd just entered. Raz sat and took in the room, not knowing how long he would be kept waiting.

The room had dark oak floors and wide bookshelves lined the circumference. In the opposite corner, several old Islamic manuscripts were framed on the wall, alluding to their importance. Raz had no clue what they said, or meant, and frankly didn't care. Every book and flat surface in the room had a fine layer of dust, and Raz wondered if anyone ever took the time to dust the shelves, or open a window for that matter. The place could use some fresh air.

After what seemed like an eternity, but was probably not more than twenty minutes, a man with black glasses and gray hair whisked into the room and took a chair opposite Rasul. He wasn't wearing any of the garb of a traditional Muslim man, just a simple gray pin-striped suit with a maroon tie. This man was all business. His clothes matched his demeanor, very western and very modern. This wasn't anyone associated with the Islamic Center at all. Rasul was not surprised.

"You did a good job, Rasul. Very professional." The man in the gray suit trained his gaze on Raz.

"Thank you." Rasul copied his serious posture.

"Did you have any problems? How did you manage to get the package on board?"

"It was easy. My old friend Andrew trusted me. I just wrapped it up like a Christmas gift, and he took it with him. I told him it was a clock, but to wait and unwrap it when he was in his home in London. He put it in his overnight bag and boarded the train with it. Of course, I was counting on the fact that being a high ranking official, he would be waved past security."

"And you don't suffer any guilt in killing your friend?"

"A little. But everyone has to die sometime. He had no wife or children depending on him, so it really isn't so bad."

"Excellent. And you have the key?"

"I do."

"Very good. The key fits locker C101 at the train station. You can pick up your package there tomorrow morning before you board your return train for London."

"Good. So, everything worked out as planned for our friends in New York?" Rasul raised his eyebrows, hoping to garner some detail to exactly how well their little plan had worked out for everyone.

"Yes, the plan worked extraordinarily well. You will enjoy your little package tomorrow. We will be in touch." The gray suited man rose from his chair opposite Rasul, shook Rasul's hand, and the man left the room. As usual, Rasul did not know the man's name or how he figured into the big picture, but what did he care? The plan had worked, and he would reap the benefits very soon. Yes, he had to lose a friend in the process, but sometimes people have to die. Rasul refused to think any more about Andrew. It was water under the bridge at this point anyway.

Rasul did not wait for the ghost man to appear again. He hated this place, and he was eager to get out. He made his own way back down the corridor, out the front door, and into the bright afternoon air. There was a chill to the air, and Rasul buttoned up his coat and wrapped his scarf snugly around his throat. So, he would have to spend the day in Oxford after all. But Rasul did not mind. He welcomed having a day to himself in the little city he loved so much.

He hurried down the sidewalk, eager to put distance between the Islamic Center and himself. He thought about what the man had said ... What did he mean about enjoying the little package that would be left for him at the train station? It wouldn't be his money, that was always handled electronically. Maybe a little cash bonus? More than likely the package would contain some information about their next project. It would be several weeks away, months probably, no doubt, but he had an inkling their next job would involve something closer to home in Paris. The prospect sounded good to him.

Rasul turned back onto Cornmarket, and decided to visit some of his old haunts in Oxford. He wanted to see if the little town that had changed him so much, had changed itself at all. Jabbing his hands in his pockets, he moved down Cornmarket, feeling once again like the young student who'd arrived over twenty years ago. The sun was warm on his face, and he pushed thoughts of Andrew Bolling far from his conscious.

CHAPTER EIGHTEEN

Eight o'clock Tuesday morning and John O'Leary had already been at his desk for two hours, rifling through the information that had poured in overnight. Two hundred and thirty bodies had been pulled from the train wreckage at this point, and sadly, the remainder would probably never be accounted for. O'Leary massaged his temples with his fingertips. It was so much death and destruction. In his twenty-seven years in Her Majesty's service, he'd never worked such a devastating crime. But with over two hundred investigators working the investigation, he was certain they would uncover who, or what group, was responsible for the explosion of the Chunnel Train, but in the meantime, it was a horrific job that had to be done.

O'Leary picked up Andrew Bolling's cell phone records and poured over them once again. Right now, the phone call naming Bolling was his best lead, although he couldn't figure out how a number cruncher from the Prime Minister's office could be linked to a terrorist bombing. What on earth would that accomplish? The guy's life seemed as clean as a whistle, but O'Leary's gut was telling him something else. Was this a coincidence that one of the Prime Minister's top advisors was on the train that night? It easily could be. Top officials were always zipping back and forth to Paris, along with a good chunk of the British population. The Chunnel Train had made Paris an easy visit. With just under two hours connecting the two great European cities, the train ran dozens of times a day, and it was almost always full. No unusual situation there.

But the phone call to Jeffrey Hunter's cell phone raised the specter that there could possibly be a link. And right now, it was still O'Leary's best lead. No one, or no group, had claimed responsibility as of yet for the bombing. The phone call to Hunter's phone was his only solid lead for the time being. He would have to take Bolling's life apart and examine it piece by piece before he could eliminate his involvement in this tragic nightmare.

Returning to the cell phone records, he studied the list. He would eventually turn the list over to his investigators for a thorough analysis, but for now, he wanted to take a look himself. Right now, he could only review the list of phone numbers associated with texts and phone calls. He would have to wait a few days for the warrants to be executed for the actual transcripts of the text messages, and of course he would probably never know what was said in the phone conversations, but for now, he had a little to go on.

Reviewing the list, O'Leary noted that on Friday, December 9, there were 147 text messages and seven phone calls from Bolling's cell. Most of the text messages appeared to be sent to members of the Prime Minister's staff, including Jeffrey Hunter; Rex Smythe, Brittan's Home Secretary; Annelise Craig, Jeffrey Hunter's assistant; and the Prime Minister himself. The remaining nine texts went to his mother and his brother in London. The seven phone calls were to most of the same people, plus one extra call to a phone number that was as of yet, unidentified. It appeared to be connected to a French cell phone company.

Saturday, December 10: just eleven texts and two phone calls. The text messages were to the unidentified French number, as well as work associates again, as expected. The two phone calls went to Annelise Craig, the assistant, again.

Sunday, December 11: seven text messages to the unidentified French number and two phone calls to Annelise Craig, again.

Strange, O'Leary thought. The French number would be tracked down in a matter of time. Probably belonged to whomever he was meeting up with in Paris. And the contact with Annelise Craig wasn't too unusual, although a bit. She was probably working on a project for him, chasing down numbers or something. He would need to question her about their ongoing work projects, O'Leary made a mental note.

As O'Leary scanned the list again, his desk phone rang.

"O'Leary . . . ," he said, picking up the receiver.

"John, the preliminary report from the lead investigating team just came in." It was the chief investigator from the Weapons & Explosives Laboratory on the south end of the building.

"Looks like it was an IED, as we guessed, probably homemade," he continued. "Nothing too sophisticated, just explosive material, ball bearings, metal fragments, the usual crap. It looks like a circuit board was attached and probably set off by a timer. The fact that it detonated inside the tunnel at a structurally vulnerable location probably set off a chain reaction, ultimately derailing the train, which resulted in the crash and the ensuing fire and tunnel collapse. It was a relatively simple bomb, but when detonated in just the right circumstances, produced immense damage. Not to mention death."

O'Leary stared down at his desk, letting the information sink in. It was just as he had suspected, damn it, some lunatic extremist. As usual, he thought to himself, the world was being destroyed by maniacs, intent on destroying other people's lives and property. It was madness, and yet it was taking over the world like wildfire. People, and those whose jobs it was to defend them, were increasingly having their lives and their peace shattered by a bunch of madmen. When and how would it ever end? John O'Leary had a few good years left in him, and he was determined to do his best to stop as much of it as he possibly could.

"Do we have any idea how it got on the train?"

"I'm afraid not, not yet," came the investigator's predictable response.

"Does the bomb lend any clues as to who made it . . . where it came from? Do we have anything to go on for suspects at this point?" John already knew what the answer would be to his question.

"I'm afraid not yet. I've got twenty-seven people working on it around the clock. We should have a pretty good idea in a matter of hours."

"OK, thank you. Just send me the preliminary report on the bomb when you have it." John hung up the phone.

Returning to Bolling's cell phone report, he picked up his phone again and called Dennis Fischer, his second in command for the overall investigation. "Dennis, I've got Bolling's cell phone report here. Bring your entire team in here and let's go over this report. There are a couple of red flags we're going to need to chase down. It all looks innocent enough, but I've got a hunch there's more here than meets the eye."

O'Leary put down his phone and studied the report once again. Picking his phone back up, he called the Prime Minister's office on Downing Street. "Jeffrey Hunter's office please, John O'Leary here."

After a few moments, "Good morning, John, how can I help you?" came Hunter's stock greeting.

"Good morning, Jeffrey. I'm going to need a couple of things this morning. First, I'm going to need access to Andrew Bolling's office. I can get a warrant if you like, or you can just assist me with access. Secondly, I need to visit with your assistant Annelise Craig – this morning, if it is convenient."

CHAPTER NINETEEN

Access to Andrew's office? Today? Jeffrey Hunter was taken aback. From the moment Andrew's name had been mentioned on that ridiculous cryptic phone call he received, Jeffrey knew that Andrew would be dragged into this ugly mess somehow. But the fact that they seemed to be focusing on Andrew at this early stage seemed like a colossal waste of time and manpower at this critical point. There were terrorists that had just committed one of the worst mass killings in history, and yet the chief investigative team wanted to waste time looking through Andrew's desk.

"Of course we want to cooperate with the investigation in any way we can, Agent O'Leary, but it just seems to me to be an enormous waste of time at this point to be chasing down a trusted government servant who was unfortunate enough to be in the wrong place at the wrong time." The fact that Jeffrey had reverted to using John O'Leary's formal title revealed his apparent irritation with the way the investigation was focusing on his friend and work associate.

"Mr. Hunter, we've narrowed down the actual origin of your phone call to within a few blocks' radius in Paris. The fact that it originated in an area with several known potential terrorist cells is a fact of utmost concern to us at this point. We're going to start with your Mr. Bolling until we can rule him out. But as it stands, this is our best lead at the moment." O'Leary was now matching Jeffrey's annoyed tone.

"Now, will I need to seek a search warrant, or will you make his office available?" O'Leary was growing increasingly impatient with Hunter's government-standard lack of cooperation.

"No, no, of course... it's yours. I'm sure Andrew had nothing to hide. Just let me know what time you'll be here, and we will make sure you have access to whatever you need."

Jeffrey Hunter pinched the top of his nose between his eyes, the usual signal that he was nearing the end of his rope. The fact that MI6's investigation was currently centered on one of the top people in the Prime Minister's administration was not what he wanted to deal with right now. Let alone the fact that the man at the focus of the attention was also one of his closest friends. He wanted to give O'Leary whatever he wanted, and then get him the hell out of his office. This was nonsense.

"And, Ms. Craig? Is she available this morning as well?" O'Leary was used to getting his way.

"Of course. I'll have her clear her schedule when you arrive." Hunter glanced out toward Annelise's desk and saw her empty chair pushed under her desk. Where in the hell was she?

It was 8:35 a.m. and Annelise was just pulling into her usual parking space behind #10 Downing. It was a full thirty-five minutes past her normal arrival time, but she was doing the best she could. In spite of the fact that she was operating on almost no sleep, she'd spent most of last night lying awake, going over the hand-written chart she'd found in Andrew's desk in her head. What could Andrew have possibly been recording on this hand-scrawled chart that seemed to record all the major terrorist hits in Britain and France over the last several years? Other than the normal concern of any British government official who was involved with global affairs, he had never mentioned any particular apprehension about terrorism on British soil, and certainly not French soil. Perhaps this was some routine analysis to do with his job. But why the cryptic mention of a train at the bottom of the list? This was the telltale fact that bothered her the most, the detail for which she had no plausible explanation.

Arriving at her desk a few moments later, she saw Jeffrey give her an exasperated look. Arriving late on a day with so much going on in the office did not look good. But at this point, just putting one foot in front of the other was an accomplishment. She mustered up a slight smile and wave for Jeffrey and mouthed "Sorry" with a slight grimace. She had been Jeffrey Hunter's right hand person for far too long for him to hold this slight indiscretion against her.

Annie slid her purse in her bottom drawer and hung her coat in the small closet opposite her desk. Turning around, she saw Jeffrey Hunter headed her way.

"Annie, John O'Leary was just on the phone. They're chasing down some of the early leads on this bombing, and for whatever reason, they're focusing on that ridiculous phone call I received yesterday morning. They want access to Andrew's office, and for some reason they want to talk to you as well, probably because of how closely you worked with him."

Annie could feel the blood draining from her face, but she managed to keep a tight smile in place as she took in Jeffrey's words. "No problem. When do they want to talk to me?"

"Actually, I think they're on their way over here now. I'm sure there's nothing to worry about. When they arrive, will you show them back to Andrew's office and make sure the door is open and everything is available for their review? He told me they will not be removing any items at this point. They just want a quick look through. I want you to stay with them as well, to confirm they don't stick their noses where they shouldn't and to make sure they don't remove anything from his office. If they decide they're keenly interested in anything, they're going to have to come back with a warrant."

"Absolutely, no problem," Annie managed to say.

It most certainly was a problem. *Damn, this is bad,* Annie thought. It now dawned on her that the act of removing that file had now been elevated to removing evidence in an investigation. If she had the file with her, she could quietly and easily go back and slide it back into position. But right now, the file was carefully positioned on the dusty shelf above her television, behind a stack of books. It was too late for retrieving and replacing the file. She had tampered with evidence from a national security investigation into a terrorist plot. Not to mention, she also happened to be having an affair with the man currently at the center of the investigation.

Annie's head was spinning. Somehow, she had done wrong, and she wasn't sure at what point she had crossed the line. She sat down at her desk and pretended to be busy as the minutes ticked by, just waiting for an investigation team from the country's top foreign intelligence service to arrive and question her. She didn't have to wait long.

At 10:25 a.m., the front doors of #10 opened, and she could clearly hear the clicking of news reporters' cameras as they snapped away shots of Agent John O'Leary arriving at the Prime Minister's office. O'Leary was all business, and didn't even pause to look in the direction of the cameras. Right behind him, his usual entourage of investigators walked in synch. Today, for the first time, they carried cameras of their own, along with thick file boxes. Obviously, they were not here to simply chat.

"Mrs. Craig, it's good to see you again, would you mind letting Mr. Hunter know we are here?"

"Yes, of course," Annie said breezily, and moved across the floor to tap on Jeffrey's door. "Mr. Hunter, Officer O'Leary is here to see you."

"I actually think they're here to see you, Annelise," Hunter said as he emerged from his office and crossed the floor to shake hands with the officer. "Good morning gentlemen."

"Annie, if you'll please take these men back to Andrew's office and make sure they have whatever they need," Hunter said with a businesslike demeanor. "You will also have privacy to talk there as well. Please let me know if you need anything else from me while you're here. We are at your service, as usual." Hunter's deadpan glare made his irritation evident. But with all of the European press just steps outside his door, he could not risk appearing to be uncooperative with MI6's lead terrorism investigator. It was politics as usual.

CHAPTER TWENTY

To Annie's surprise, the investigative team was not in Andrew's office for long. They rifled through his desk, took photographs of the desktop, his credenza, his bookshelves and even the pictures on his desk. After a cursory glance through his files, O'Leary ordered the men to collect the files and other government-owned file storage. They removed all of his files, along with his calendar and schedule book, and stuffed them into a large square leather briefcase that looked more like a suitcase. Annie was too stunned to remember Hunter's words about alerting him if they tried to remove anything from the office. She simply stared at the officers as they worked, while her mind worked to assemble a plausible narrative of exactly what her relationship with Andrew entailed. What could she say that would reveal nothing, yet not put her in jeopardy of lying to a government investigator? They unplugged his desktop computer and placed it in a large cardboard box marked *evidence*, keyboard and all. For a moment her mind raced ... was there anything that linked her to an office affair on that computer?

She and Andrew had always been extraordinarily careful to not email or communicate via the office communications system or email about anything other than ordinary office business. Andrew's office computer should be clean of any incriminating evidence that would link Annie to an elicit office affair. Now, Andrew's cell phone was an entirely different matter, but right now, that cell phone would be buried seventy-five meters below the seafloor in a collapsed tunnel.

But even as she told herself this over and over, her heart raced at the thought that some tiny incriminating piece of information might be hidden within the guts of that computer that would blow her whole world wide open – as if it hadn't been already. Her breathing grew shallow and she knew her face must be pale as she watched the team gather up most of the remaining pieces of Andrew's life and haul them out of the office.

As the team wrapped up its work, O'Leary asked Annelise to take a seat. As she lowered herself into the blue suede wingback chair across from Andrew's desk, O'Leary pulled out Andrew's desk chair and rolled it around the desk so that he could face Annie without any obstacles between them. Annie hated seeing O'Leary in that chair. She hated seeing anyone in that chair except for her beloved Andrew. She felt her jaws tighten as she worked to appear at ease and casual about the whole scenario playing out in front of her.

As O'Leary began pulling out his notes to begin the questioning, his team of investigators gathered behind him. Half a dozen men positioned themselves along the wall behind their chief. One man in a long gray coat pulled up another side chair, took out a laptop computer, placed it carefully on his knees, and appeared to be taking notes. Annie suddenly felt like a dying animal with a flock of vultures looking on, just waiting on her to give up or die. She suddenly wondered if she should have insisted on having an attorney there with her, but she knew that would make her look guilty as hell. She was just going to have to play the part of naïve assistant, and do it well. She crossed her legs, trying to appear casual, and leaned back in the chair. She pasted a small smile on her face and tried to appear helpful and cooperative, although in reality she felt anything but.

O'Leary began, "Ms. Craig, I know that everyone in this office is intensely busy right now, but we appreciate you taking time out of your schedule to talk with us this morning. As you know, this is not a formal investigation of any type. We are here simply trying to piece together some loose ends after Mr. Bolling's name was mentioned in a suspicious phone call that was received by Mr. Hunter on the morning after the terrorist bombing."

"Yes, I'm aware of all of that. I'm not sure I can be of any help," Annie gave the officer her best blank look.

"Perhaps not, but you probably know as much about Andrew Bolling's official work here at the Prime Minister's office as anyone," O'Leary forged ahead. Annie nodded with a polite smile.

"Can you tell us what the nature of Mr. Bolling's work was with the P.M.'s office, and any special projects he might have been currently working on?"

"He's an Economic Analyst and advisor for Mr. Wellington's administration. Their friendship goes back to their time at Oxford. Mr. Bolling was a key architect of the P.M.'s economic policy and advised him on all things related to the British economy, and the strength of the British pound overseas. Basically, he was a number cruncher. Always studying charts and analyzing trends. Real boring stuff, but I guess very important."

"I see." O'Leary jotted down something on his notepad, and the man in the gray coat behind him tapped away on his laptop computer. "Was he working on any special projects at the time of his tragic death?"

"Not that I know of," Annie shook her head for emphasis, eager to play up the naïve assistant angle.

"OK, I see," O'Leary glanced back at his notes, and made a face.

"So, I notice that Mr. Bolling made several phone calls to you from his cell phone over the weekend that he was in Paris. Can you tell me what those calls were regarding?" O'Leary quickly looked up at Annelise to watch her reaction to the latest question.

"Oh really?" Annie tried to appear surprised and confused, but she knew her acting skills probably weren't passing muster with this crew.

"Um . . . let me see." Annie looked across the office and studied the portrait on the wall of Winston Churchill that had probably hung there for decades. She studied the line of dust along the ridge on the frame, and wondered how long it had been since anyone had dusted the old portrait. Annie had never been a good liar, and right now, her head was spinning with a dozen different potential answers she could offer the investigator, all with varying degrees of truthfulness and believability.

"Ms. Craig?" O'Leary was becoming impatient with Annie's short answers and her seeming lack of information.

"Oh, I'm sorry, I was just trying to remember what it was we must have been discussing . . . ." In reality, her mind was swimming with the little comments and laughter they had shared during the few calls he made to her on his weekend in Paris. She remembered what he told her about how Raz was acting distant, and about how disappointed he was that Charlie and Jorge had backed out at the last minute of their little Paris reunion weekend. She remembered his funny story about how Raz was acting so serious, but had forgotten and left his coat in a men's room in a Paris restaurant, causing them to have to run in the rain back to the restaurant to retrieve it. She could still hear his laughter as he retold the story about how dripping wet they had become.

"Ma'am?" O'Leary slammed his notebook shut.

"Oh, I'm sorry. Um... I think he was just asking about some numbers I had pulled for him regarding the value of the pound overseas. I guess he was trying to get a little work in while he was in Paris. He was kind of a workaholic like that, I guess."

"Ok that's about all for today, Ms. Craig," O'Leary stood up and started stuffing his notepad and papers into his leather bag. The cadre of men behind him began to file out of the office, and Annie knew she had not given them anything they wanted to hear. It would have to be enough she thought to herself. They weren't getting anything else from her. This was all a fool's errand anyway. Andrew had been viciously murdered along with more than four hundred other innocent people. Why were they here, and not out looking for the terrorists?

O'Leary stopped on his way out the door and shook hands again with Hunter. Giving a gruff, "Thank you, Mr. Hunter, we'll be in touch," he was out the door. He positioned himself into the back seat as his team loaded their boxes and bags into the back end of their black Chevrolet Suburban. Slamming the doors, they pulled away from #10 Downing and headed back toward Vauxhall to plan their next step.

As the black SUV pulled away from the P.M.'s office, O'Leary turned toward the gray coat investigator and announced what was already obvious to everyone in the car.

"She's lying."

CHAPTER TWENTY-ONE

Jeffrey glanced at his watch, 11:20 a.m. He wondered how long O'Leary and his crew would keep Annie back in Andrew's office grilling her for information. This was crazy. There was no way in hell Andrew Bolling was involved in this disaster in any way, shape, or form. O'Leary was chasing a thin lead because he had nothing else to go on. Until a group claimed responsibility, the investigation turned up some evidence, or someone came forward with a stronger lead, they would just have to cooperate and put up with O'Leary's team putting them under the microscope.

At that moment, O'Leary and his group emerged from Andrew's office and made their way down the long corridor toward the front door. O'Leary stopped to shake hands with Jeffrey, but had very little to say.

"Thank you, Mr. Hunter. We've got all we need for now. We'll be in touch."

O'Leary was out the door before Hunter could quiz him on any new information about the investigation, or if they had any new leads. O'Leary was too smart to ever reveal too much, and Hunter knew he would get very little out of him today.

With O'Leary gone, Hunter wheeled around looking for Annie. Her desk was vacant, and there was no sign of her in the lobby or halls. From his vantage point, he could see through almost to the back of the offices, and there was no Annie in sight. He wanted to know from her what O'Leary was looking into, so he went to find her.

Glancing around as he walked toward the back of the building, there was no trace of his assistant, but he could feel eyes on him. The staff knew who O'Leary was and why he had been there. Damn, this place was worse than Fleet Street when it came to office gossip and rumors. Still, Annie wasn't showing her face.

Stopping in front of Andrew's door, he turned the handle – locked. What the hell? Why was this door suddenly locked?

Trying the door knob once more, he suddenly heard something coming from inside the office – a soft sound like a whimper or a moan. He looked around, no one was currently paying any attention, or at least they were hiding their interest very well.

Knocking softly, Jeffrey was annoyed that his assistant might be holed up in the office.

"Annie?" he said quietly through the door.

Inside, the noise stopped. In a few seconds, the doorknob turned, and the door slowly opened a few inches. Jeffrey was bewildered to see Annie's face, tear-streaked, looking back at him through the narrow opening.

"Annie, what's going on? Are you OK?"

For a moment, Jeffrey was completely baffled at what could have upset his assistant like this. But in an instant, he realized that with the terrorist bombing and their good friend dying, he had been suppressing his own feelings for two days now, and he shouldn't be surprised that some were beginning to crack under the pressure.

"I'm sorry Jeffrey, come in."

Annie stepped back and pulled the door open another two feet. Jeffrey stepped in, feeling a little awkward to be intruding on Annie's private breakdown.

"No, I'm sorry to intrude. I just wanted to check on you – to see if O'Leary let on to what direction he's taking this investigation, or anything else I need to be aware of."

"Oh, no, nothing. I mean there's nothing new. They took Andrew's files and his computer. I guess you gave them permission to do that. They took pictures of a lot of his belongings and the contents of his desk. This is just all so absurd. I don't know why they're wasting their time on Andrew. There are terrorists out there planning their next attack on all of us, and the chief investigators for the British government are in the Prime Minister's office photographing a desk. It's just ridiculous."

Annie's grief was now turning to anger... Anger at O'Leary, anger at MI6, anger at the British government, anger at Andrew for being on the stupid train in the first place, and right now, anger at herself for getting so wrapped up in an extra-marital affair, and entangled in this horrible mess.

Suddenly, Jeffrey Hunter slammed his hand on the desktop with such force that it stung, and his face went red with anger.

"Damn it! O'Leary told me they wouldn't remove anything today. He intentionally led me to believe they wouldn't take anything so that they could get in here and rifle through his office before we could look everything over. Since it's all subject to open records, I couldn't have stood in his way, but I damn sure could've delayed it. This has already gone way too far!"

"I'm so sorry Jeffrey, I totally forgot you told me to let you know if they tried to remove anything. I guess with everything going on, I dropped the ball."

Jeffrey went back to clenching his jaw, too angry and frustrated to say anything more about the computer and files.

"Annie, why did O'Leary want to question you? What in the hell did he think you could shed light on?"

"I don't know. Right now, I'm just feeling a little sick over everything." About this, Annie wasn't lying. Her stomach had begun to churn again and she felt again like she might be sick. Her neck was so stiff from anxiety that she could hardly turn her head.

"Everything's crazy around here right now, but we don't have time to fall apart. I'll call O'Leary and find out exactly what the hell he thinks he's doing. Take some time to compose yourself, and I'll see you later this afternoon. We need to go over the updates from the recovery operation and get ready for the next press briefing this afternoon."

"Ok. Thanks." Annie grabbed a Kleenex off the credenza and dabbed at the corners of her eyes where she knew mascara was probably making its way down her cheek. She had to get hold of herself. As Jeffrey turned to exit the office, Annie suddenly felt an overwhelming urge to tell someone – not everything, but something.

She just needed someone to understand what she was feeling. Someone to share some of the load of the grief she was carrying around.

"Jeffrey... we've worked together a long time. I consider you a friend, and not just my boss."

"Thanks, Annie, I feel the same way," Jeffrey gave her a quick smile and reached out to give her a hug. It was not his normal manner for the office, but nothing around the office was normal anymore.

"There's something I'd like you to know, as a friend, and in confidence."

"Of course."

Annie turned and faced the desk, looking away from Jeffrey. She could not bear to see his face when he heard whatever it was she was about to say. And she hadn't entirely decided what that was going to be just yet . . . .

She took a deep breath. "I hate to tell you this, but over the past few months, Andrew and I had grown very close."

"Okay..." Jeffrey held his breath. He couldn't believe what Annie was saying.

"We were very close friends. Well, maybe more than that."

"I see." Jeffrey was in shock. What the hell was she saying? They'd been carrying on an affair? His close friend and his assistant? Right here beneath his nose? Fury rushed over him, but he remained outwardly calm, breathing slow measured breaths.

"Annie, are you telling me you were having an affair?"

Annie was horrified at what she had already said. What was she doing? This wasn't going to solve anything and it wouldn't bring Andrew back. It was only going to make matters worse – in fact, she already felt much worse.

"Oh no, no, no. It wasn't an affair. Nothing sexual, or anything like that! There's no way. We both knew the repercussions of anything like that. No, it was more emotional. We had just become very, very close. Probably too close. My husband would be devastated. Jeffrey, please tell me this will remain confidential."

Jeffrey stared at the back of her head, doubting her story. But right now, he didn't want to know any more. He never wanted to know any more. This wasn't his business, and for both personal and professional reasons, he never wanted to hear more about this. It was a closed subject, as far as he was concerned.

"I understand. Yes, of course. This goes no further. I'm very sorry for your loss. I guess I understand now why you've been unusually upset over this whole thing. This stays between us. Please tell no one else."

"I have no intention of ever telling anyone. I know you loved Andrew too, as a friend. I just needed to tell someone."

"Of course."

Finally, Annie turned back around and Jeffrey could see fresh tears streaking down her face. With this, he understood that indeed, Annelise Craig had loved their friend as well, but in a very different way than the college buddy friendship he and Andrew had shared.

Well damn, this changes everything, Jeffrey thought to himself. He gave Annie a quick hug – not very professional he knew, but he awkwardly didn't know what else to do – and bolted from the room. He was angry, confused, and irritated, all at the same time. He didn't have time for this nonsense. He made a beeline back to his office and before he realized what he was doing, slammed the door behind him.

CHAPTER TWENTY-TWO

Rasul made his way down Cornmarket Street, now feeling much lighter than he had earlier this morning. He was glad that his meeting at the Islamic Center was over, and he could have a little fun. He eyed the pretty co-eds shopping along the pedestrian boulevard, and thought again how much he missed college, with its languid days and crazy nights. It was seriously the best time of his life, he thought to himself.

As he approached the building that had housed his old college apartment, Raz couldn't resist the nostalgia he felt for his college days. The Starbucks on the first floor was bustling with business, and the warm pungent aroma of coffee wafted out the doors every time a customer entered or exited. Next to the coffee shop, he eyed the small side door that allowed entrance to the staircase leading to the apartments above. He tried the narrow door and found it unlocked. The lock was probably broken, he thought to himself, much like it had been for most of the years he lived in the upstairs flat with Andrew and their roommates. He took a risk and quietly walked up the tiny staircase that rose from the small grubby alcove. Each step he took up the rickety staircase made its own unique creak or squeak to announce his ascension up the stairs. Hopefully, no one in the building was home, and he could poke around without causing a commotion.

Throwing caution to the wind, at the top of the stairs, he gave two quick knocks on the door of this old apartment. Thinking better of his actions, he turned and started to make a fast retreat back down the stairs. Just as he started to descend the staircase, he heard the door open, and a dark headed student that looked to be of Indian descent stuck his head out the door. He'd obviously woken the young man up, and in an instant, Raz regretted his entry into the building.

"Yeah?" The sleepy student was fumbling with his glasses, and eyeing Raz with an irritated gaze.

"Oh, I'm sorry to disturb you. I was just . . . um . . . looking for someone. Well, actually, I was just looking at the building. I used to live here. This was actually my apartment a hundred years ago."

Raz gave the student a small smile, half expecting a happy homecoming welcome back to his old stomping grounds.

"Oh, yeah, cool." The Indian student was tired and unimpressed.

Raz turned to go, and then on a whim, spun back around. "Um, would you mind if I just looked around for a second? For old times' sake? I'll only be a minute . . . . "

"Um, yeah, I guess so," the student shrugged, and opened the door a bit wider. He was too groggy to care what the middle-aged Middle Eastern guy did. The young man looked to be in his mid-twenties, probably a graduate student, Raz thought.

Raz made his way into the dark apartment and waited for his eyes to readjust from the bright sunlight outside. The apartment was strewn with clothes, books, pizza boxes, and discarded plastic cups all over the place, much as it had been for most of the two years Raz had lived here. Raz could see that the two-bedroom apartment seemed to be occupied by only one occupant, as the second bedroom looked sparse and largely vacant, with nothing but a bed and bare mattress visible from the doorway.

Raz walked over to the window and looked out at the exact same view he had looked over twenty-odd years ago. Below, he could see the old roofs of the ancient buildings on Cornmarket, with their colorful roof gardens and patios. Beyond, he could see the Thames River as it meandered along the edges of town, and wound its way around on through the countryside. For a moment he felt transformed and was looking at the view with the same eyes he had had as a young, naïve student, looking over his own little corner of the world for the first time.

He thanked the young man and made a hasty exit from the building, before the student completely woke up and threw the middle-aged stranger out of his small apartment.

In a moment, he was back on the street, heading south. He decided to walk toward the university and wander through some of his favorite buildings in the world, so he made a quick left onto Market Street, which transitioned into the campus at Brasenose Lane. It was all exactly as it had been for hundreds of years, like a mythical city, surrounded by surreal buildings. Rasul Aziz loved every square inch of it.

As he entered Radcliffe Square, he gazed up at the majestic Radcliffe Camera, its round edifice still rising like a cathedral on the university lawn. As usual, students and tourists strolled around the grassy square, oblivious to the hundreds of years of history that had taken place in the shadow of the magnificent structure. Radcliffe was a gorgeous library and had been standing here since the mid-1700s in all of its glory. It was all just as he remembered it, and he was mesmerized by the beauty of all of it.

Crossing Catte Street he approached the wrought-iron gates of All Souls College and walked up to the magnificent gilded gates that stood sentry at the entryway. He pressed his face to the cold black and gold iron and peered through to the expansive green lawn and twin spires of All Souls Quadrangle. Something about these gates, and the entrancing view, had always drawn him. He had gazed through their black and gold vines and arches a thousand times, peering through at the Gothic structure across the lawn that dated back to the 1700s.

Stretching out in front of the glorious buildings was the pristine green lawn, usually devoid of human inhabitants. Rasul had always thought that looking through these gates, with his face pressed to the iron like a little child looking through a storefront window, was like staring into a medieval still life painting. Today, as always, the gates were locked tightly shut, only allowing passersby a small window into the ethereal world.

Rasul had often thought that looking through these gates was a lot like how he felt going through life. He could always look at the pristine world of the British high society around him, almost touch it in fact, but he could never really be a part of it. He had done everything he was supposed to in life, and he had the impressive academic resume to prove it. He was smart enough to be admitted to Oxford on a full scholarship, allowed to have a small taste of what life was like on the inside of British aristocracy, but he was always an outsider, never truly a part of this world. It was an inaccessible dream. He knew he would never have the connections or networks to truly gain entrance to this upper crust British life, but his fascination with the place was something more. Something he had never been able to put his finger on. So just as he had as an undergraduate, he stood at the gates and peered through at the unattainable world beyond.

Raz spent most of the rest of the day trolling the streets of Oxford, eating dinner in another pub, and watching football in a sports bar over several more pints of local beer. Growing tired, he knew he would need to find a cheap place to sleep for the night before his early departure and return train to London and then back home tomorrow. Before finding a hotel, Raz decided to stop by the train station and check out locker C101. He knew it would be empty tonight, but was confident that sometime in the wee hours of the morning, a package would be left for him, contents still unknown. He would just find the locker tonight, check his key, and then find a place to lay his head for the night.

Fifteen minutes later, he entered the busy train station and looked around for the locker area. Enquiring at the information desk, he was directed down the staircase and into a damp basement area that smelled of mold and dirty clothes. As he made his way down into the smelly basement space, he thought to himself that it seemed no one had been down here in months, maybe years. Why would they choose this rat hole of a space to drop his package? Why not just hand it to him this morning or deliver it to his bookshop? The methods of those in his group were getting strange indeed.

Once in the dingy basement, he found rows of rusty lockers, and a cement floor lined with trash, dirty solitary socks, and empty food bags. Looking around, he spotted C101 and tried his key. Weirdly, the key wouldn't slide into the lock. Turning it upside down, he tried it again, only this time to have it stick in the lock. He tried to force it out, but no luck. Banging on the lock, and pulling with all of his might did nothing. It was stuck as if it were soldered awkwardly into place. It wasn't budging. He went back upstairs and complained at the information desk, but was told they would report the problem to maintenance. Irritated and tired, Raz determined he had no choice but to return to the Islamic Center for instructions. He was frustrated at the incompetence of his liaisons, but realized he had no alternatives. Leaving the train station, he turned north, determined to cut through the more modern neighborhoods of Oxford, taking a short cut to the Islamic Center.

It was growing dark as Rasul descended the stairs in front of the modern station, and the evening crowd closed in around him. Suddenly, he felt the jostle of someone right behind him, moving against him at the foot of the stairs. Always on guard against pickpockets, Rasul shifted quickly away as he glanced back over his right shoulder at the man bearing down on him.

Rasul heard the quiet "Whusssshhhh" of the silencer before he felt the hot ripping of the bullet as it entered his body. In an instant, he realized he'd been hit. Sinking to his knees, he felt the intense deep pain in his right side as the bullet wedged between his ribs. With horror, he looked down at his white shirt as a bright red circle of blood spread across the cloth, the shirt soaking up his blood in an almost perfect circle, just below his right shoulder. His head hit the ground with a thud as pain ripped through his body.

Laying flat on the ground, with his head at an unnatural angle, Rasul looked up overhead at the dim Oxford sky as he hit the ground, and caught sight of the face of the Ghost Man's white robes billowing in the winter breeze as he darted quickly away. His eyes no longer appearing blank, the Ghost Man glared directly at Rasul, confirming he had hit his target. Darkness closed in around him, and the sound of the crowd's shrieks and murmurs grew faint. His head cocked awkwardly on the pavement, Rasul's eyes were transfixed on the site of Oxford's ancient street. A panic broke out among those in front of the station, and he could see the crowd separate around him, moving back, away from him as he lay gasping on the pavement. He heard a lady scream and then a man's voice as he yelled for someone to call the police. As he hovered on the edge of blackness, Rasul could hear the bells of Tom's Tower ringing out in the distance – 101 strikes of the bell, just as it did every night at exactly this time, 21:05 sharp, Oxford time.

CHAPTER TWENTY-THREE

Annie stood motionless as the sound of Jeffrey's office door slamming reverberated through the offices of #10 Downing. Her head pounding, she realized that she had just made a huge mistake. Jeffrey Hunter was the epitome of professionalism and decorum. He was her friend, but was not necessarily her close friend, and she didn't really know how far she could trust him to protect her. And now she had just told him the biggest secret of her life. Had she said too much? Would he be able to read into her words and see the reality of the situation? Had Andrew ever told him anything? Her legs were weakening from the pain of everything that had happened, and she thought she might just collapse right there on Andrew's office floor.

Annie had to get some air. She had to get out of the building, at least for a while. The grief of losing Andrew, and now the knowledge that she'd just let the truth slip out to her boss was just too much for her to bear at the moment. She needed space and time to think. Glancing down at her watch, it was now 11:40, close enough to lunch. She bolted for the back door.

In ten minutes, she was speeding down Victoria Road in her red Volvo. At a stoplight, she decided she'd better text Jeffrey and cover for her hasty exit. With everything still going crazy at the office, this was a terrible time to be gone, but some things just could not be helped. She had to get out of there.

Pulling up Jeffrey's name on her phone, she typed out a quick message. *"Took an early lunch to take care of an important errand. Be back soon."* She pressed send.

Driving east along Victoria Drive, she passed by Victoria Station and had to swerve to avoid hitting some self-absorbed Americans standing in the middle of the intersection snapping selfies. *Damn tourists.* Turning right onto Grosvenor Place, she decided to head toward Hyde

Park. She would park and walk for a few minutes, get some air, and give herself some time to think. Everything was crashing down in her mind, and she didn't know how much more she could take.

Her phone dinged, and she looked down to see a text from her husband, Richard.

"Hey, honey, how's your day? Don't forget I have that meeting tonight. Be home about 9. Love you."

Annie cringed at the text, and a wave of guilt washed over her. For a brief moment she actually let her thoughts focus on Richard, as she so rarely did. She loved Richard, she did. Just not in the same way she had loved Andrew. She hated lying to him, cheating on him. It would crush him to know that she had fallen in love with another man, and yet she never wanted to hurt Richard. She didn't want any of this. And now Andrew was gone. He would no longer be a factor in her life. Maybe she could fix it . . . . Fix her marriage, and her whole life. She just didn't know how. Maybe she could put all of this behind her, put Andrew behind her. She would repair the damage to her marriage and focus her future on Richard. Maybe she should get pregnant....

At that moment, she suddenly felt a tremendous jolt to her car. Now traveling down Knightsbridge, she was driving only about 40 mph, but suddenly her car lurched forward, and for a moment she struggled to regain control of the steering wheel. Swerving left and right, she barely missed a row of compact cars parked at the entrance to Hyde Park, and heard her tires squeal as she fought to get back in her narrow lane.

At that moment, she felt another hard bump from the rear of the vehicle. Again, she momentarily lost control and realized for the first time that someone had somehow bumped into the back of her car as she motored along Knightsbridge.

"What the hell?" she said out loud as she once again brought the car under control. Angrily glaring through her rearview mirror, she searched for the drunk or hapless idiot who was driving like a lunatic. She could see nothing but a teenage girl in a little yellow Volkswagen just ahead in the lane beside her as she slowed to a stop at the red light at Knightsbridge and Queen's Gate. Surely that little blonde girl wasn't the culprit. One glance had told her that the girl seemed more interested in her radio than anything around her, and besides, Annie doubted the little Volkswagen could have hit her that hard.

As she waited for the light to turn green at the next intersection, suddenly Annie felt a third hard blow from behind. Her car skidded forward again, this time a good ten feet into the intersection. Her head hit the steering wheel hard and she was dazed as she noticed the little yellow Volkswagen speed away in her peripheral vision. And then she saw him.

In the rearview mirror, she realized in shock what had hit her. A large black BMW sedan loomed large in her mirror. She could see the little BMW hood ornament was hanging loose from its wired footing, now dangling from the repeated hits. As she sat stunned, staring at the BMW in her rearview mirror and trying to make sense of what had happened, a large, bald man wearing a long black coat emerged from the driver's door, and was moving quickly into the intersection toward her car. Her first thought was that he was coming to talk to her about their collision, maybe to check on her and exchange insurance information if necessary. But the look on his face was menacing, which didn't add up. As she stared in her rearview mirror in confusion trying to figure out what was going on, she saw the flash of metal in the bald man's hand. She studied the hard black outline against his tan gloves, and in a moment, realized he was holding a black handgun. The bald man was looking right and left as he darted through the intersection, moving quickly toward her driver's side of the car.

Instinctively, Annie pressed the gas pedal to the floor, and her Volvo almost lifted off the ground. She raced away from the intersection and drove as fast as she could, too afraid to even check the rearview mirror. Speeding past Hyde Park, she reached the A4204 and took a hard right, disappearing into traffic. She had to get the hell out of the area.

After a few minutes, and with her heart still racing, she made a quick left onto Notting Hill Gate and another quick right onto Pembridge Road then Annie drove into the small, quaint residential streets of Notting Hill. She slowed her speed, and it was not until then that she dared look into the rearview mirror. No one was in sight. She pulled to the side of the street and waited to see if any cars turned down the narrow lane lined with parked cars. No one came. She had lost the bald man in the BMW. But she was scared to death.

As she sat on the side of Pembridge Road, her car parked against the curb between a white Audi and a black Mercedes, she could no longer hold everything in. She sat with her face in her hands, tears washing down her face and her mascara streaming down her cheeks, as the sobs came in waves. First the horrible terrorist attack where hundreds of people had died, then realizing she'd lost Andrew, MI6 questioning her, and now this. Who was the bald man and why was he after her – first hitting her car, and then coming after her with a gun? Was it another case of random road rage or what? Why would someone attempt to shoot her? What the hell was going on?

Annie thought about the file she'd taken from Andrew's desk, and a cold chill went down her spine. The chart on the paper had been so succinct: The list of terrorist attacks, and then the words "Train" printed out so neatly on the list. How could Andrew have known there was going to be a train bombing? How could anyone have known? Could Andrew have been involved somehow? Was someone now after her as well? Annie realized she was holding her breath. She let out a long sigh, and dabbed her face with an old Kleenex she found in the glove box. She realized she had to do something. This was getting all too scary and complicated. Even though she hated that she had told Jeffrey as much as she had, she simply had to tell someone what had just happened, and about the file, and the truth about Andrew. Someone had to help her make sense of it all, and right now the only person that could be was Jeffrey Hunter.

But first, she had to get the file. Jeffrey would want to see it, and if she was going to come clean about everything, she was going to have to show it to him sooner or later anyway. She decided to stop by her flat in Chelsea on her way back to work to pick up the file and give it to Jeffrey.

Pulling onto Elm Park Gardens Road, she pulled around to the back of her flat to the tiny car park behind the house. Her small neighborhood was inhabited by young, dual career couples, so it was usually deserted this time of day. With everything that had happened, she had an eerie feeling getting out of her car. There was no sound except the faint sound of traffic on Kings Road further down the Lane.

Approaching the back door, she was surprised to see the screen door ajar. She usually left before Richard most mornings, and today had been no different. He left it unlocked from time to time, usually on the days when he had to put out the trash, and would forget to secure the lock on this exterior door. But today wasn't a trash day. She pulled open the screen door, and realized that not only was the screen door ajar, but the door to the house was standing wide open. Someone had broken into the house. Stunned, and before thinking better of it, she rushed inside to see what had been taken.

The front room had been ransacked. The cushions on the couch were thrown aside, several chairs were turned over, and the drawers on the entertainment center had been pulled out and dumped on the floor. Running into her and Richard's bedroom, everything had been scoured and searched. Drawers had been pulled open, and half of her lingerie lay strewn across the floor. Her jewelry box was gone, as was her television, and the camera bag that always sat on the side table. Returning to the living room, she realized their personal laptop had been taken from the desk, and Richard's antique coin collection was gone from the display case on the wall. Their house had been broken into and robbed, and Annie felt an overwhelming sense of invasion sweep over her, as if she'd been personally assaulted.

And then she remembered the file. Before she even looked up, she knew it was gone. Of course, it was gone.

"That's what they came for in the first place," she said aloud to herself, before she realized what she was doing.

Then the idea that had been lying low in the background of her mind came roaring to the foreground; she was truly in danger. She didn't understand why, or who was after her, but it suddenly dawned on her that the man with the gun was no random case of road rage. Someone was after her, and they knew where she worked. And now they knew where she lived. She was in danger, just like Andrew's life had been in danger. And now he was dead, she shuddered at the thought.

Bolting from the house, she jumped back in her car and spun out of the driveway before she could think what to do next. She knew only one thing at this point, that someone was after her, and it had something to do with that file – Andrew's file. She had to get away. She had to figure out what to do. She sped toward King's Road, not sure where she was going to go next.

CHAPTER TWENTY-FOUR

The MI6 building at Vauxhall Cross is a white monolith, perched on a low hill overlooking the River Thames. Built to house Her Majesty's Secret Intelligence Service, its Modernist facade is both loved and reviled by Londoners. John O'Leary had been working in this building since he joined MI6 in 1997, three years after the building was opened. After a dozen years as a Detective with London's Metropolitan Police Force's Counter Terrorism Command, his reputation for extraordinary investigative talents was almost legendary. After being heavily recruited by the top brass at MI6, he moved across town to Vauxhall Cross as a Special Officer in the Foreign Intelligence Division. In twenty years, he'd steadily moved up in the ranks, and had led investigations that detected and averted numerous impending attacks on London and the British Aisles. He had saved hundreds – perhaps thousands of British lives in his tenure – and every investigator at MI6 knew it and wanted to work alongside him.

At one o'clock, O'Leary called a special meeting of his top staffers to discuss the investigation into the EuroStar bombing and the agency's strategy for moving forward. Crime scene investigators were still on the scene deep in the tunnel looking for bodies, gathering evidence and documenting the crime. They would be there for weeks, but O'Leary wasn't about to await their findings before figuring out who was behind the biggest terrorist hit in British history. He would follow the leads – and his instinct – to their natural conclusion. The physical evidence was important of course, but following his gut was always his initial course of action in the beginning of an investigation. Everything else was just secondary in his opinion. In most regular cases O'Leary knew to follow the money, that was usually the most direct line to figuring out who the chief suspects were in any crime. But in cases of radical terrorism like this that had swept the world in recent years, money usually had nothing to do with it, which made the motives and suspects in cases more difficult and obscure to decipher. These people weren't normal criminals, they were zealots, radicals, extremists whose motives and tactics were based on a twisted worldview based on hate and fanaticism. In investigating acts of terrorism, O'Leary had had to revise and modify everything he knew about investigative work. When it came to terrorists, he had to throw out the old rulebooks of investigative work and go with his gut.

In his vast experience, he had always found that in the end, the crime scene evidence would either confirm or obliterate the soft evidence – his own personal strategy for unraveling the motives and the actions of the suspects surrounding the case. And in his experience, the two almost always dovetailed into a very solid case. And this time was no different.

O'Leary's office was located on the sixth floor of Vauxhall, with a wide window and an enviable view of the Thames below. Outside, a light December snow was falling, and a long cargo barge was slowly making its way up the river, weighted down with crates carrying everything from toys to car parts into Central London. A river boat packed with tourists was also cruising past, with a hundred-plus tourists snapping pictures of the spy agency as they moved up the river. Movies had made his building – and not to mention his job – the stuff of Hollywood legend. But O'Leary didn't care about any of the myths surrounding his job at MI6. He cared about one thing only; he wanted to keep London safe, and secure the British Homeland against its enemies and would-be terrorists – there was nothing glamorous about it as far as he was concerned.

Seated around O'Leary's large conference table were most of the agencies' best and brightest. He had also called in three men from the Home Office with expertise in Counter-Terrorism. He knew he was going to need the expertise of a broad range of government agencies, and getting them on board early on was important.

O'Leary called the meeting to order at exactly 1 p.m. He wasn't used to wasting time.

"Okay, let's get down to business. We've got a lot to discuss this afternoon."

The room grew quiet and all attention was focused on the red headed man at the head of the table.

"As you know, the first responders are still working the site. At this point, we have two survivors and we've recovered 235 bodies. The recovery teams are still working but we really don't anticipate pulling any more bodies out of the wreckage at this point. That leaves 160 men, women and children unaccounted for at this time, and probably will never be recovered. The fire that broke out after the explosion made recovery almost impossible. We're lucky we recovered as many as we did."

Jennifer Hawthorne, O'Leary's protégé was sitting immediately to his right. With auburn hair and green eyes that matched those of her boss, there was a long-standing joke around the agency that O'Leary was her long lost dad. Given their friendly and almost affectionate relationship, the joke wasn't too far off base. Jennifer was smart, intuitive, and hard working. Her boss relied on her for her innate discernment and sharp eye for incongruities. She was one of his best investigators, and John O'Leary trusted her implicitly.

Without hesitation, she jumped in. "John, I know they're there to recover bodies at this point, but have they found any evidence of the explosive device, or any chemical residue we can work with? Can we pinpoint a source of the explosion yet – or at least a workable theory from the investigators at the site? Have they found anything we can work with?"

"No, Jenn, I just got the latest report an hour ago. We don't have anything at this point that definitely identifies a source for the detonation. They've pretty much wrapped up the recovery operation, and they're still in the final stages of documenting the crime scene. But as soon as we have all the data in, we'll send the evidence team in tomorrow morning and start turning over everything to forensics. I hope to have a workable theory on the source of the explosion within a couple of days. This situation is exponentially more difficult of course, given the depth and length of the tunnel. They're working as fast and efficiently as they can."

Jennifer's mind had already moved far beyond what was being discussed in the meeting at hand. Like most meetings, it was just a formality to disseminate information and formalize the real work being done behind the scenes. She would leave the science and the details to the forensic teams who would scavenge every trace and remnant from the blast in search of evidence that would lead them back to a suspect. They would likely bring in explosive experts from around the world with expertise in terrorist bombings. This was a British and French tragedy, but it was a global problem, and experts from around the world would be on hand to help solve it.

"For the present moment, we're focusing on just a hand full of leads that we have so far." O'Leary turned around to the large white board on the wall behind him, and in all capital letters wrote *ANDREW BOLLING* on the board behind him. In small letters just below, he scrawled *Annelise Craig.*

"As most of you are aware, right now we're focusing on Andrew Bolling, Special Advisor to the P.M., who was killed in the bombing. An anonymous call connected his name to the attack, and with the limited amount of digging we've done so far, we're finding vague links to a suspected terrorist cell operating out of Paris. We don't know right now what his involvement might be, if any. But it is the focus of our investigation at the moment. Right now, it's all we've got."

A junior investigator standing behind the table, and eager to join in, piped up, "And who is Annelise Craig?"

O'Leary was his usual gruff self, "She's a staffer at the P.M.'s office. Worked closely with Bolling, and we have several phone calls between she and Bolling in the days leading up to the attack. We interviewed her briefly this morning, but her story seems weak. We think there's a lot more that Ms. Craig may know. We're not done with her yet."

Jennifer Hawthorne was already devising a plan in her head to get more out of Annelise Craig. The two had never formally met, but Jennifer had seen Annelise at several government functions that involved Wellington's office in the past few months, including a reception for some MI6 top brass just a couple of months ago. Jennifer had noticed Annelise's striking appearance with her strawberry blonde hair and hazel eyes and had taken special note of the friendly way Annelise moved in and around the Prime Minister and other members of his top staff. She was obviously a trusted member of their team.

Jennifer had also already figured out that she and Ms. Craig must live in the same neighborhood. A few weeks ago she looked up in a Pilates class to notice Annelise entering a workout studio in London that they both frequented. Jennifer remembered noticing how quiet, yet intense, she seemed. She had always stood out to Jennifer because she wasn't the normal type-A personality who usually served on the P.M.'s top staff and seemed a bit out of place in the rough and tumble world of British politics. She remembered thinking that they probably had a lot in common. Both of them young women who didn't fit the mold in their respective high intensity careers, but who were both obviously incredibly good at those jobs. And like Jennifer, Annelise probably used that misperception to her advantage.

Jennifer was hatching a plan to get a little more out of Annelise Craig, and she thought she might know just how to find her. While the meeting droned on with O'Leary outlining possible links to the known terrorist cells in Britain and Paris, Jennifer popped open her laptop and punched in the search bar: "*Sloane Square Fitness Pilates schedule*". The Sloane Square gym's bright blue website popped up on Jennifer's screen. No one seemed to notice, except for the new guy on Jennifer's right.

Sam Sagar, the handsome male investigator who had just joined the team four months prior glanced over her shoulder and watched her type in the words with a puzzled expression. When the evening's Pilates class schedule popped up on the screen, he gave Jennifer an annoyed look. Jennifer noticed his expression and shot back a look of equal irritation. She didn't have time to explain herself, nor did she care to.

As soon as the meeting broke up, Jennifer waited for the room to clear and then grabbed O'Leary's arm as they exited the room.

"I'm going to take a crack at Annelise Craig."

"I don't think she'll talk to you. After our little visit this morning, I'm fully expecting her to be accompanied by a lawyer next time we see her. She agreed to talk to us this morning on an informal basis, but she wasn't giving us the full and complete story. I'm quite sure she won't make that mistake again."

"But she might open up to a friend over drinks. Women like to talk, especially to other women. Right now, she's not a suspect, just a woman possibly needing a friend. And I'm very friendly." Jennifer gave O'Leary a cunning smile as she exited the conference room.

Jennifer stopped by her desk and picked up her purse and shoved it into her black leather tote bag along with her thick government issue laptop. She grabbed her long red coat and headed for the elevator.

"Where you going?" O'Leary gave her a confused look.

"Pilates. I've got work to do," Jennifer shot back, along with a smirk directed toward O'Leary as she stepped onto the elevator.

O'Leary just laughed and turned back toward his desk. He knew she was up to something, and he knew better than to doubt her methods.

CHAPTER TWENTY-FIVE

Speeding down Kings Road, a thousand thoughts were flying through Annie's mind. Was someone really after her? Had she somehow become a target? But why? How was all this related to Andrew and to the train bombing? Why was Andrew even on the train that night when he had specifically told her he was taking a plane? Was all of this somehow linked together? What in the hell was going on and how did all of this have anything to do with that file?

The questions swirled around in her head as she pulled to a stop half a mile from the office. Sitting at the red light, she realized she had no idea what was going on, and worse than that, she really had no idea who she could trust. O'Leary's office was already sniffing around, and chances were, they would probably discover the truth about her relationship with Andrew at any time. There were probably clues everywhere – receipts, text messages, office gossip – and the more they focused on Andrew, the likelier they were to start uncovering the clues to their relationship. She knew they would be back again to talk to her, and at some point, they were going to press her against the wall about her relationship with Andrew. She knew she couldn't deflect their questions for long.

Once that happened, the truth about their relationship would become public knowledge. She would likely lose her job, at a very minimum - and she would surely lose Richard. And if someone was after her because of her relationship with Andrew, she could become an open target. Right now, she didn't know where she was even safe. She needed information, and she needed advice from someone she could trust.

Without thinking, before the light could turn green, she made a quick right into the Belgravia neighborhood, and then another left onto Ebury Street. She had always loved this street, with its quaint rows of genteel homes and offices. She had grown up near here, and she had often walked these streets with her dad. Many of the old row homes had been converted into hotels, and the area still held an air of old London sophistication.

Pulling into a small spot, she turned off the engine and tried to think what to do. Who would know what might have happened to Andrew that weekend? Why was he not on the plane as he had told her but was instead on a late train back to London? A train that blew up far below the English channel, killing Andrew and more than four hundred other innocent victims? And who could she trust at this point? With no one to trust, and no one to talk to, she got out of the car and began walking toward Victoria Station, the hub of so much of the transportation into and out of London. She knew Victoria like the back of her hand, and she knew from this vantage point she could get to almost anywhere in England in a few hours' time. Heck, she could be anywhere in Western Europe within twenty-four hours from here.

With no forethought or plan, Annelise Craig entered Victoria Station. She entered the main ticket hall and then disappeared into the pedestrian tunnel leading down to the Tube Station below the historic train station. Without even a glance at the diagram on the wall that laid out London's spider web-like underground transportation system, she stepped onto an underground subway headed for King's Cross. With each step her situation became clearer to her and a plan began to emerge. She knew now exactly where she needed to go.

In just a few minutes, Annelise Craig emerged at King's Cross station, and zigzagged past the hordes of students and tourists who seemed to constantly crowd the old station twenty-four hours a day. Businessmen and women were bustling around trying to get back to their offices after lunch, and a parade of university students headed for the McDonalds on the corner were crowding the turnstiles headed for the exits.

Annie crossed Pancras Road, dodging the long line of taxis, and entered directly into St. Pancras Railway Station. As she entered the building, she glanced into her purse and felt the interior pocket lining for the familiar outline of her passport. Like every staffer at #10 Downing, she carried her passport with her at all times. Working for the Prime Minister of Britain carried with it an important responsibility to be ready for every eventuality at all times. She had only ever used her passport once under such circumstances, when an important meeting in Frankfurt was moved up a day to accommodate the German Chancellor's last-minute schedule change. She, along with Jeffrey, Andrew, and a small cadre of top-level staff had accompanied the P.M. for the daylong meeting, with no prior warning. She carried the passport now as routinely as she did her driver's license or credit cards. Today she was extremely glad she did.

Security around the train concourse was tighter than she'd ever seen. Large signs posted in front of the ticket counter warned of increased security measures, along with a long list of prohibited items on the train. Since she carried no luggage, she breezed past the signs without concern. She stopped at the ticket machine and inserted her debit card into the slot, punching the button for Luton Airport, a short twenty-two minute ride out of London.

Ticket in hand, she boarded the commuter train for the short trek out to Luton. Annie had been through the airport dozens of times, and like many Londoners, used the airport as easily as she jumped on a train. As the shuttle train pulled out of the station, she pulled out her phone and dialed Richard's cell number.

As expected, her call went straight to voicemail, as it usually did. Richard was notorious for not picking up his calls, and sometimes she wondered if he ignored her calls in particular. After the short beep, Annie left her carefully crafted message for him to pick up later:

"Honey, everything at the office is crazy with the investigation, and the search and recovery teams are working around the clock at the tunnel site. They're sending me out of town on an emergency trip, and I probably won't be back until tomorrow. I know you're working late and probably won't get this message until tonight, so I'll call you later and give you more details. Love you."

She clicked off the phone. Richard would be home later tonight, and he would find the break-in at their home. She would never let on that she had already discovered the burglary first. She would have to just let him handle it for now, because she simply couldn't entangle herself further. She couldn't become part of another police investigation and involve herself in everything else that was going on. Richard would call the police, and it would be handled like a routine robbery, at least for now. Maybe someday she would explain everything to him.

With Richard handled, for the present, she moved onto Jeffrey. Punching the green Messages icon on her phone, she composed a text message for Jeffrey:

"Jeffrey, I've got a family emergency. I'm so sorry, but I've got to leave town. I should be back tomorrow. I'll be in touch."

She pressed send. Pretty vague and unprofessional, she knew, but it was the best she could do under the circumstances. Everyone was just going to have to understand, and give her some space and time to get herself out of this mess.

In just a few minutes, she arrived at Luton Airport, a small airfield outside London used for quick flights to nearby European cities. She loved this airport because it allowed her to bypass the hordes of international travelers at Heathrow and Gatwick. Without even checking the flight schedule, she laid her debit card and passport on the EasyJet counter.

"Hello, I need a one-way ticket on your next flight to Paris."

CHAPTER TWENTY-SIX

It was 2:30 p.m. and Jeffrey Hunter was pissed. After their awkward conversation, his usually professional and diligent assistant had disappeared. She'd texted that she was leaving for lunch, but that was hours ago and since then he'd heard nothing. He had a press briefing to prepare for and Annie Craig was nowhere to be found.

Picking up his cell, he was about to text her when Annie's text arrived, telling him she was called out of town by a family emergency and wouldn't be back until tomorrow.

What the hell? First of all, there is her shocking admission that something had been going on between her and Andrew, and now she's leaving town without warning or adequate explanation. The train bombing was enough to shake him to his core, but with the realization that two of the people closest to him where having an affair, and might somehow be linked to the terrorist attack, it was all more than even he could handle. Andrew and Annie had been two of his closest associates and confidants. Without either of them right now, he was losing focus. And right now, that was the last thing he could afford to lose.

He texted back:

"Annie, what the hell is going on? Are you OK? Let me help you."

He pressed send, and waited, staring down at the little screen, but there was no reply.

Jeffrey grew more agitated. He had a country to help run, damn it. He didn't have the time or energy to waste worrying about his assistant, or how one of his oldest friends might be somehow linked to this horrific act of terrorism.

Everything was spinning out of control, and he needed perspective. Sadly, the two people he usually relied on weren't available now. Surely there was someone else he could talk to about this. Get their input, their opinion. With that, he suddenly remembered that he'd asked

Annelise a couple of days ago to find Rasul Aziz's number in Paris. Surely, he must have it somewhere.

In a moment, he pulled up the interoffice email he'd received from Annelise on Monday, giving him Rasul's number in Paris. Apparently, he worked in a bookshop, or owned it, or something. He and Rasul had not really stayed close through the years since college, but they'd kept in touch. There had been holiday cards, occasional Facebook posts, the usual communication between two people who wanted to stay in contact, but really didn't want to make time for each other. He dialed the number, and wasn't surprised when it went straight to voice mail. Even though it had been months, maybe years since they'd actually spoken directly, once the message started to play, Andrew recognized the voice of his friend from college right away.

"Hello, this is Rasul Aziz. Leave a message and I'll get back to you." The usual *beeeeep* played through the phone, and Jeffrey had two seconds to compose his thoughts.

"Rasul – this is Jeffrey. Jeffrey Hunter. How are you? Um, yeah, I was just trying to reach you. I'm sure you've heard about Andrew. It's terrible. Anyway, I know you and Andrew spent some time together while he was in Paris over the weekend, before the ... the tragedy. I just wanted to talk with you about that. See what, if anything, he might have told you. Please call me back when you get this message."

Jeffrey punched the 'end' button and stood staring at the telephone. This was all so odd. What did Andrew and Rasul end up doing in Paris over the weekend anyway? Jeffrey knew he was catching up with old college friends, which no doubt included Rasul, but did anyone else show up? And why hadn't Rasul reached out to him already? If your mutual friend is killed in a bomb blast, and you were the last to see him, wouldn't you reach out to his family or work associates to make contact and tell them what you knew?

And more than that, why would Rasul Aziz be working in a book shop in Paris in the first place? That seemed an odd choice for such a smart guy. The guy was brilliant, and one of the sharpest political minds he had known at school. The Rasul – or Raz – he knew would hardly be content wiling away his days in a dusty book shop on the outskirts of Paris. This was all beginning to feel very peculiar to Jeffrey, given the strange sequence of events. The people around him, the people he most trusted, were disappearing. And now with Annie gone, he had no one to turn to, no one to bounce his thoughts off of. Annie and Andrew were his friends and confidants, and now Jeffrey could not ignore the growing sick feeling in his gut.

He picked up his phone and dialed John O'Leary. Someone else needed to know what was going on.

O'Leary picked up on the second ring.

Jeffrey Hunter skipped the niceties. "We need to talk."

"You're damn right we do. But I must warn you, if you know anything at all about any involvement your assistant Ms. Craig, or Mr. Bolling had in this situation, you'd probably better hang up the phone right now and call a lawyer. We're done playing games here."

"I'm not playing any games," Hunter snapped back.

"Look, I know Wellington has asked you to head up the investigation for his office, but this is my department, and this is my territory. I won't have you getting in the way, and I won't pull any punches regarding any of your people being linked to the investigation...."

"Yes, I want to work together on this. That's why I'm calling you right now. My assistant, Ms. Craig has left town, and I have no idea where she's gone."

* * *

Jennifer Hawthorne was halfway to Sloane Square Fitness when her phone dinged. Looking down at her phone, she saw that it was from O'Leary.

Jennifer knew all along that she wouldn't catch Annelise Craig at a workout class. That had never been her plan. But women talk, and Jennifer felt sure that Annie had befriended enough employees at the workout center that maybe someone knew something. If Jennifer talked to the right people, maybe she could pick up some gossip about her. Did Annie come there with friends? Did she have a boyfriend? Were there any rumors floating around that Jennifer could use to glean some information about Ms. Craig's life?

At the next red light, she glanced at the text from O'Leary: *"Just got off the phone with Jeffrey Hunter at the P.M.'s office. Annelise Craig has left town. Said she had a family emergency. I think we need to put a tail on her."*

Jennifer's fingers were flying: *"I'm on it. Do we know where she's at or where's she's headed?"*

"Let me do some checking. I'll get back to you."

Jennifer traveled the five minutes to her flat on Cumberland Street in Pimlico. She shared the apartment with two roommates who were almost never home. Laura and Katherine were both friends from college and were now flight attendants for British Air. They wouldn't be back for a couple of days. She parked in front, and within ten minutes she had a small bag packed. It had been a while since she'd tailed anyone, but her tenure at MI6 had taught her a few things. On top of her jeans, skirt, and a couple of blouses, she threw in a short black wig and a pair of glasses, along with her passport. She didn't think Annelise Craig would recognize her, but at this stage she couldn't take any chances.

Before she could lock the front door, her phone lit up with a phone call from O'Leary.

"This is Jennifer."

"Hello, Jenn. Ok, we ran her passport, and not surprisingly, she just checked in for a flight at Lupton. She's headed to Paris it looks like. EasyJet flight leaves in half an hour, and will land at Charles de Gaulle at 4 p.m. After that we obviously have no idea where she's headed."

"I can't believe she's going to make it this easy for us." Jennifer responded. "I don't think I can make the EasyJet flight. Can you have someone check flights to Paris out of Gatwick? I'm near Victoria, and I can take the Gatwick Express and be at the airport in 30 minutes or so. Have them book me a ticket, and I'll pick it up at check-in."

"Good plan. Let me know when you're on the plane." O'Leary clicked off the call.

Jennifer knew better than to deal with her own car and parking near Victoria. She jogged down the block a hundred yards to Sutherland Street where dozens of London's black cabs traversed back and forth day and night. She raised her arm, and was climbing into the back seat of a taxi within two minutes.

Five minutes later, she exited the cab at Victoria Station. She made her way through the enormous main hall, down the tiled corridor and climbed aboard the Gatwick Express, the shuttle train that makes dozens of trips everyday between the hub at Victoria, and London's second largest airport. She knew that within thirty minutes she would be at Gatwick and would be on a plane bound for Paris within the hour. Annelise Craig may have a one hour lead on her, but she was gaining fast. Jennifer knew that it was critical that she locate Annelise before she exited the airport at Charles de Gaulle because after that, the odds of finding her would shrink exponentially.

John O'Leary was thinking the same thing, and wasn't going to take any chances. Right now, the Andrew Bolling/Annelise Craig angle was his best lead, and it was getting more and more promising by the minute. He picked up the phone and punched the number for Sam Sagar, his rookie investigator who was still learning the basics of investigative work. He thought pairing Sam and Jennifer on this leg of the investigation would be a good way for Sam to learn the ropes from one of O'Leary's best and brightest. O'Leary had high hopes for his new hire, but he knew that Jennifer wasn't so keen on Sagar. O'Leary, in his usual brusque way of doing business, liked Sagar's confidence and swagger, but Jennifer had said that he always seemed cocky, as if learning the basics of investigative work was beneath him. Of course, Sagar was the one who had tried to shame Jennifer during the meeting for her perceived interest in that evening's Pilates schedule, yet O'Leary still believed in the guy. He wanted to give him every opportunity to learn and prove himself, so he forged ahead with his plan to have Sagar learn the ropes from his favorite operative.

Sam picked up his cell on the first ring, "Yes sir?"

"Sam, I've just put Jennifer on the tail of Annelise Craig from the Prime Minister's office. Jenn is on her way to Gatwick right now and plans to intercept Craig at Charles de Gaulle in the next couple of hours. We can't lose her trail if she leaves the airport before Jennifer arrives. I need you to get one of our guys in Paris to put a post outside the EasyJet terminal and keep an eye on her until Jennifer lands. She should be on a plane landing soon after hers. You can get a picture of Craig from the file and send it to whoever you put on post so that they don't miss her."

"Certainly boss, I'm on it." Sagar punched the button hard with his finger, annoyed that he was once again one step behind the action.

Sam immediately called Harry Jasper, a long time freelance operative in Paris and gave him the assignment to find and follow Annelise Craig when she landed at de Gaulle. Harry had worked little jobs on and off for the agency for about forty years, and word was, he was getting more than a little foggy in the brain cell department lately. Sam immediately emailed a bad photograph from the file to Harry, along with a brief description of what they knew about her travel itinerary. Happy to get the assignment, Harry Jasper left immediately for de Gaulle to find Annelise.

After finalizing the details with Harry, Sam Sagar excused himself to the open-air balcony on the other end of the building, past the employee cafeteria and conference rooms.

Sagar was pleased to find himself alone on the balcony. He took out a cigarette as he often did and positioned himself far away from the building, where the smoke would be carried away with the breeze, out over the Thames. A very bad habit he'd picked up years earlier, cigarettes helped him relax, but more importantly, often gave him a handy excuse to escape undesired situations. In fact, through the years, he'd found that the nasty little habit had a lot of good uses, today's little smoke break being one of them.

After verifying again that no one was joining him on the smoking balcony, he pulled a little burner phone out of his coat pocket and dashed out a quick text.

"Craig headed to Paris, Charles de Gaulle, EasyJet, ETA around 4 p.m. Final destination unknown. MI6 has put Jennifer Hawthorne on her tail, she should arrive about one hour later. You take care of Craig, I'll handle Hawthorne." He pressed send and slid the little phone back in his coat pocket.

CHAPTER TWENTY-SEVEN

The bells of Tom's Tower rang on insistently. As Rasul drifted in and out of consciousness, he could hear the persistent lament of the bells, compelling him to hang on. Around him, he could hear the muffled shrieks of the people gathered around. The crowd had immediately scattered as soon as Rasul hit the ground, but a few kind souls had made their way back to him as they realized someone had been shot, and was lying there on the pavement with blood seeping out onto the sidewalk in the cold evening air. In the distance, he could hear a lone siren as a police car was no doubt making its way toward the train station and the solitary man lying motionless on the sidewalk in front. Once again, everything went black.

When Rasul Aziz opened his eyes again, he immediately had to squint his eyes to protect them from the bright lights glaring down on him. For a moment he thought he was dreaming, or dying, or floating somewhere in between. He instinctively thrust his left hand to his face and tried using his hand to shield his eyes from the unrelenting lights. He then realized he couldn't move his right arm. He tried to move his body, but it would not budge.

Light poles were positioned around his bed, with bright lights glaring down, and Rasul could hear machines emanating a low hum around his head. It took Rasul only a few moments to realize he was lying in an emergency room of some sort, although not a very large or modern one. His mind was still scrambled from the alcohol he'd consumed all the previous day, and he'd also lost a lot of blood. They had obviously given him some sort of pain killers as well, and his gut was reeling from the mixture of it all. Lying on the table underneath the unrelenting lights, he tried to remember where he was, and how he got there. The last thing he could remember was the white robes of what appeared to be a ghost wafting away from him, but he could not place where or who it could have been. Was it a hallucination? Was it an angel? Who would wear white robes like those in his dream?

He laid there, his mind in a fog, staring at the ceiling and trying to make sense of where he was. Slowly, the previous day began to replay scene by scene in his mind. He remembered arriving in Oxford and his peculiar meeting at the Islamic Center. He remembered his glorious afternoon walking around campus, and watching sports in the pubs. He remembered his little visit to his old apartment and the Indian student who answered the door. It was all replaying in his mind like a dream. But it still didn't make sense how it connected to where he was now.

Slowly, the full memory of his return to the train station, the locker, and the horror of being shot outside the train station started to replay in his mind. In an instant, he realized that the man in white robes wasn't a hallucination or even a dream, it was a real man – the ghost man from the Islamic Center. In his mind he remembered the man's eyes staring menacingly at him as he made his getaway through the crowd. The realization that the ghost man wasn't blind at all made him shudder. It had been a set up all along. He had been summoned to the Islamic Center not to receive some kind of reward for his work, but to be taken out by that killer. The scene at the train station wasn't some pickpocket, it was an assassination attempt, and none of what had happened to him was a mere coincidence. It was all a set-up, and they wanted him dead.

He was a good man, he thought to himself. He knew that sometimes he had to do bad things, and he felt a little bit bad about that. But in a war, sometimes people have to die. And often in war, some smart people invariably get rich. At least for those who know how to profit from the conflict.

Lying on the table, realizing for the first time that some of his own people now wanted him dead, Rasul recognized that he had never really harbored a lot of radical or self-styled noble motivations for his actions. He had never been a true believer in any extremist causes like some others in his neighborhood who believed they were in a war against the West. He certainly harbored his share of anger toward Americans, Brits, and others who he believed had mistreated his countrymen and brothers. But for him, it had never really been about any cause or political agenda. He had simply reasoned to himself that he might as well get rich anyway from the natural consequences of that war. He didn't really care for lofty causes or motivations, but he did like money. For him, it had always been about the money. That, at least, was crystal clear in his own mind.

Rasul also realized that no matter what motivations or justifications for his actions he made to himself, he was now a hunted man. What happened to him on the steps of the train station wasn't mere attempted murder – it was a hit by a trained assassin. The people who he thought were his friends, his co-conspirators, his comrades – the very same ones who had been a part of the plot that had spawned his actions that resulted in a trainload of innocent people being killed – these were now the very people wanting him dead. Rasul knew the full extent of the plan, he knew all the players, and he had been the one who carried out the biggest component of the plan. And now, they were going to kill him because of it. As the principal agent who had executed the most important part of the plan, his continued existence made them all more vulnerable to capture. They obviously wanted him eliminated.

And now they very likely knew he wasn't dead. They would be back for him. They weren't going to take any chances at this stage, especially after they had tried and failed to eliminate him. He knew these people... they didn't take chances, and they didn't leave loose ends unattended. If they wanted him dead, they would stop at nothing to make sure it happened – there was too much at stake. If he was to survive, he would have to take extraordinary measures to escape. He had to get the hell out of there, and out of Oxford. Now.

As he attempted to swing his legs off the bed, a piercing pain ripped through his mid-section, reminding him that he'd been shot. He threw back the covers and examined his abdomen, which was now securely wrapped in a large surgical dressing. A light wrapping covered the dressing from just below his collar bone to a few inches above his navel. He looked a little bit like a mummy he thought to himself. His right arm was numb as well and was of little use.

On cue, a short overweight woman in light blue scrubs came in, holding a clipboard.

"Oh good! You're awake!" she said in a chipper voice.

"I am. What happened to me?" Rasul tried to make his voice sound polite.

"Well goodness, you were shot! Witnesses said someone was trying to rob you, and then they shot you! Left you for dead right there on the sidewalk. Thank goodness some kind people called the police, and an ambulance brought you here straightaway. Otherwise, well . . . ," and she let her voice trail off. The nurse went back to studying her clipboard, while taking glances at her patient to ascertain his current status.

"But am I going to be OK?"

"Oh yes sir, I believe you are! But you gave us quite a scare. You lost a lot of blood, but the surgeon was able to remove the bullet and patch you right up. You're a very lucky man."

"Um, yeah. Thank you. How bad is it? I mean, any permanent damage?" Rasul couldn't believe he was talking this casually and calmly with this strange woman about an assassination attempt on his life.

"That's why you are so lucky." The nurse gave a little laugh and smiled at him as she patted his arm and then went back to her clipboard. "I'm Melissa, by the way. The bullet entered your body near your right shoulder, and just missed your heart by a few centimeters," she said while making an exaggerated grimace on her face.

"Dr. Mason was able to extract the bullet without doing further damage. You've lost a lot of blood, but you're a very fortunate man. Well that and you had an excellent doctor. And nurse, I might add." With that, she gave another little high-pitched laugh.

Rasul closed his eyes and pondered the information. He'd been shot. The guy was aiming for his heart, trying to take him out with one fatal bullet. The fact that he'd missed by mere centimeters made Rasul shudder. Obviously, the fact that he had jerked away from what he thought was a pickpocket attempt had in reality, saved his life. He let the information wash over him as Melissa, the lighthearted nurse took his pulse.

"I think the police want to talk to you first thing in the morning, sir. This was obviously some sort of robbery, and the police want to know if you have any idea who did this. Maybe you got a good look at the guy..." The nurse gave him a sideways glance. "Oh, and the lady from Admitting will be here shortly to get all your information. We didn't find any identification on you, so right now, you're just a number, unfortunately, Mr. . . . ?"

"Oh yes, certainly." Rasul gave a forced smile. "And I'm Joe. What time is it right now?"

"Um, 4:35 a.m." she said, checking her watch. "I get off in a little less than an hour, but Margot will be here with you when the police come. I expect they'll be here early, probably before 8 to see if you're awake. Margot is really sweet. She'll help you with anything you need."

"OK. Thank you, Melissa." Rasul gave her a weak smile, and wished she would go away already.

Melissa gave him a quick smile in return and another pat on the arm. She made a few more quick notations on her clipboard, and then placed it back in the plastic bin hanging on the wall near the doorway.

"OK, I'm back on shift tonight, so I will see you then. In the meantime, get some rest. You're going to be here a couple of days at the very least, so you might as well enjoy it. It was nice meeting you Mr. . . . Joe." With that, she was out of the room, and Rasul could hear her rubber soles squeaking on the linoleum as she made her way down the hall.

Rasul looked again at the ceiling, and listened to the clock on the wall ticking off the seconds. His side was throbbing, and he felt woozy from the painkillers, but he knew he had to get out of there by whatever means possible. Right now, the hospital staff thought he was the victim of an attempted robbery. Little did they know that the man lying in their emergency room was actually the target of a global manhunt for the largest terrorist hit ever on the British homeland. On top of that, he was being hunted by his own accomplices, who wanted him eliminated.

Gritting his teeth under the pain, he gently peeled off the surgical tape on his forearm and extracted the IV needle that connected him to a bag of painkillers and antibiotics. He slowly slung his legs off the bed and stood up. His head was swimming from a blend of pain, blood loss, and the fog of painkillers. Struggling to put one foot in front of the other, he made his way to the supply cabinet in the room. He pulled out a drawer with his good left hand and found a spool of large surgical tape. He methodically wrapped it around and around his chest, securing the surgical dressing into place. He grabbed a handful of sterile bandages and stuffed them into his pockets, along with more tape and a bottle of antiseptic solution.

He found his pants hanging in the small closet, along with his shoes, and pulled them on to his body as best he could. He realized his shirt, covered in blood and cut off of his body, was stuffed into a plastic trash can in the corner. His bag, carrying his passport and other belongings was nowhere to be seen. Shirtless, he stumbled over to the door and glanced down the corridor. It was still pre-dawn, so most of the hospital was quiet with few signs of human activity. Aside from a light at the end of the hall illuminating what was probably a nurses' station, the halls were dim and vacant.

Outside his hospital room door, he found another larger supply closet, and helped himself to a nurses' large blue scrub top. Someone's brown sweater was hanging on the hook inside the closet, so he grabbed that too and pulled it on over the scrubs.

Giving one more check down the hallway, he hobbled down the hall and out the side exit. Cold early morning air still enveloped the small city, but the area around the hospital was brightly lit up with night lighting. There was a large sign in front of the parking lot welcoming people to Churchill Regional Hospital. Wrapping the sweater tightly around his chest, he staggered away from the building toward a dark grove of trees that lined the hospital property. He was going to need to find a place to lay low until daylight. Then he would need to figure out a way to get back to Paris.

The sun would be up in an hour or so, and Raz knew he needed to find someplace to stay warm and hide out until he could move about the city without attracting too much attention. Reaching the trees, he looked back toward the hospital exit. No one seemed to be following him. The overnight nursing staff was scarce, and since they'd just checked on him, he probably had an hour or so before anyone noticed his absence. With any luck, he would be long gone before anyone grew suspicious about the Middle Eastern guy with no identification.

Hiding in the trees, he noticed a faint light coming from a small building a few hundred feet away in the opposite direction from the hospital. Edging out of the trees, he realized he was standing on the edge of a golf course, and the small building with the light appeared to be a groundskeeper's hut. Raz recognized he must be standing on the edge of the greens of the Oxford Golf Club, a place he'd heard about, but never actually laid eyes on. He'd never been in this part of Oxford before; he certainly never had reason to be. But right now, the groundskeeper's building was exactly what he needed.

Hobbling across the well-manicured lawn, he saw no one around, except for a lone red fox keeping a close eye on him from along the edge of the fairway. He reached the groundskeeper's building and peered through the small dirty window. Inside, the small hut was entirely black except for one small desk lamp that provided the warm glow he had seen through the window. The Oxford Golf Club was deserted except for him and the little fox.

Making his way around to the door, he tried the handle. It was locked, but he could tell from the flimsy way the doorknob rotated back and forth that it was a simple push lock standing between himself and the hideout he so desperately needed. Taking a step back, he winced as he raised his right leg and gave the door one heavy roundhouse kick. The door swung open.

Once inside, Raz pushed the door back into closed position and secured it in place with a brick that had obviously served as a doorstop before. His eyes took a moment to adjust as he stood back to survey the room.

Instantly he could tell that his new little hideout wasn't inhabited too frequently. No telling how many hours that little lamp had been shining away, lighting the room for no one. No wonder its bulb was growing dim. It could blink off at any moment, he imagined.

Rummaging around the room, he found a lawn mower, maintenance tools, and no less than seven ancient golf bags, replete with irons that were laced together with spider webs. On the desk he found a calendar from two years ago, a can of short pencils, and a rusty stapler. Then he spotted it – unbelievably – on the file cabinet next to the desk was an old black desk telephone that looked like it hadn't been receiving any calls in a while.

Holding his breath, Raz lifted the receiver to his ear, and as clear as crystal heard the loud dial tone, as if it had been sitting there for ages waiting for someone to make a call. Looking out the window, Raz could see the darkness starting to recede as morning was growing near. He knew he had no time to waste, and there was only one person he could call right now.

Dialing the international toll free number he knew by heart, he felt a little like an idiot. He knew this was a ridiculous way to make contact for such an important call, but without his wallet, his cell phone, or any way to charge the call, it was his only choice. What's more, it would be the middle of the night in New York at this hour, but right now, he had few options.

After three rings, a recorded voice came on the line.

"Hello, and thank you for calling Hazelwood Investment Services. At this time, all of our New York offices are closed. If you know the extension of the party you are trying to reach, and would like to leave a message, please enter that extension number now. Otherwise, please call back within our normal business operating hours. If you do not know your party's extension, simply enter the first three letters of the last name of the party you are trying to reach."

The buttons on the phone were dingy and faded, but Raz firmly punched in T-U-R. In a moment the familiar voice recording came on the line:

"Hello, this is Charles Turner of Hazelwood Investment Services. I'm not in the office at the moment. If you would like to leave a message, please do so at the tone."

After a long buzz, Raz almost hissed into the phone, "Charlie, I've got to talk to you. I'm in . . . uh . . . outside of London and in trouble. I need your help. I'll call you at 8 a.m. your time. Be available." He clicked the phone off. Looking out the dingy little window again, he noticed the first rays of sunlight out the window peeping up over the horizon. It would be dawn soon.

CHAPTER TWENTY-EIGHT

At 4:05 p.m., Annie emerged from the EasyJet terminal at Charles De Gaulle. She had spent the short flight from London's Luton airport to Paris mostly staring out the window, examining the little French hamlets below and wondering about the simple lives of the people who made their lives in the little towns that dotted the French countryside. Somewhere down there, just a few nights ago, her beloved Andrew had crossed the French landscape in a speeding train, probably reading the *Sunday Times,* thinking about work, and staring out the window. And she liked to imagine that he had been thinking of her. She already missed him terribly. The idea that she could not talk to him, that she couldn't touch him, that she couldn't ask him about the file, and this whole mess almost drove her crazy. She couldn't help but wonder, was he involved in this somehow, even unintentionally? She knew Andrew. There was simply no way he was overtly involved in anything immoral, unethical, and certainly not anything criminal. But how did his private notes, outlining the terrorist strikes of the past few years, seemingly predict a train bombing? Had he somehow been working to thwart the attack?

Her only idea at this point was that maybe the last person to see him might somehow provide some clues. Maybe one of his oldest friends, Rasul Aziz. might offer some information; some inside knowledge that could help her make sense of all of this. Not quite as altruistically, she also hoped that maybe he had spoken about her to Rasul, and she could glean some comfort from the words and thoughts that he had shared about her with his old friend. At this point, she felt she was losing her mind a bit, and was willing to grasp at anything to bring some solace and peace to her heart.

Annie exited the terminal and made her way through the main corridor, past the kiosks and counters selling *I Love Paris* T-shirts, umbrellas, books, and every imaginable incarnation of the Eiffel Tower. The concourse was crowded with travelers of every conceivable variety: businessmen and women, mothers with small children, old people, students, and the ubiquitous tourists. The American tourists were always the easiest to spot with their loud clothes and even louder voices. She made a special effort to avoid all of them.

Making her way down the long corridor toward the main exits, she still wasn't sure where she was headed. She had Rasul Aziz's phone number programmed into her cell phone, but she had not attempted to make contact yet. She wasn't sure that Andrew would have even told him about her, and so she hadn't yet figured out how to introduce herself – or how to explain her presence here in Paris for that matter. Even if Andrew had told his old friend everything, he likely would not have approved of Andrew having an affair with a married woman. And now Andrew was dead, and the married woman was showing up on his doorstep. It suddenly dawned on Annie that this all might be a very bad idea. Yet here she was, in Paris, headed for the taxi stand. Her desperate need for information about Andrew was overriding her better judgement, and she began to walk even faster down the corridor.

As Annie hurried down the main airport corridor, just twenty paces behind her, a lone man had fallen in lockstep behind her. Young, dark headed and handsome, his designer jeans, expensive belt, and white shirt with a casual jacket over his shoulder made him appear like every other young professional landing at Charles de Gaulle that afternoon. He tucked a copy of today's *Le Figaro* under his arm and carried a small leather bag and briefcase to complete the look. As they walked in tandem down the long hall leading to the exits, he never took his eyes off of the back of Annie's head.

The cold winter air slapped Annie in the face as she stepped outside the airport terminal. Always much colder than London, she cursed as she realized she had not thought to grab a coat before she bolted out of London. It was freezing, much colder than normal in Paris, and Annie clenched her small jacket around her neck as she searched for the taxi line.

As Annie entered the taxi que, Akeem, the man who had been trailing her eased up behind her and snapped open his newspaper. Pretending to read the cover stories, he watched Annie carefully out of his peripheral vision. She wasn't noticing anyone around her right now. Annie was lost in thought as she spun through her contacts on her cell phone, oblivious to anyone around her.

Akeem's handsome face did not divulge his mix of Eastern and Western European background. Born in Istanbul to educated, but very poor Muslim parents, he had worked his way west and found himself mixed up in a variety of low-grade criminal activities, just to keep food in his stomach and a roof over his head. His current gig as a part-time errand boy to one of the largest criminal networks in France kept him very busy. They provided nice clothes, pocket money, and often excellent meals in exchange for a variety of tasks that he usually didn't understand, and didn't question. Today was no different.

Positioned beside Annelise, he made a big show of checking his watch, and shuffling his feet, as if he were agitated and in a hurry.

"These taxis are always late and ridiculously expensive!" He said under his breath.

Annelise continued to stare at her phone.

After a minute, he opened his fingers and let the newspaper slide to the ground, on top of Annie's foot.

"Oh, I am so sorry. Please forgive me."

"Oh no, no problem." Annie gave him a quick smile and bent down to help him gather up the newspaper that had fallen past his grasp. She gave the handsome man a quick smile and went back to her phone.

"This your first time in Paris?" A stupid question given the fact that she obviously had no luggage, but Akeem could think of nothing else.

"Oh no, no. I'm just here from London for a couple of days, visiting a friend." For the first time, Annie noticed the man's good looks and expensive clothes. Obviously, a well-heeled businessman here for quick trip in the city, she thought, noticing his leather bag and briefcase.

Annie turned back toward the taxi stand, and wondered how much longer she'd have to wait. She contemplated calling Rasul, or maybe texting him first, just to break the ice.

"I'm sorry, but I'm in a terrible hurry to get to a late afternoon meeting. Would you be interested in sharing a taxi into the city?" The young man smiled and seemed harmless enough. Besides, she didn't mind splitting the fifty plus Euros fare it would cost to get into the city center.

Annie smiled back at him again. "Sure, that sounds fine."

For the next five minutes they made small talk about Paris weather, Paris traffic, and the constant bother of tourists clogging the streets around Christmas and in the summer. Soon they were loaded into a yellow taxi and travelling the forty-five minutes toward the center of Paris.

"Where you going?" the driver said after they exited the airport.

Akeem motioned to Annie to speak first. Annie realized she still hadn't decided.

"Um, Boulevard Saint-Germain, please." Caught off guard, Annie called out the name of a favorite street in her favorite Arrondissement, near the Sorbonne where she had studied the summer after her junior year in college.

"Awe, what a coincidence! I am going to the Sorbonne." Akeem gave her a big smile.

Annie again returned his smile, and pretended to study the buildings along the highway as they sped down the motorway. He was a nice enough man, but Annie had no need of new friends right now. Heck, she didn't need anyone who could place her in the city today anyway.

Akeem pulled out his own phone and fired off a brief text to Sam Sagar back at MI6: *"In the taxi with AC, headed toward Paris."*

"Perfect. Keep me posted," came Sam's quick response.

Akeem gave Annie another quick smile and gazed out the window as well, working hard to appear nonchalant and lost in thought.

CHAPTER TWENTY-NINE

5:10 p.m. and Jennifer Hawthorne's plane was finally pulling up to the gate at Charles de Gaulle.

Damn, why doesn't Sam text me back? Jennifer was preoccupied with her cell phone, wondering if there was a problem with its ability to connect to a signal in the French network.

As soon as the plane's wheels had touched the ground, Jennifer had fired off the text to Sam back at HQ. That had been eight minutes ago, and still no response. She didn't have time for this kind of nonsense, she thought to herself.

As soon as she was off the plane and in the terminal, she stepped into a quiet corner, behind a row of waiting area chairs, and dialed Sam's office number. No response.

What am I supposed to do now? Annelise Craig has already been on the ground more than an hour and I have no idea where she's gone. What in the hell is going on?

Jennifer decided that Annie had to be headed into the city, there was no other explanation for which way she could have headed. Proceeding in that direction was the only thing that made sense... she would deal with Sam Sagar and his irresponsibility soon enough.

Jennifer was halfway through her forty-five minute ride into Paris before Sam finally responded to her text.

"So sorry Jenn. I was working on another matter. Couldn't be helped. I just heard from our post who was stationed at de Gaulle. He's in a cab following Craig, and she has just been dropped off at a restaurant in the 19th Arrondissement. It's called Le Rond Parc, near the Bassin de la Villette."

Jennifer stared down at the text. Weird. The 19th Arrondissement? Why in the hell would Annelise be headed way over there? Far from the more glamorous shopping and tourist areas, it was more known for its high rise public housing projects and 19th century former slaughterhouses. It seemed an odd place for Annelise Craig to be meeting anyone for business, pleasure, or anything else for that matter.

She googled the restaurant and gave the address to her driver. At this point, she figured, she had about twenty minutes to figure out just what she was going to do with Ms. Annelise Craig when she found her. Just follow her? She hadn't done anything like this in years, and she realized her skills at espionage were probably a bit subpar at this point. But right now, she was the only asset Her Majesty's Government had working this lead, so she had to get it right. She unzipped her little overnight bag and pulled out the short dark wig. She pulled it on her head and used the driver's rear view mirror to adjust the hair piece and smooth out the bangs. Checking the mirror, she was satisfied that Annelise Craig would never recognize her.

The driver shot her a puzzled look back in the mirror.

"Just meeting an old boyfriend," she smiled back. "He always used to prefer my hair short and dark."

The driver gave her an even more puzzled look, gave a short laugh, and averted his eyes. He had seen stranger things in his taxi. No big deal.

As the taxi turned onto Avenue Jean Jaures, Jennifer could see the little restaurant *Le Rond Parc* perched among the buildings and shops at the edge of the road. Across the street, she could make out the glistening water of the beautiful Bassin de la Villette, the narrow artificial lake that had been providing water to Parisians since the early 1800s. Just eight hundred meters in length, and seventy meters wide, it was originally used for drinking water, but over time had transitioned into being used for everything from commercial purposes, to now harboring little boats and other recreational uses in recent years. Tonight, on this chilly winter evening, it was beautifully lined with vacant boat docks and taverns. The setting sun was starting to disappear behind the buildings lining the little reservoir, and the last rays of sunlight glistened as they bounced off of the thin layer of ice that was beginning to form on its surface.

Jennifer payed the taxi driver and departed the taxi. Stepping out onto the Avenue Jean Jaures, she fired off another text to Sam back at the office, *"I'm here."* She wrapped her long red coat even tighter around her body and readjusted the awkward wig on her head. People were bustling by, pulling their jackets up around their ears as the evening breeze and disappearing sun made the cold air even more frigid. Jennifer had always loved Paris, but this trip was growing worse by the minute.

Above the little brasserie, red neon letters spelled out the name *Le Rond Parc.* Outside on the pavement in front, four little metal tables with two chairs each sat vacant on the sidewalk. Nobody in their right mind would be sitting outside in this frigid air. Jennifer opened the door and went in, happy to see most of the tables occupied, which would take the attention off of her. She found her way to a little table along the far brick wall, and quickly took a seat, avoiding eye contact with any of the other customers. She didn't want to draw any undue attention to herself at this point. She grabbed a menu and buried her face in it, searching for something to order that she could easily pronounce without advertising her Britishness in this decidedly non-touristy part of town.

In a few moments the waitress stopped by her table and raised her eyebrows with a half-smile. Jennifer understood that this was her attempt to take her order.

"Um, just a croissant and coffee please," Jennifer said with a smile. The waitress gave a smirk, turned and left. Jennifer's smile turned into a frown. The waitress obviously wasn't happy with Jennifer's meager order. She never got used to the French.

Why hadn't she heard from Sam again? she thought to herself. What in the hell was going on back at HQ?

After waiting a couple of minutes, Jennifer decided it was safe to scan the room and see if her target, Annelise Craig happened to be one of the customers surrounding her. She glanced quickly around the room, and noticed two older couples, a couple of French students, two men arguing over a couple of pints at the bar, and a young woman trying to feed cheese sandwiches to two small blonde children. No Annelise Craig.

Two minutes later, the waitress returned and slid the small plate with a croissant and two small packets of butter onto the table. She set down a steaming cup of coffee Americano and a tiny pitcher of cream and motioned toward the packets of sugar already on the table. After laying down the paper ticket, she turned and disappeared into the kitchen again.

With nowhere to go and no one to watch, Jennifer decided her only option at this point was to sip her coffee slowly and wait for Sam to deliver further instructions. She had no idea why everything was dragging out like this.

In a few moments, the door to the little dining room opened, and a new customer entered. Large build, with a dark bushy beard and little knit cap on his head, he took a seat at the counter facing away from Jennifer. He picked up a menu off the counter and began studying his options for dinner. Jennifer took out her phone and fired off another text to Sam:

"Sam, I'm waiting on instructions. What's the hold up? Do we have a current location on AC? No sign of her here at Le Rond Parc."

Glancing up from her phone, she took a quick look around the room again. Just as her eyes were rounding the room, her stomach flipped as she caught the gaze of the new man at the counter. He was staring at her in the reflection of the mirror mounted just above the counter. Involuntarily, she did a double take to confirm he was actually looking directly at her. And there again, in the mirror, his steely brown eyes met hers, and then looked away. Her stomach felt like a pit, as she realized this strange man had been staring intently at her.

Her gut was telling her to get the hell out of there, but she pretended to study the picture on the wall next to her table and stalled for a full two minutes, so as not to appear to bolt out of the room. She willed herself to take her time, studying the bill the waitress had left. Realizing she didn't have any Euros on her, she fished a five Pound bill out of her purse and laid it on the table. The waitress would be annoyed, but what else was new? Dabbing her mouth with the napkin, she took every pain to appear unrushed and unconcerned. She grabbed her purse and made her way out the door and into the cold evening. It was dark outside now, a light snow had begun to fall, and the street was now devoid of pedestrians along the waterfront.

As she walked quickly away from *Le Rond Parc*, behind her she heard the soft jingle of the bell on the restaurant door as another patron exited the building. Too afraid to turn around, Jennifer hurried away down the sidewalk, walking quickly into the dark Parisian night.

CHAPTER THIRTY

Jennifer quickened her step as she made her way up the Avenue Jean Jaures. It was growing darker now, and the streets were largely deserted. A frigid winter blast had driven most Parisians indoors, leaving her essentially alone walking the street. Sam Sagar was being inexplicably slow with instructions and giving her scant information, and her uneasiness with the situation was growing more acute. Her anxiety was increased exponentially by the echo of footsteps ricocheting behind her as she made her way up the street.

She had walked two blocks, and yet the footsteps steadily remained a hundred meters or so behind her. On one occasion she stopped and pretended to inspect the heel of her shoe, using the occasion to look under the crook of her arm and behind her at the figure trailing her down the dark street. Unable to make out any discernable features other than the general size of her anonymous companion on the street, she straightened up and continued down the block. She was pretty sure the dark figure was a large man, and her instincts told her it was the stranger from the counter at *Le Rond Parc*. She began to walk faster. She decided that it was high time she needed to lose this guy.

Crossing the Avenue Jean Jaures, she made a hard left onto the Rue de la Moselle and headed toward the Bassin de la Villete. As she approached the man-made lake she turned right and headed north east, skirting along the park-like banks of the long narrow canal. Taking advantage of the wide open spaces, she swung around to take in the view, and took the occasion to search the landscape for her stalker. With a sigh of relief, she saw no one, and decided she had inflated the whole situation in her head, making a big deal out of nothing.

The inexplicable situation with Sam was a different matter. He was being blatantly reckless with the lack of information and directives for the entire assignment – yet it was her neck on the line with this operation. She didn't really know Sam that well, he'd only been with the agency a few months, and she had little experience working with him. Why O'Leary put him in charge of this part of the assignment was beyond her. She was going to talk to her boss about Sam's incompetent handling of the operation as soon as she got back to London. If they lost Annelise Craig in Paris completely, it would be squarely Sam Sagar's fault.

She texted him again: *"Sam, what the hell? I've had to leave Le Rond Parc. Now heading northeast along the Bassin de la Villete. Concerned I may be being followed. Please advise AC's location. I need to move."*

As Jennifer continued to walk along the canal, the air was frigid, and she was growing colder and more uncomfortable by the minute. She could not stop the gut-level feeling that she was in danger, although currently she seemed to be out of harm's way. With the wind gusts whipping at her red coat, Jennifer decided that she really had to get out of the cold weather. A light snow had turned heavier now, and the night was now pitch black with little light around the artificial lake. Somewhere along the way, she realized she'd lost her short dark wig, and her long auburn hair swung freely, and was soon covered in a dusting of snow.

Across the canal, a hundred yards or so beyond the banks of the reservoir, she spotted a small pub that looked welcoming enough. The lights were still on and she could make out a glowing red "open" sign glowing in the window. She decided to make her way to the pub, and then she would text John O'Leary directly for further directions. This whole operation had spun out of control and she needed to apprise her boss of how Sam Sagar was incommunicado and putting the whole mission at risk.

She looked up and down the canal for a place she could cross to the other side, and spotted a sign that she was approaching Pont de Flandre, with its beautiful high arching bridge, a few hundred meters up the canal. The sign said that the bridge had spanned the canal since it was built in 1808. As she approached the historical structure, she marveled in the dim moonlight at its beauty, and the fact that it had been standing here, allowing Parisians to cross this reservoir for over two hundred years. Running parallel alongside the beautiful metal arch bridge, she noticed an antique and antiquated lifting bridge on Rue de Crimee, the last of its kind in Paris. Another marker noted that the lifting bridge still rises more than two dozen times a day to allow barges and large boats on the canal to pass beneath it. The lifting bridge, and the fixed arching foot bridge next to it, both had ice crystals beginning to form on their metal architecture that sparkled in the night air. Together they made a stunning site over the canal on this cold winter night. While she admired the beauty, Jennifer was distracted by her strong desire to get across the canal and away from whomever she feared might be following her in the night.

As Jennifer hurried toward the steps leading up and over the bridge, she heard the muffled sounds of a cough behind her. Instinctively, she spun around, and this time, trailing her by just twenty meters or so, was a large man with the hood of his jacket pulled up over his head, and a black scarf wrapped around the lower part of his face, presumably to shield him from the wind. Above the scarf, she recognized the same menacing brown eyes that had watched her so intently from the mirror above the counter.

Jennifer's stomach dropped, and adrenaline raced through her body. In an instant, she realized she was in danger. She rushed toward the bridge as her heart beat out of her chest, and then realizing the man behind her was gaining on her, she broke into a dead run toward the arch bridge. Her eyes desperately searching the landscape around the bridge for someone walking the banks of the reservoir in the cold night, she saw no one, and so fixed her eyes intently toward the only place in that moment where she thought she might find refuge – the little bar across the canal.

Reaching the bridge, she mounted the metal steps two at a time. In her peripheral vision, she could see the man's black scarf waving in the wind as he advanced toward the bridge behind her. She could hear his guttural cough as he trailed her, and for a moment, she thought she might be widening the distance between them. Another moment passed, and then she could hear his heavy breathing over her shoulder as she realized he was almost upon her.

As she reached the top of the arched bridge, she was suddenly yanked backward as the man grabbed a handful of her long auburn hair and pulled her backwards toward his enormous chest. She was able to emit one high-pitched short scream before the man's other arm circled around her head and clamped down across her mouth. As the man seized her, she felt herself being pulled down onto the top of the metal bridge, and as she desperately fought to escape the man's tight grip on her body, she frantically wondered if someone might be watching all of this – watching as she struggled for her life. She fought with everything in her, but his arms felt like iron clamps on her small frame. Fighting with all of her might to free herself, she realized in horror that his massive hands were moving up across her chest, until they finally locked in around her throat. Desperately trying to scream for help, she realized quickly that with every sound she made, she was releasing air that could not reenter her body. He was strangling her, and no amount of struggling or wrenching could free her from his tightening grip. His chest was heaving for air from chasing her. She could feel his hot breath hitting her face, and smell putrid coffee with each exhale. His eyes bugged out as he squeezed her thin neck with all of his might.

Frantically looking up at him, her eyes begging for mercy, she could still see his raging brown eyes, fixed in a cold stare on her face as the last gasps of breath escaped from her lungs. She grabbed the metal rails of the bridge and tried with all of her might to wrench her body up, but the man pushed her head back, hard against the metal rails. As her head dropped back over the top railing, she was staring at a crazy upside down view of the city and the canal below. As her last breathe escaped her body, her eyes fixed on the moon glistening off of the ice on the canal below.

Once he was sure she was dead, the brazen killer lifted Jennifer up over the railing of the bridge, and dropped her lifeless body twenty-five feet to the thin sheets of ice below. The weight of her body easily broke through the surface, and her slim frame disappeared beneath the thin veneer of black ice. Her heavy coat quickly saturated with cold water and the weight tugged her body down below the surface. As she descended, the man watched the outline of her vibrant red coat as it faded from view under the dark water. The ice would certainly refreeze by morning, and no trace of Jennifer Hawthorne's body, trapped in the cold canal below the ice would remain. It would be weeks before the ice would begin to thaw, and only then would Jennifer Hawthorne and her red coat float to the surface.

CHAPTER THIRTY-ONE

At 6:30 p.m., John O'Leary burst into Sam Sagar's office at MI6.

"So what's going on? Where are we at? Has our post picked up Annelise Craig at Charles de Gaulle? And where is Jennifer? I told you to keep me updated on this!" O'Leary was firing off questions rapid fire at Sam, who could only hold his breath and wait for him to finish before attempting to answer.

"Yes sir, I just got off the phone with Harry Jasper, I put him on post at de Gaulle. I'm sorry to report that he wasn't able to locate Annelise Craig, and I think he's failed to rendezvous with Hawthorne as well, he said with feigned exasperation. "I have no clue how he missed them both. We need to fire his ass."

"Well damnit." O'Leary had no patience for incompetence. Harry Jasper would be fired immediately. There was no room in his organization for this kind of lazy stupidity. People's lives were on the line.

"Are you in contact with Jennifer? Has she made contact with Craig? Where do we stand right now?"

"Yes, I'm in constant contact with Jenn. We caught a lucky break. She spotted Craig in the airport concourse. She's trailing her in a taxi right now into Paris. Last report was they were headed for the Champs Elysees. Who knows, maybe she's just there for some shopping!"

Sam Sagar was delighted that his little plan was working so beautifully.

Sam gave O'Leary a weak smile, doing his best bit to act deferential, but O'Leary just scowled at him. Sam Sagar had only been with the agency for a short time, but he was now testing O'Leary's patience. Jennifer had razor sharp instincts and she'd already planted some doubt in O'Leary's mind about Sagar's trustworthiness. O'Leary was quickly deciding she might be right.

O'Leary turned to leave, unhappy with what he'd been told. "Tell Hawthorne I want to talk to her personally as soon as she is able. Tell her to call me on my direct line, it doesn't matter what time. I want to talk to her myself."

"Certainly John. I'll let her know right away."

O'Leary slammed the door behind him, as he often did when he wasn't happy. Sam Sagar smirked and turned back to the papers in front of him. Pulling out the bogus headshot he'd pulled from the files and sent to Harry Jasper, he laughed to himself at the thought of poor Harry Jasper running all over the airport looking for the woman in the picture who he'd never find. He slid the photograph into his shredder, and checked his watch. The text messages from Jennifer were mounting up, but he'd wait another half hour or so before responding. It didn't matter, she'd be dead soon enough, and knowing how the boys on his team worked, no one would find her body for a few weeks yet.

Sam smiled again at the thought of how well his little assignment was going. Of course, he didn't know the big picture of the whole plan – he never did – but he knew the operation was going well. That's the way things usually worked. No one in their ad hoc organization ever explained exactly what was going down to him. He was a bit player and he knew it, but his post at MI6 was critical, and he enjoyed his little part in the larger plan. The money wasn't bad either.

Hesam Sagar, or Sam as he went by now, had been recruited online months ago in a chatroom for Muslim singles for his current job. Although he was Muslim by birth, he didn't care much for religion. He adhered to most Muslim customs for his family's sake, but he wasn't a true believer. The only thing he believed in was money. The man who recruited him for his current double life had promised him 20,000 English Pounds in exchange for some simple tasks. Nothing too strenuous, nothing too difficult. He simply had to follow directions, orchestrate a few situations, and coordinate some unfortunate deaths. He wasn't crazy about the work, but the pay was excellent. All he had to do was follow directions.

So much of his work was still a mystery to him. He knew there were some heavy hitters masterminding some very big schemes in this organization, but who was behind all the activity, and what their primary motivation was still was not clear to him. What's more, how he'd wound up in his current position at MI6 was still a mystery to him as well. Two years ago, he had been just a low-level clerk in Britain's foremost spy agency, when he first joined a new website, 'Muslim Mingle,' looking for a girlfriend.

He met Naim, a beautiful dark-eyed girl from East London, right away. Hesam fell hard and fast for her. After only a couple of dates, Naim started talking a lot about politics, and how Muslims weren't treated right in English society. Sam didn't care much about the issues, but he played along if it meant spending more time with Naim. Soon, she introduced Sam to her brother, Rasul Aziz who lived in Paris and was a member of a loose network of criminals who did low level jobs like car thefts, burglaries, and some jobs that entailed acting as a courier for items he knew nothing about. He began earning some serious money by helping out and participating in the petty crimes around London. Soon though, the group graduated to more serious activities, and Sam got deeper involved. A couple of times Sam was asked to 'eliminate' people – that's what they called cold blooded murder – who were causing problems for the network. He did those jobs too, but didn't like it much. Sam knew better than to ask a lot of questions. He just worked for the money and kept his head down.

Sam was heartbroken when Naim broke up with him just a couple of months later, but by then he was a full fledge member of the network. About that time, the network started asking Sam to do tasks related to his job at MI6. In the beginning, he just provided information to Rasul, who passed it along to others that Sam never met. But in the last couple of months, Sam could tell something larger was going down, and his role had been increased dramatically. His last cash payment was for €20,000, and he was expecting much more after orchestrating Jennifer's little drowning accident in Paris. His plan was to work another six months or so for the network, and then he'd make his exit from both of his jobs. He appreciated the money, but even Sam knew this was a dangerous business, populated by dangerous people. He wanted to get out before he wound up at the bottom of some French canal himself.

CHAPTER THIRTY-TWO

Rasul's head was pounding. The right side of his chest was throbbing with pain. He needed food and a place to rest, his body still reeling from the loss of blood. Rummaging through the desk drawers in the dirty groundskeeper's shed he found a granola bar with an expiration date of two years ago and a candy bar of indeterminate vintage. He ate both, and found a faucet and water hose outside that afforded him a long drink of water. Raising his borrowed scrubs, and pulling back the bandages, he inspected the stiches on the right side of his chest. There were twenty-one stiches by his count, all neat and tidy in a row, but Raz could see a bit of fresh blood oozing from the end of the incision. Raz was pretty sure walking around town just a few hours after being shot and having surgery to remove the bullet was not what the doctor ordered. The last thing he wanted was to pass out in this dirty shed. He decided he'd better find somewhere to rest and recover for a couple of days. Once he was in better shape, he would have to figure out a way to get back to Paris, to some kind of protection, and far away from whoever was trying to take him out.

With sugar from the candy bar giving him a bit of new energy, Raz decided he'd better get off the golf course before the sun came up and some eager early morning golfers stumbled upon a half dressed man with obvious injuries holed up in the groundkeeper's shed of the esteemed Oxford Golf Club. Shuffling across the greens in the early morning light, he decided that he needed to avoid the hospital area at all costs. He headed southwest away from the Golf Club, weaving his way through small residential streets, crossed the Thames on a well-traveled bridge, and then made his way back into Oxford proper on the A4144. Buttoning the stolen sweater up high on his chest, he tried to give the air of a gentleman out for a brisk morning walk. Underneath his sweater, however, the stitches had begun to pull and hurt, and he imagined his chest opening up at any minute and blood gushing from the deep wound. He couldn't go much further. But where in the hell could he go?

With each step, the dream-like sequence played out in his mind over and over: The image of the ghost man, with his white robes waving in the breeze as he darted away, looking back at his victim as he lay dying on the sidewalk in front of the train station. In an instant, almost before he comprehended that he'd been shot, Raz realized that the ghost man was not blind at all. He replayed the image of the ghost man's eyes scanning the scene of his crime, confirming the kill he'd just accomplished. He remembered the look of bemusement and satisfaction on his face: A job well done, he'd thought.

Raz knew of course, that he could not go back to the Islamic Center. It was they who had tried to kill him. But why did they want him dead? He was a good soldier, always doing exactly as he was told. Hell, he had just helped to pull off one of the biggest terrorist attacks in world history. Delivering a lethal bomb that had killed hundreds of people, including one of the only real friends he ever had. And now they were trying to kill him too? He had turned his back on everything he had ever held dear to prove himself to these people – discarded his friends, his family, his beliefs, even his religion. And this is how they repaid him? What the hell was going on?

The questions reverberated through Rasul's mind as he made his way back into town. He was careful to walk as naturally as possible, and did everything in his power to blend in with the crowd moving down the street. As he walked along, however, he could feel his head swimming again, and the stitches felt as though they were coming apart. He couldn't go much further, he knew he had to find a place to rest, to recover for a few hours at least.

Instinctively, he turned down the one street in town he knew best, the wide avenue he'd known as home for most of his time at university. Making his way down Cornmarket Street, he quickly found his old building and this time, didn't pause before pushing open the door on the street entrance. His energy quickly slipping away, Rasul struggled as pain darted from his chest with each step up the flight of stairs. At the top, he lightly tapped on the door that was so familiar to him. This time no one answered. With all the energy left in his body, Raz threw his weight against the old door. The flimsy lock gave way with just one hard shove, and the rickety door flung back on its hinges.

The room was dark and quiet, and Rasul quickly scanned the room for an inhabitant.

"Hello?" There was no response. "Hello? Anyone here?" There was no sign of the Indian student.

Raz stumbled into the front room and gave the bathroom and kitchen a quick check. The second bedroom appeared to be empty as well, save for the bare mattress, as it had been before. No lights were on, and no sign that anyone had been around recently. Breathing a sigh of relief, he moved back into the bathroom and flipped on the light. Raising his stolen scrubs, he saw that the wound had indeed opened a few millimeters toward the edge, and blood was oozing out.

Raz found a faded washcloth under the sink and a bottle of alcohol. Dabbing the cloth on top of the bottle, he pressed the cloth against the incision. The sting of the alcohol on the incision was almost worse than the gunshot had been. He let out a howl of pain, and his head began to spin again. For a moment Rasul wondered if he might pass out.

Holding the cloth tight to his chest, he went into the kitchen and threw open the refrigerator. Inside was a virtual laboratory of bacterial species, covering everything from cheese, to old fruit and an indecipherable black blob that must have been some sort of meat. There were two beers and a bottle of water. He downed the water in one long gulp, and then opened one of the beers, sending it spewing all over the ceiling and across the counter. He drank the beer fast, letting the overflow spill down over his chin and dribble onto the floor. After he had finished them both off, he then let out a long burp, so loud he feared he might actually rouse the neighbors.

Making his way to the couch in the front room, he lay across it, and pulled a dingy blanket off of the back of the couch and yanked it over his legs. Still clutching the cover to his chest, he laid his head back on the armrest, and was out cold in a matter of seconds.

CHAPTER THIRTY-THREE

Charlie Turner stood at the window of his office in Hazelwood Tower and stared down at the people on the sidewalk, eighty-three stories below. They looked like ants. What's more, they behaved like ants, Charlie thought to himself. Each ant just following another one in lines, moving off to do their work, coming home at the end of the day. Always just marching along, never questioning the meaning of it all, never questioning anything for that matter. Charlie wasn't like that. He questioned everything. He was never content to just march along to the sound of some commanding drummer. Instead he was always looking for a shortcut, a way to outmaneuver the other guy, to grab the prize without playing by everyone else's rules.

That's how he wound up in this business. Both businesses, actually. His day job was a constant game to outsmart and outmaneuver the financial markets and profit off of unseen market forces. But that was just peanuts. The real money – and the real fun – was in his growing resume of "side projects".

What started back on Cornmarket Street in Oxford as just a bunch of college guys making a few extra dollars doing day trading, had over the years morphed into a brilliant strategy for making millions of dollars off of the inevitable fluctuations of the investment markets. The key of course was knowing when those "inevitable fluctuations" were going to hit. Everyone knew, of course, that there were always instantaneous and dramatic – sometimes even devastating – market swings immediately following cataclysmic events. But the problem, of course, was knowing when and how to capitalize on those market fluctuations. That, of course, was the unknown variable. If he could just learn how to predict those pivotal events that drove the markets, he could practically mint money at will.

Had the original brainstorm for the idea been Charlie's? Or was it Jorge's or Rasul's? Andrew had been involved in the beginning, when they were just learning the ropes of day trading. But Andrew wasn't motivated by money and had moved on to his interests in politics and other pursuits long before their strategy morphed to controlling the events that affected the markets. Among the remaining three, there was constant debate about who actually came up with their unique spin on the original plan. But everyone agreed that it started the day back in college when one of their gang noticed how the value of the British Pound took a beating in the hours after an Irish Republican Army bomb blew up near London's Canary Wharf, killing two people and doing extensive damage to the surrounding area.

During those days – often referred to the as "the Troubles" – the IRA was in an underground campaign to win Ireland's independence from British Rule. The IRA was a Terrorist group by every definition, eventually causing the deaths of over fifty people in their thirty-year campaign. At its height, it was a guerilla war that utilized car bombings, assassinations, and explosions in public buildings and transportation routes. The IRA attacks sometimes came as frequently as monthly, or even weekly, and the little group of Oxford College buddies began to notice that market dips were often a direct result of the attacks. The bigger the hit, the bigger the market fluctuation.

At some point, one of the group jokingly suggested that they could make a lot more money if they could only predict the IRA hits. They all laughed, until somehow one day, after a few beers, they began to talk seriously about the idea. Of course, they had to leave Andrew out of their little scheme, even from the beginning. He was too honest, too scrupulous and honorable to ever consider making money off of tragedies that befell others – even early on when no one was getting hurt. It took a few years to really get the ball rolling, but that was the beginning of what Charlie considered to be their brilliant investment strategy. Kind of like minting money, he thought.

And that was how it all began. The Cornmarket Conspiracy, as their little group liked to call it – born right there in their little shared college flat on Cornmarket Street, an ingenious strategy for making money. Charlie loved the money, of course, but what he really loved was the feeling of outsmarting everyone else. That had been his lifelong pursuit, winning the game, at all costs. Now THAT was a reason to get up every morning.

Now it was Wednesday morning, three days since the train explosion in the English Channel Tunnel. Charlie looked at his watch... almost 9 a.m. The call from Raz had not come. He'd received the voice mail as soon as he got into his office that morning at 7:15 a.m., and had spent the last couple of hours distracted; trying to figure out why in the hell Rasul was trying to call him. Hell, how was Rasul even alive? He was supposed to have been taken care of by now. He was supposed to be dead. A non-issue. Somehow the plan had gone awry, and that made Charlie nervous. There were too many loose ends at this point, and Charlie didn't like it.

Sliding both his personal and business phones into his jacket pockets, Charlie locked his office door and took the express elevator to the lobby. Out on the street, he walked a few dozen feet in the morning crowd, and then turned down an alley that he often used when he needed complete privacy for his phone calls. Secure in the narrow alley between two buildings, and out of the wind, Charlie pulled out his personal phone and dialed the London number he had memorized. As with all calls on this phone, Charlie had to remember and manually punch in each phone number – this phone had no contacts or phone numbers saved.

As expected, no one picked up, but the automated voice response politely asked that he leave a message.

"Yeah, this is Charlie. I received a voice mail early this morning from our French associate. What the hell is going on? I thought he was supposed to have been taken care of by now. We have too many loose cannons on deck. Call me back."

Charlie stared at the dirty brick walls of the alley, letting his mind race with the permutations of all the possible outcomes of his current situation. He had a hell of a lot of money in the bank. Maybe he should just cut and run now. His passport was good; he would have no trouble getting out of the country. He could be on Grand Cayman by this afternoon if he left now. Or better yet, he could be in Switzerland by tomorrow morning. From Switzerland, he could be anywhere in the world in a couple of days. His condo in Phuket was situated only a stone's throw from the beach in one of the most beautiful resorts on the small island off of Thailand. If he closed his eyes, he could hear the waves lapping against the beach and could almost smell the lemongrass and lime of Tom Yam Goong drifting up to his second-floor bedroom at the beachside condominium complex. For a moment, he was laying on his soft silk sheets, listening to the sound of the ocean through the trees. It was heaven.

With the blast of a taxi horn, Charlie was quickly back in the dirty alley off of Wall Street, the cold December air now whipping through the alley entrance and blowing his coat open, allowing the freezing air to chill him down to his soul. Right now, the world was a very cold place, and he was standing at its frozen core.

The reality was, he couldn't go anywhere. He was the brains of this organization, or at least he liked to think he was, and he couldn't go running off, chasing down loose ends that needed attention, right here on top of their biggest scheme ever. He whipped out his private phone again, and this time typed out a quick text to Jorge, still ensconced eighty-three stories up in Hazelwood Tower.

"Come meet me on the street for a quick conversation. I'm waiting now." He pressed send and leaned back against the wall, away from the wind. Jorge had better get his ass down here fast.

Inside of three minutes, Charlie looked up to see his friend's quizzical face peering down the alley. Standing up straight so as to be seen, he motioned for Jorge to join him. It had been a while since the two had met in this little dark alley. Their conversations about their side business usually took place in delis and at coffee counters, using code words and vague references, but today there was no room for vagaries or inferences. Charlie wanted to be crystal clear with his old pal, and there could be no miscommunication.

"What's up Charlie?" Jorge said as he sauntered up. He was, as usual, clueless.

"We need to talk." Charlie motioned Jorge to step back into the shadows behind a filthy dumpster.

"Okay, shoot," Jorge said, with no indication of irony. Charlie rolled his eyes.

Charlie spoke quickly, staring at Jorge with intensity as he spelled out the situation.

"Here's the deal: Rasul is alive. I don't know how, and I don't know exactly where he's at. Our guy was certain he had taken care of him at the train station, but he somehow survived. I'm certain he's still in the U.K., probably still in Oxford, but I'm sure he'll be doing everything possible to get back to Paris as soon as possible. Either way, he's been shot, so I don't think he can travel very far or very fast."

"Damn, that's bad." Jorge said, always good at stating the obvious. "So, what do we do now?"

"Well, I've put in a call to our friend in London, but I haven't heard back. I've decided we can't afford to wait on him. He's a fool, and it probably won't be long before he's got the police all over him. We can't wait on him any longer."

"OK, tell me what to do." Jorge said in his usual naïve, yet eager way.

"You've got to go to Paris, immediately. If Rasul isn't already there, he will be soon enough. Figure out what happened, where he's at. And when you find him, you've got to kill him yourself."

"What the hell, Charlie? No way. No way in hell am I killing anybody. I've been with you from the start on this, but I never signed on to actually eliminate anybody myself."

"What the hell do you think we've been doing here, Jorge? You've already killed hundreds of people. You are a full partner in this, and we've all got blood on all our hands. You're as guilty as any of us. You killed all of those innocent people on the train, you killed Andrew, and now you're going to kill Rasul, unless someone else gets to him first. Either way, you've got to go to Paris and take care of this. I can't go,

I've got to stay here and handle the money, and make sure everybody else is doing what they're supposed to be doing."

"I can't Charlie. . . I just can't. I can help plan, I can work the details, but I can't kill somebody with my bare hands. It's where I draw the line," Jorge's eyes were welling up with tears. For a moment, Charlie almost felt sorry for his pathetic old friend. Damn, in a minute he'd be crying.

Charlie stiffened his back. "Jorge, shut up. You don't have a choice in this. None of us do. We're too far in, and we cannot afford to let this get out of control. Do you want to wind up with your face plastered all over the world on the Interpol Most Wanted lists? Do you want to wind up on Death Row?" Charlie was glaring at him, and by now, only inches from his face. And then the tears actually did begin to roll down Jorge's face. Charlie was disgusted.

"Look friend...," Charlie spat out the words with disgust. "I'm onto your little drug problem. I know you've got a stash up there in your office right now. I know you need the stuff bad." Jorge looked back at his friend in horror. "Unless you want your entire world to come crashing down right now, I suggest you get moving."

"Go upstairs, tell your assistant you've got to leave on a family emergency. Have her get you a ticket on the first plane to Paris. Get your passport, and get to the airport. I want to hear from you before the end of the day that you're there, ready to move."

Jorge stood speechless, staring into his oldest friend's steel blue eyes. They were hard, cold, and there were no traces of their old friendship. They had crossed a line together, and now there was no going back. They were not the same boys who had played baseball together back in Dallas. They were killers, mass murderers, terrorists. Jorge nodded at Charlie in recognition of what they had both become.

As Jorge turned to walk out of the alley, he wiped away the tears sliding down his cheeks. He wrapped his coat tightly around his body as he made his way back to Hazelwood Tower. As he walked, he dialed his assistant from his business phone for a flight to Paris.

He had a lot of ground to cover in the next twelve hours.

CHAPTER THIRTY-FOUR

"Mademoiselle, we are very near the Boulevard Saint-Germain. Exactly what address do you need?"

Annie was jolted out of her thoughts as the threesome in the cab entered the quaint streets of Paris's left bank. These streets held so many memories – the carefree summer she spent in college studying abroad at the Sorbonne, and then the long weekend she and Andrew had spent here a few months ago when she was able to slip away for a few days, telling Richard she was going to meet an old friend from college days. Paris had never held anything for her but wonderful memories of lazy days exploring the museums, walking the cobblestone streets of the left bank, and wiling away the hours over French coffee in sidewalk cafés. In her mind, Paris was nothing more than a series of hazy happy memories. But not anymore.

"Mademoiselle?"

"Oh, I'm sorry, um, please take me to the intersection of Boulevard Saint-Germain and Rue Bonaparte."

"Very well," the cab driver said, and pressed on the accelerator.

Annie knew she needed a plan, because right now she was just aimlessly calling out directions to one of the only points in Paris where she felt at home: her favorite local haunt, Les Deux Magots. The little café was gorgeous, historic, and in many ways a tourist trap, but it was also a place she could gather her thoughts, order coffee and perhaps something to eat, and figure out a game plan. So far today she had been questioned in a terrorism investigation, blurted out her private life to her stunned boss, almost been shot on the street in London, made an ill-advised escape from work, jumped on a plane, and was now trolling the streets of Paris with no master plan. She desperately needed to stop and think.

"And sir, where would you like to be dropped off?" The cab driver had turned his attention to Akeem. Annie had all but forgotten about the handsome businessman sharing the back seat beside her. He had been strangely quiet the last half hour from the airport, allowing Annie to get lost in her thoughts.

"Oh, the Madison Hotel please," said Akeem. The fact that he was referencing a location just a few hundred yards past her own stop did not appear to catch Annie's attention. Once again, she was lost in thought.

As the cab pulled to the curb at the corner of Boulevard Saint-Germain and Rue Bonaparte, Annie gave a quick glance toward the meter and pulled out 25 Euros and handed it to Akeem. For the first time since they left the airport, she turned and looked directly into Akeem's eyes and was struck again at how handsome he was. "It was so nice to meet you Mr. . . . , oh I am so sorry, I don't think I ever got your name."

"Oh I apologize, it is Tom. Tom Khan."

"Well, it's been very nice to meet you Mr. Khan. My name is Annelise Craig. Perhaps we will run into each other around the Sorbonne," Annie said with a smile as she stepped out of the cab.

"Yes, it has been a pleasure Ms. Craig," Akeem smiled back. Annie slammed the cab door shut and turned back toward Les Deux Magots. Akeem watched her walk quickly away from the vehicle, and the cab slowly pulled away from the curb and back into traffic.

As soon as Annie disappeared into the crowd around the front doors of the café, Akeem called to the cab driver, "Oh excuse me, I think I've decided to go ahead and get out here. Please pull over."

The cab driver gave him a quizzical look in the rearview, and weaved the car over to the curb. Akeem added another 30 Euros to the money Annie had handed him, and dropped it over the seat, with a quick "Thanks." In an instant, he was out on the street and headed back through the crowd, headed for the small café on the corner. Annie should just be finding a table, he thought. *She's making this very easy.*

He allowed himself a little smile as he dodged the crowd on the sidewalk.

Akeem stopped outside the cafe and pulled out his phone. Pulling up Sam Sagar's message thread, he typed out a quick update: *"At Les Deux Magot, AC is inside. Will wait here until she exits. I'll keep you updated."*

Akeem scanned the crowded tables along the sidewalk. No sign of his cab companion. He found a small table among those on the sidewalk, still covered with empty cups, glasses and dirty plates from the previous occupants. The table was pushed back in the shadows of some large potted palms, and looked like it had been neglected by the wait staff for a while. Taking a seat, he positioned his chair so that he could eye every person entering and exiting the small restaurant. He picked up a newspaper from an adjacent vacant table, and popped it open to give him partial cover. Picking up the small cup of espresso still sitting on the table, he took a gulp of the cold liquid. He needed to blend in, and didn't want the added attention of the wait staff, so adopting the leftover food and drink on his abandoned table seemed the smart thing to do. He settled in for a long wait, not knowing how long his new friend would loiter inside the restaurant. He could wait all evening if need-be. Darkness would serve him and his plans better anyway.

* * *

Inside Les Deux, Annie stood just inside the door, using the heavy burgundy velvet curtains as a shield while she peeked out at the intersection in front of the restaurant. *Tom Khan – bullshit,* she thought. Surely he could come up with a better name than that.

Although she had no clue who he was or what he wanted, Annie realized instinctively that Tom Khan was a fraud, almost from the moment she met him. The events of the last few days had served to sharpen her mind even further than it already was, her discernment earned from years of working in a world with imminent terror threats on a daily basis. While she had to admit she wasn't on to him at first, they hadn't been in the cab more than five minutes before she realized that Tom Khan was a fraud and that she was in danger.

What tipped her off? Perhaps it was his shoes. No educated, professional man in Paris would be caught dead wearing shoes as scruffy as his. His clothes were expensive and looked brand new. His shoes, however, were cheap, faux-leather, and there was a visible hole wearing on the outside panel where they were worn to a thin covering. Or perhaps it was the way he struck up a conversation and claimed to need to get to Paris immediately for a "late meeting." What meeting would be going on at the Sorbonne after 6 p.m. in mid-December, when the campus would be deserted for winter break? His story had seemed fishy from the beginning.

Watching intently from behind the velvet drapes, Annie's heart jumped as she saw the man appear in the crowd, and look clearly in her direction as he stepped off the curb and headed precisely for her location. She did not wait another second. Turning quickly, she almost ran through the restaurant, and came within inches of running directly into a waiter carrying a large tray of entrees. She swerved to miss the tray, but ran headlong into one of the large white columns positioned throughout the beautiful dining room. The column hit her square in the middle of her forehead, right above her eyes, and almost knocked her flat on her back. Stunned, she mumbled her apologies, and made a beeline for the back door. This place hadn't changed in almost a hundred years, let alone the twenty years since she'd been a regular. She knew where every table and door was, and where she could make her quickest escape.

Out the back door and headed toward a rear sidewalk, Annie moved quickly down the Rue Bonaparte toward the Seine. Her head still throbbing from her run in with the pole, she knew she needed somewhere to stop and think now more than ever. More than that, she wanted to get off the street, where she felt vulnerable and in full view of whoever could be watching for her. At that point, she had no clue where she could go, or who she could trust. She only knew that someone – or some group – was after her.

Andrew's death had only been a small piece of a much larger and much more sinister puzzle. She realized that now. She understood now that all of it –the terrorist hit on the Eurostar, Andrew's death, the break-in at her home, the man chasing her through the streets in London – all of it was connected. Andrew had somehow been involved, and now she was involved too. What's more, someone knew of her connection to Andrew, and someone was trying to come after her too. They no doubt wanted her eliminated, just as they had killed Andrew. Most frightening, whoever they were, they had detailed inside information about her location and her movements. Someone was hunting her, and they weren't likely to stop until she was dead.

CHAPTER THIRTY-FIVE

7:30 a.m. Wednesday morning, and Jeffrey Hunter had already been at his desk at #10 Downing for over an hour. *Where in the hell was Annie?* he thought again to himself for the one thousandth time. Torn between a desire to protect whatever secret she and Andrew shared, and a dread that he was increasingly becoming suspicious that they may have somehow been involved in the train explosion, Jeffrey was furious that he had been put in this situation. Annie had been gone for almost twenty-four hours, and yet he had not heard one word or text from her since she abruptly disappeared. He was sick with worry for where she might be and what might have happened to her, but at the same time, he was livid that she and Andrew's irresponsible behavior had put them in the middle of all in this mess. Whatever happened, it would be a huge scandal for the administration, and could easily cost him his job as well, in light of his close relationship to two people who somehow were tied to the biggest terrorist tragedy in British history.

It was too early to contact John O'Leary's office for an update. He doubted they would tell him much anyway at this point. In spite of the fact that he was one of the top ranked people in the British government, as it stood now, because of his close relationship with both Andrew and Annelise, he was probably on their list of persons of interest. He doubted they suspected him of any nefarious behavior, but his close link with both of them had no doubt cast doubt on his story, and his possible connection to the tragedy. Jeffrey realized that he needed to be very careful from here on out who he said what to. The circle of people he believed he could trust had always been small, but it was growing smaller by the hour.

Distractedly tapping his pen on his desk, he tried to think of someone he could talk to. Someone who knew all the people involved in the escalating situation, who might have some good advice on how to proceed. Of course, it had to be someone with security clearance, and someone he could trust. Checking the interoffice communications system, he could tell who had checked in for the morning, and who hadn't come in yet. As expected, one of his most trusted colleague's light was already on.

Jeffrey punched out a quick interoffice email, which would go straight to his computer screen. *"Hey Fletch, got a minute? There is something I want to talk to you about."*

"Sure, come on back," came the immediate response.

Fletcher LaForge's office was in the back of the building near Andrew's office, where all the Prime Minister's top Advisors, number crunchers, and support staff had their offices and cubicles. Jeffrey's office was up near the front, near the P.M.'s office suite, where all the action took place. Fletcher LaForge didn't come up front much. As Deputy National Security Advisor, his job consisted mostly of communicating with his counterparts in Western Europe and the United States, researching potential threats, and advising the National Security Advisor and the Prime Minister on impending situations and preemptive action that needed to be taken to keep the country safe. He liked to keep a low profile, and most of the press didn't even know who he was. He was expert at flying below the radar, which suited his job well.

Along with the others, Jeffrey had also known Fletch since Oxford as well. A few years older than Jeffrey and his friends, he had never run in their circles at university. He was Professor LaForge back then, Adjunct Professor of Economics and Public Policy. Fletcher had worked at his London Investment office during the day and took the train out to Oxford two afternoons a week to teach a couple of upper division classes. Jeffrey and the Prime Minister had both taken his classes, where they both scored A's, and the P.M. had been LaForge's Teaching Assistant their final semester before graduation.

LaForge was the fourth member of 'The Oxford Crew' as Jeffrey, Prime Minister Wellington, and Andrew were mockingly referred to around the office. Their upper-crust education, and now their high government positions, always gave them the trump card in any office argument or in any intellectual debate. While Jeffrey Hunter, Andrew, and P.M. Wellington usually downplayed their elite education with humility and self-deprecating humor, LaForge was regarded by most on the P.M.'s staff as a bit of a jerk – pompous and arrogant by most of the people around the office. Regardless of the common perception, Jeffrey Hunter still respected LaForge. Even though Hunter thought LaForge's actual job performance was mediocre at best, Hunter and most everyone on the P.M.'s staff regarded him as a brilliant analyst, and his razor sharp mind afforded him a decent measure of respect. Yes, he could be difficult at times, but he seemed to be decent at his job, and could usually be counted on to help out during a crisis. Regardless, the P.M. trusted him, and that had cemented his position on Downing Street. Hunter still sought out his advice from time to time, and their common history was enough to provide for a nostalgic conversation over an occasional pint after work, even if he still found him to be a little obnoxious at times. In politics, half the people he knew were obnoxious on occasion anyway.

"Come in...," LaForge sounded like he was already distracted by work at 7:35 a.m. when Hunter knocked on his door. The back section of the P.M.'s office complex was already abuzz with work on this early morning, as it had been almost around the clock since the attack.

Jeffrey stuck his head in the door, and LaForge waved him in.

"Come in, Jeffrey... have a seat." LaForge rose to clear the stacks of notebooks and files off of the only two chairs available for visitors. Jeffrey, ignoring the chairs, paced the floor in front of the desk, unsure how to broach a subject that was so sensitive and potentially explosive.

"Fletch... I've got a situation. I'm not sure how to deal with it. I need your advice."

"Sure, Jeffrey... I'm happy to help with whatever," he said with his usual air of condescension.

"It's not business... well, sort of, but not really."

"OK tell me what's going on."

"It's Annie... Annelise Craig. She disappeared yesterday afternoon. Well, I mean she told me she had a family emergency, but it's a lot more than that, I know."

LaForge made sure his facial expression looked concerned, yet helpful. "What do you mean? Is she OK? Do you know where she might have gone?"

"No, not really. She said she'd be back in a couple of days, but I'm afraid it's rather complicated. Fletch, I know this goes without saying, but this needs to be completely just between us. I think she may be in some kind of trouble."

"Absolutely," Fletcher LaForge was nodding his head, making sure that the proper concerned look was affixed to his face.

"Before she left, she told me that she and Andrew Bolling – he paused, searching for the right words – had a thing going on. She claimed it wasn't sexual, but I'm doubting that. A few weeks ago, Andrew had hinted that he had a new girlfriend that he cared for a lot, but he would never divulge her name. I'm betting his new girlfriend was my married assistant."

Fletcher changed his facial expression to appear mildly shocked.

Jeffrey continued, "On Tuesday morning, MI6 was here, questioning her. They know she had been in frequent communication with Andrew the weekend before the explosion. And as you know, MI6 is looking into Andrew's death as part of its investigation into the terrorist attack. They think Andrew might be involved, all because of that phone call I received Monday morning. They think it's all related somehow."

"Damn it, Jeffrey, this isn't good." Fletcher shook his head.

"Yeah, I know. I've told John O'Leary at MI6 everything I know, so I'm not withholding any information. Well, except for the part about their relationship, but Annie has told me the bare minimum about that, so most of that is just conjecture on my part anyway."

Jeffrey stopped pacing and stared at Fletcher LaForge. "Anyway, I'm sure I don't have to tell you that this whole thing has the potential to explode into a mushroom cloud of scandal. If Andrew was a target or involved somehow, this entire administration is going to be scrutinized for blame. The British people want someone to bear responsibility and if a member of this administration can be linked to the person, or people who did this, if they can be held even just partially responsible for hundreds of people dying, they'll do it.... And then they'll take down Wellington, this administration, and our whole ship will go down with him. Everything we've worked for the past several years, and everything we had hoped to accomplish will be destroyed."

Jeffrey was pacing again, "And then there's Annie's immediate situation... I'm just concerned about her, where she is, and her safety. She's been out of touch for almost twenty-four hours. She sent me a text right before she disappeared, but I haven't heard from her since. I don't have to tell you that this is completely out of character for her. If this train explosion was in fact a terrorist attack, which I firmly believe it was, and if Andrew was targeted for some reason, then maybe Annie really is in danger."

LaForge pressed his hands together in a steeple formation and held them in front of his chin like he always did when he was thinking. "I agree Jeffrey, this could be potentially catastrophic for the administration, not to mention incredibly dangerous for Annie. Any idea where she could have gone?"

"O'Leary says they traced her movement using her passport to Paris. Annie studied at the Sorbonne back in college, so I'm betting she's staying somewhere around there. They had a female agent on her tail, one of their best, but they've lost contact with her too. I have no idea why she would go there unless it has something to do with Andrew's activities the weekend before he was killed. She must know something. The more I think about it, the more I believe she must be in trouble. Of course, I've tried to reach her, but she's not responding to any of my texts or phone calls."

"You're not in contact with her at all?"

"No, but I'll keep trying."

"I think you're right to be concerned Jeffrey. I'd like to help. I think it's in all of our best interest to find her and get her back here and sort this all out before MI6 finds her first and brings her in for more questioning. They can talk to her after we know what we're dealing with so that we can control the damage politically. I have some people on the ground in Paris, people who I work with on occasion who might be able to track her down and talk some sense into her, but I would need a lead on where she's at."

"I'll let you know when and if I hear from her, Fletch. I knew you would be able to see how important it is that we protect the Prime Minister's office from any links to this disaster, and of course do all we can to protect Annie. I appreciate your help more than you know."

Fletcher LaForge walked around his desk and Jeffrey Hunter gave him a slap on the back like he would have if he'd run into him in a pub back at Oxford. LaForge stuck out his hand, they shook hands like old college mates, and Jeffrey hurried out the door.

The investigation of the crash scene was still evolving, and there was still much to do. Without his assistant, he was pivoting in a thousand directions to respond to the crisis: every hour brought news as he monitored the recovery process, assembled updates and channeled information to the Prime Minister, and spent hours communicating with the media and fielding questions from the press. The Prime Minister's office was in turmoil, and somehow one of their own seemed to be at the epicenter of it all. As usual, Jeffrey Hunter buried himself in his work.

CHAPTER THIRTY-SIX

The sound of police sirens woke Annie from a deep sleep. For a full ten seconds she did not know where she was, or how she had gotten there. Staring at the peeling wallpaper on the ceiling of the cramped hotel room, she gasped and sat straight up when the memories of the preceding day came flooding over her.

Flashbacks of running through the streets of Paris the previous evening came rushing back. Her mind went back to yesterday late afternoon, peering out the window at Les Deux Magots, and watching the man from the cab hurry toward the restaurant. Once she had seen the man emerge from the crowd, step off the sidewalk and walk directly toward Les Deux Magots, she knew she was being pursued. And she had no doubt that just like Andrew, whoever this man was who had worked his way into her taxi, or whoever he was associated with, wanted her dead. She fled the restaurant through a back door and didn't stop running until she ran directly into the low walls along the Seine River. Stopping to catch her breath, she had searched the streets behind her for the man from the cab.

She waited there next to the Seine for what seemed like an hour, and only when she was absolutely certain that no one might be following her, she had allowed herself to relax a little. She was fairly certain that she had escaped the area without him realizing that his target had spotted him, and had escaped out the back door. Annie thought that he probably waited outside that restaurant for hours before realizing she had escaped somehow undetected.

After she was certain she was no longer being followed, she made her way through back streets and alleys, and circled back around the Sorbonne neighborhood to this small, non-descript, little two-star hotel, the *Hotel Venue*, on Boulevard Saint Michel. It was cramped and shabby, but the front door was guarded by a rather large twenty-four hour night manager, the hotel took cash, and her room had a lock on it. Right now, that's all she needed.

Looking around at the garish room, all four walls, and much of the ceiling was covered in faded floral wallpaper. The little room had obviously been cut out of the attic space, as the sloped vaulted ceiling and dormer windows provided little space. The bed was small, and the only other items in the room were a tiny velvet chair and an old trunk that served as a table at the foot of the bed.

Her purse was on the trunk where she had left it, and her clothes were lying across the chair undisturbed. For a few minutes, she allowed herself to drift in and out of sleep, relishing the safety of the attic room.

Another siren soon passed outside her hotel on the Boulevard Saint Michel, rousing her at last from her sleep. Getting up, she took a quick shower in the tiny pink tiled bathroom, and redressed in the same clothes she'd had on the day before, the only clothes she had with her. Glancing at her watch, she realized it was already 9:30 on Wednesday morning. The office back in London would already be in full swing, and Jeffrey was most probably very angry at her by now. But she couldn't think about that now. There was a man somewhere outside this hotel in the streets of Paris hunting her, and undoubtedly planned to kill her if he found her.

Annie's stomach growled and tightened from hunger and she faced the fact that she couldn't stay holed up in this hotel room forever. She knew she needed to find something to eat, and then try to make contact with Rasul Aziz. Whether she was being followed or not, she knew that she must talk to the man who was probably the last person to see and talk with Andrew. She had to find out what he knew, if anything, about what happened to the man she so desperately loved. Maybe he could provide some clue as to why Andrew was on that train, and if he had some knowledge, some bit of a warning, that a train attack might be imminent.

Picking up her cell phone from the table where it had been charging all night, she scrolled back to the email where she had sent Jeffrey Rasul's contact number. She added Rasul to her list of contacts, and then punched the call button on her phone. As the phone began to ring, she realized she had no idea what she was going to say. Would he even know who she was?

After the fourth ring, she heard the recorded deep voice of a man with a slight French accent, but it was laced with something else – Arabic? She knew nothing about Rasul except that his nickname was Raz, the name that Andrew always called him by. She realized that other than that, she knew almost nothing about him. She had no idea where he was from, or what his background was. Andrew had friends from all over the world; Raz was just one name from his distant past. But right now, he was the only possible key she had to uncovering what or who may have wanted Andrew dead. The beep on the recording prompted Annie to speak.

"Um, hello . . . Hi, this is Annelise Craig, I'm a, work associate of Andrew's . . . Andrew Bolling. I'm in Paris and was hoping I could talk with you about Andrew and his, death. I'm so sorry to be calling like this out of the blue. If you could just give me a phone call back when you have a moment, I would really like to meet you. Thank you so much."

She punched 'end' and stared at her phone. *Well that was awkward.* What do you say to someone whom you've never met, when your only connection is someone who has been tragically killed? She pushed the phone into her purse, and decided it was time to find something to eat and figure out where she was going next.

Out on the street, she immediately spotted a Patisserie across the street, and darted in for coffee and something substantial to eat. She ordered a Ham and Swiss croissant sandwich and a large black coffee. She found a place to stand at a counter near the window, where she could keep a watch on the front door and outside as well, as she figured out her next move. Keeping her eyes on the street, she knew she would not feel safe again for a very long time. What if she did not hear back from Rasul? What if he never even checked his messages?

She suddenly remembered her conversation with Jeffrey on Monday afternoon about Rasul. Something about where he worked. Where was it? A library? Jeffrey had said something about how surprised he was about where Rasul worked. It's a bookstore! Annie's sharp mind quickly recalled the information she'd found when she hunted down Rasul's number for Jeffrey. It was a shop with a funny name... Paramount? Paradox? What was it? She knew herself well enough to know that the correct name would come to her eventually. The name was stored somewhere in the memory folds of her brain and it would surface soon enough. In the meantime, she needed to make contact with Jeffrey. If she didn't try to get in touch with him soon in some way, she was certain she would have no job to return to in London anyway. Dialing his direct number, Annie was startled when Jeffrey Hunter picked up on the second ring.

"Annie, where in the hell are you? Are you OK?"

"Jeffrey, I'm so sorry. Yes, I'm OK. I'm in Paris, on Rue Saint Michel, near the Sorbonne actually. I flew here last night and checked into a little hotel."

"Thank God you're OK. Listen, Annie, whatever all this is about, let me help you. I know Andrew must have had some involvement with this, either voluntarily, or involuntarily, but this situation involves dangerous people. Your life might be at risk. You need to get back here to London where we can protect you and help you unravel this mess."

"Yes, Jeffrey I realize that. I came here to try and help uncover the truth, but I've realized that Andrew's involvement must be bigger than I'd realized."

"Annie, I've known Andrew for over twenty years. I know he would never get involved in anything criminal or illegal, or certainly anything that would hurt anyone. I just think he got mixed up in this somehow, and now you are getting dragged into this mess as well. We need to figure this out, but you've got to come back here, where we have the resources to solve this together and protect you."

"Jeffrey, I think I'm already much more involved than I realized. I wasn't planning to tell you this, but . . . I think someone's following me here in Paris. Actually, I know they are, for a fact. He followed me from the airport. I've managed to get away from him, but I'm not sure where to go next. I've made contact with Andrew's old friend Rasul Aziz ... the one we talked about on Monday, but he hasn't returned my call. My plan is to meet with him and . . . "

Looking up, through the windows of the little bakery, Annie's eyes fixed on a man coming down the street, walking toward her little hotel. She could only see him from the distance, but his walk, his clothes, his scruffy shoes; she immediately realized he looked very much like the man from the cab. How could he be here? How did he find her?

"Jeffrey, I've got to go . . . someone is . . . here."

Annie clicked *End* on her phone, disconnecting the call with Jeffrey. Outside, through the window, the man was still a couple of hundred meters or more down the street, but getting closer. Then her eyes fell on the man's leather bag, and she knew in an instant it was him. She stood transfixed as she watched him hunt for the front door of the hotel. She realized he wasn't sure where he was going. He seemed uncertain. He must not know for sure where she was, or if she was even at that location. When he spotted her hotel, his pace quickened, and he made his way for the door. She waited, and as soon as he disappeared into the hotel, she was out the door of the little Patisserie, and made a quick left and disappeared down an adjacent alley within seconds. She didn't look back or even pause to see where he might be headed next. Once again, she was running, as fast as she could go.

This man obviously was tracking her somehow. How in the hell did he know where she was? Had he been checking every hotel and boarding house in the area since last night? Paris wasn't safe. Hell, no place was safe if he was somehow tracking her every move. She needed to get back to London. She needed to find a cab, or a bus, or something headed away from here.

And then as she ran, her mind delivered the name, Paradigm! It popped into her head just as she knew it would. Paradigm Books — that was it! That was Rasul's bookstore. Now that she knew the name, she knew she couldn't leave Paris without at least trying to talk to Rasul Aziz, Andrew's friend. If Andrew trusted him then she knew that she could trust him too. Maybe he could help her.

She punched the name of the bookstore into her Google Maps, and quickly pinned down the location. It was a quite a distance from where she was, halfway across Paris, but she could be there within the hour. She would find Rasul, talk to him, and find out anything he knew about Andrew or what happened to him, and then get the hell out of Paris. She could be back on a plane by late afternoon, if she played her cards right. With that, she emerged onto a wide boulevard a block away from the Hotel Venue, and raised her arm to signal a taxi. Within moments, she was safely ensconced in the cab and headed to Paradigm Books across town. Surely, she thought, Rasul Aziz would help her.

CHAPTER THIRTY-SEVEN

Rasul Aziz was walking up steps leading to a great white stone building on the Oxford campus. At the top of the steps he could see his old friend Andy Bolling standing, gazing down at him with tears in his eyes. Rasul felt sudden and instant sorrow that his good friend Andy was dead, and wanted to tell him how sorry he was for everything that had happened. But somehow, with his each step, Andy got further and further away from Rasul until he had all but disappeared. Rasul looked everywhere in and around the building for his friend, and he felt a wave of extreme sadness at the realization that he could not find him anywhere.

Rasul's mind was in a fog as he awoke from the dream, but a vague feeling of deep sadness still hovered over him as he opened his eyes. Hearing footsteps approaching from outside, his dream faded from consciousness as the steps grew louder. In an instant, his brain snapped awake, and he realized that the footsteps he was hearing were not part of some hazy dream, but the sound of real footsteps ascending the stairs outside his old college apartment where he was still lying on the broken down couch.

Jumping to his feet, he suddenly felt a shot of pain rip through his right shoulder. Grabbing the incision on his right side of his chest where the fresh stitches still stung, he stumbled into the second bedroom, pulling the dingy cover along with him. He stepped into the empty closet and stood motionless as the listened to the sound of the Indian student enter the apartment.

"Tatti," the Indian distinctly said under his breath, just loud enough for Rasul to hear him in the second bedroom. Rasul recognized the Indian swear word and realized that the young man must have found the broken door lock and was thinking that he'd been robbed. Rasul listened as he moved around the room, opening drawers, inspecting this apartment for anything missing. Rasul's mind raced, trying to think of any evidence he'd left that there had indeed been someone in the apartment, or that he was still there.

And then Rasul remembered the empty water bottle and the beer can. Damn, he thought to himself. He would surely see those in the kitchen.

From the second bedroom, Rasul could hear the faint *bink, bink, bink, bink* of cell phone buttons being pushed. From the tones, Rasul realized the student was calling someone.

The next words he heard were indecipherable, and Rasul realized that the Indian student was speaking Hindi. He must have called someone from home. Rasul was relieved for a moment that no police had yet been summoned. In between the Hindi words, Rasul could pick out "no, no, no" and "it's okay." Rasul took that to mean that the Indian would not be calling the police. As the young man said his goodbyes, Rasul held his breath for the sound of a second phone call. It did not come.

In a few minutes, Rasul could hear the squeaking sound of water faucets being turned on in the shower, and the young man pulling back the shower curtain. Rasul waited until he was certain the guy was in the shower, and snuck back out the door and down the stairs. On the street, he walked around for a few minutes and wondered how long it would take a twenty-five-year-old college graduate student to take a shower. Ten minutes? Fifteen?

After twenty minutes or so, Rasul climbed back up the same staircase, making sure to create a fair amount of noise so that he was sure to be heard. At the top of the stairs, he knocked three times on the door, which was still swinging free from the broken lock. In a moment, he heard the bathroom door open and the young man calling from the bathroom. "Yes? Who is it?"

"Oh hello, it's me again, from yesterday." There was no response. A full minute passed.

Rasul was beginning to think that the guy must be hiding in the bedroom, afraid to come to the door. But in a moment, the student's dark head emerged from behind the front door, a quizzical look on his face.

"Hello, I'm so sorry to bother you again." Rasul tried his best to appear friendly and unthreatening. The young student's enormous dark eyes just peered at him.

"As I explained yesterday, I'm in Oxford on business, but I used to be a student here at Oxford. This was my apartment." The student gave him a slight nod, but the quizzical look remained on his face. Rasul had no choice but to forge on with his story.

"I know this sounds a little crazy, but after I left here yesterday, I was mugged at the train station. They took my wallet and my bag, along with my cell phone. I have nothing. I've called my company and they are wiring money into my account, but for the time being, I have no money, and I know no one in the city anymore. Well, other than you. Would you mind terribly if I stayed here for a little while, at least until the money hits my account? I could pay you .... I mean, when my money comes in, I'll give you one hundred Euros."

The student continued to just stare at him, and Rasul was convinced he was about to slam the door in his face. But in a moment, the young man stood back and opened the door wider.

Rasul smiled to himself. He could still spin a lie faster than anyone else he knew. He entered the apartment, and waited for the guy to speak.

"Hi, I'm Himmat," the young man stuck out his hand.

"Hello, I'm Rasul," and Raz shook his hand.

"Have a seat. Would you like some water?" Himmat walked toward the kitchen, and Rasul took a seat on the same dirty couch where he'd been lying all day.

"No, thank you. And thank you again for letting me stay here for a while. I'm hoping the money will come quickly, but the banks close very soon. If the money doesn't arrive within the hour, I may have to find a place to stay for the night."

The young man gave no immediate reply to Rasul's remark, but paused outside the kitchen to chat with his unexpected visitor.

"I'm sorry you were mugged. Things like that happen all the time around here. You must be more careful." Himmat was obviously feeling very comfortable with his new visitor.

"Yeah, I need to be more careful," Raz's shoulder was beginning to hurt again, probably from running up the stairs and all the activity of the last twenty minutes.

"You want a beer?" Himmat didn't wait for a reply this time. He spun around and headed for the kitchen. He seemed grateful for the company, even if the Middle Eastern man's presence seemed a bit odd to him.

Just as Himmat turned toward the kitchen, Rasul panicked. He again remembered the beer cans, but now it was too late. At that exact moment, Himmat spotted them. Himmat stopped dead in his tracks and stared at the empty cans lying on the counter, spilling their last remnants of beer in a neat circle around each can. Rasul saw Himmat tilt his head ever so slightly to the right, as if trying to make sense of the cans' presence on the counter.

In one swift motion, like a cat attacking its prey from behind, Rasul was on him. As his left hand grabbed the grad student by the left shoulder, his right hand swung up and around his head and grabbed the young man by the face. With all the power he could still muster in his upper body, Rasul snapped Himmat's head to the right with one hard jolt, forcing his head in to a contorted hard right angle, until he heard his neck snap. He held him there, listening to him gurgle his last breaths while he held the young student's body in a vice. Himmat's body twitched and convulsed. When Rasul was sure he was dead, he let Himmat sink to the floor of the kitchen and lay there in a limp heap on the linoleum floor.

Rasul felt a new wave of pain sweep over him, and he went to the bathroom to inspect his incision once again. Fresh blood was oozing from the stitches. He felt a little bad about the grad student. He hadn't planned or wanted to kill him, but when it was obvious he was starting to put two and two together, Rasul had no choice, he reasoned.

Rasul knew he needed to get out of Oxford, and fast. He needed to get far away from this city, from London, the Ghost Man, and whoever else wanted him dead. He needed to get back to Paris, his own neighborhood. But how? He'd lost his passport, his identification, and he would need an airline ticket as well.

Rasul knew he could not hide out here in Oxford. The news that he had survived the attempt on his life was no doubt common knowledge at this point in a town this size. News of the shooting would have been widely reported, along with information about him being taken to the hospital. The Ghost Man had probably already paid a visit to the emergency room at Churchill Hospital looking for him. The streets of Oxford could not hide him for long.

Of course, he knew that the Ghost Man was not his ultimate enemy. He was just a small pawn in this whole conspiracy, just as Rasul realized he was as well. They were both pawns, and now Rasul understood he was expendable as well. Obviously, the command to have Rasul killed had come from someone much higher up. Rasul realized as well that as is so often the case, the easiest way to control possible leaks and unpredictable variables in a conspiracy is to have them eliminated. Rasul had just helped pull off one of the largest terrorist hits in history. Now, the people who masterminded the whole operation – the people he thought were his friends – wanted him dead, just like the people on that train. He was just a tool, a tool whose usefulness was no longer required, and that needed to be discarded as fast and as efficiently as possible.

Rasul reached across the dead body on the kitchen floor and grabbed the last cold beer from the refrigerator. Returning to his spot on the couch, he downed the beer in three long gulps and sat staring out the window. He needed to get back to Paris. He needed more medical attention, away from the suspicious eyes here in this small town. In Paris, he would be back on his home turf, in his own neighborhood. The people there were used to watching out for each other. He could be safe there. People would help him. But how could he get back to Paris? His bag and belongings were long gone. His passport had been lost somewhere between the train station and the hospital. Besides, after being almost shot to death and then disappearing, he was certain he was now the subject of intense interest with the British police. With the terrorist bombing, every traveler – especially travelers with a Muslim surname – would be scrutinized. His passport was useless to him now anyway.

Rasul took another look at the lifeless heap on the floor, and suddenly an idea struck him. Getting up, he rolled the body over, and leaned down to take a hard look at the dead student. His lifeless brown eyes stared straight up at Rasul, as if eyeing him in return.

Twenty-five or so years old, brown eyes, dark brown hair, darkish skin, yeah, it just might work, Rasul thought to himself. Suddenly Rasul hatched what he thought was a brilliant idea.

Rasul made a beeline for the bedroom, and methodically went through each drawer, sorting through the old pens, folders, random homework assignments and other paraphernalia of student life. In the bottom left drawer he found a metal box, and pulling it out, was delighted to find a navy blue passport with a sleek gold imprint on the cover, *'Republic of India.'* Opening the front cover, Rasul read the full name of his unfortunate new friend, Himmat Tushar Patel. The rest was in Hindi, but studying the black and white photograph, Rasul confirmed that most of their physical characteristics were a match. The single biggest problem of course was the twelve-year age difference, but Rasul convinced himself that with the right clothes and demeanor, he could pull it off. The photo, of course, was another problem. The guy didn't really look much like Rasul in the face, and that was going to have to be fixed.

Fortunately, Rasul had a bit of experience with falsifying identification from his college days right here in Oxford. Generating fake I.D.s is a common task for college students, and Rasul was convinced that with a new passport photo, he could slice the laminate cover along the edge of the page and slide his new photo imperceptibly into position. Of course, he was counting on the fact that few people would be scrutinizing passports of young people moving between

Britain and France anyway, especially one of an Indian graduate student. Even though England had left the European Union months before, most of the trappings of easy travel between the countries were still in place. Chances were, border patrol would barely glance at the passport of an Indian graduate student, and if he played his cards right, they might not even open it at all.

Rasul was convinced his plan would work. He grabbed Himmat by the legs and pulled his lifeless body into the second bedroom, stuffing his body far up under the bed. Rasul was careful to close the apartment door as he left, and jimmied the broken lock so that it would hold the door in place. Easing down the stairs, he knew just where a pharmacy was that could produce a new passport photo for him in half an hour. With any luck, he'd be back within an hour, and could make quick work of doctoring up Himmat's passport. If everything went according to plan, he could hopefully be back in London and on a plane back to Paris by late this evening.

He would grab some new clothes out of Himmat's room, steal his wallet and credit cards, and don his new identity as Himmat Patel. Rasul went to the bathroom and smiled at himself in the mirror. Making his best impression of an Indian graduate student, Rasul watched himself in the mirror as he practiced his lines, with his best Indian dialect: "Hello, my name is Himmat Patel. I am traveling to Paris for the weekend to visit my grandmother."

CHAPTER THIRTY-EIGHT

Damn. Jeffrey stared at his phone. What in the hell was going on? What did Annie mean when she said that someone was there?

To Jeffrey, nothing was making sense. Everything in his life was in a freefall of confusion and stress, and yet the people he counted on the most were disappearing one by one. His country had just experienced the biggest global terror hit since 9/11. Andrew was dead, and then he was stunned to find out the revelation that Andrew and Annie, his two closest confidants had been carrying on an affair on some level – the details for which he hoped he'd never have to hear. And now Annie had disappeared. His job as Chief of Staff to the Prime Minister was to help sort all this mess out, help coordinate a massive rescue and recovery mission to retrieve the victims, and to aid and help expedite the investigation to find the evil person or people who did this. No group had yet claimed responsibility for the terrorist attack, yet so many of those closest to him seemed to be involved. It didn't help either that with Annie now under the microscope, he was being personally dragged into the investigation as well. Jeffrey was a very strong man, he had dealt with a lot, but all of this was all almost more than he could bear.

As Jeffrey turned all of the information over and over in his head, he got a sick feeling in his stomach. Like some sort of tortuous game with a myriad of clues, but no clear answer, his brain was working overtime, trying to connect the dots. Making matters worse was the fact that, as is so often the case when people you care about are involved, his own personal thoughts and feelings were clouding his perceptions and his judgement. His talk with Fletch LaForge hadn't really helped clear anything up either.

He picked up his phone and dialed MI6.

"Yeah, uh, John O'Leary please." Jeffrey Hunter waited for the investigator to pick up his line. There was a click, and then John O'Leary's Scottish brogue came on the line.

"O'Leary here."

"Good morning John, Jeffrey Hunter. I was just wondering if you have any updates on Annelise Craig's whereabouts in Paris – or what she's doing there – anything. Have you had any luck reestablishing contact with the agent you had following her?"

"Hello Jeffrey. I'm afraid we've hit a wall on Ms. Craig's location. We still have an agent on her tail, one of my very best investigators, but still have not had any contact with her since last night. We've triangulated the agent's cell phone signal, and tracked her last location to somewhere in the 19th Arrondissment, which makes no sense. I'm worried as hell about her too at this point. I've got two more agents trying to track her down now, and we're checking all the hotels in the city center of Paris, especially around the Sorbonne, which takes time. Of course, we're betting Ms. Craig is going to try and make contact with Rasul Aziz, the man Andrew was visiting last weekend, so we have his apartment staked out. Right now, that's about all I can tell you."

"I appreciate it John. Listen, I'm worried as hell about her too. Listen, I've actually heard from her. I received a short call from her this morning, and she told me that she's still in Paris. Our conversation was brief and then she cut it off. What really concerns me is that she told me someone might be following her, although I'm thinking that whoever she saw was one of your agents on her tail. She's no dummy, she would spot someone following her in a heartbeat."

"I don't know, Hunter, we've had no reports from any of our agents that they've spotted her..." O'Leary's voice trailed off with skepticism.

Hunter brushed off his words and continued his train of thought, "And you're right, she mentioned that she planned to try and meet up with Rasul Aziz. Please keep me informed, and let me know when you've caught up with her. I want to be informed of every detail."

"All right, Mr. Hunter, thank you for contacting us. Please contact me as soon as possible if you hear anything additional. And we will contact you as soon as we locate her. You'll be the first to know." John O'Leary hung up the phone.

Jeffrey Hunter touched end, and sat down in his chair. Swiveling his chair toward the window, he sat staring out at the tiny courtyard outside his window, and thinking about all that had transpired. In his mind, he replayed the whole scenario, starting with the night he received the phone call from Annie telling him about the train explosion. He replayed all the events in his head after that, the morning phone call, the grueling rescue and recovery operation, Andrew's death, his conversations with O'Leary concerning MI6's investigation, his conversation with Annie about her and Andrew, and now Annie's disappearance.

His cell phone rang again on the desk, and Jeffrey was brought back to the present. Glancing at the phone, he was puzzled to see *"Out of Area"* appear on the screen. After the last call, O'Leary's team had set him up with the ability to record any more suspicious calls that came in. He punched two buttons on his phone to initiate the recording, and then hit the button to answer the call.

"Jeffrey Hunter," he said in his most imposing sounding voice.

There was no one there. Jeffrey stared at the screen. Okay, now I'm really getting paranoid, he thought to himself.

He laid the phone on his desk and tried to refocus on the recovery reports in front of him, when once again, he heard his phone. Although this time, it was the ding of a text message coming in. The screen identified the text as coming from Annelise Craig.

"Jeffrey, I need your help. Meet me at 17 Rue des Carmes, Paris, tonight, 22:00. Tell no one, and please come alone."

Jeffrey studied the text. This didn't sound like Annie at all, but then she was obviously under some sort of distress. He went back to his list of recent calls and saw the recent *"Out of Area"* at the top of his list. He pressed redial, but only heard the familiar *beep-beep-beep,* signaling that the call could not be placed. He stared again at the text message, gritting his teeth. He knew he was being entangled in a situation that was very obscure and hazardous, but at this point, he was beginning to feel that he had no choice.

Annie was in real danger; there was little doubt about that. He also knew that he needed to get to her before O'Leary and his team did. Of course, the whole truth would need to come out at some point, but it was Jeffrey's intention to do everything he could to keep the administration from being dragged down in the investigation. If he could intervene, perhaps he could keep the whole administration from being tied to this nightmare, putting the Prime Minister, their long fought-for agenda, and all of them at risk.

But what was he supposed to do about this text message? Paris? Tonight? How was he supposed to drop everything and fly to Paris tonight? He had a job to do, damnit, a very important one. People were depending on him. Hell, the Prime Minister of the United Kingdom was depending on him. He didn't have time to be flying off to Paris for the evening when dozens of bodies were still trapped in a train explosion far underground, the financial markets were still reeling, all of England was feeling terrorized, and one of his country's most important trade routes had been destroyed. Not to mention his critical responsibility to keep the Prime Minister constantly updated, informed, and out in front of every potential ramification from the tragedy.

And then he thought again of Annelise and of Andrew. He knew they were involved somehow, but he knew in his gut that their involvement was unintentional. They had somehow been pulled into this nightmare through no fault of their own, and Jeffrey needed to help drag them out, preferably without damaging himself or the administration in the process. Whatever involvement they had, it could spell catastrophe for the administration. He realized that at this point, keeping Annie out of danger was the same as keeping the administration out of danger. It was one and the same. He had to find out where Annie was and get her back to London safely, before the police found her, and before the dangerous people who were hell bent on destroying all of them found her.

The immediate situation was that Annie was now in real danger. He realized he had no choice. He had to get to Paris, now. But how? The train was out, of course. Most of the time, his official travel was via the Royal Squadron, the short-range airplanes and helicopters reserved for official travel by members of the Royal family and senior politicians. As the situation stood, it wouldn't be hard to commandeer a VIP plane for a quick trip to where the ill-fated Eurostar had started its last Chunnel journey. He could make a quick trip to "inspect" the emergency operations on the other end of the line, and no one would question his movements.

Jeffrey picked up his phone and dialed the transportation office. Within minutes, he had a BAE 146 plane reserved to pick him up at the London City airport for the quick trip over to Paris. He told them his return flight would be standby, pending his ability to wrap up his business in Paris.

Jeffrey ordered a car to pick him up and deliver him to London City Airport at 6 p.m. His plan was simple and expeditious. He would meet up with Annelise in Paris tonight, talk some sense into her, put her back on the plane with him, and be back in London around midnight. If he played his cards right, he would be back before anyone missed him. He could not deal with this whole mess while Annelise was out wandering around Paris, putting herself and the administration at risk.

Jeffrey picked up his phone again, and typed out a response to Annie. *"OK See you at 22:00."* He pressed send.

Down the hall at #10 Downing, Fletcher LaForge looked down at his cellphone screen, watching the rolling dots as Jeffrey Hunter's response was being composed. In a moment, the familiar 'ding' signaled Jeffrey's response was received: "*OK See you at 22:00.*"

Fletcher LaForge smiled to himself. Yes, Jeffrey, we will indeed see you tonight in Paris at 10 p.m.

CHAPTER THIRTY-NINE

Annie looked down at her watch: it was ten minutes until 9 p.m. She looked up again through the window of the coffee shop on Rue de Crimee' and squinted at the sign across the street, above Paradigm Books. The light over the sign was still on, as she assumed it would be until 9 p.m., the posted closing time for the shop. She had been sitting here, on and off, almost the entire day, watching the storefront. The paper sign taped to the inside of the front door of the shop said the owner would be back in fifteen minutes. Although that was obviously not the case today, she felt sure he would make an appearance at some point today, and so Annie had no choice but to wait. She was too hungry for information to question the meaning of the sign much. Too afraid to venture too far, she was convinced that Rasul Aziz would materialize at some point, and she could talk to him about Andrew, hopefully piecing together what happened to the man she loved. She needed to glean any information she could uncover about Andrew's life: what did he know about any terrorist attacks, what the file had meant, and why he had been on the train that night. Rasul was the last person in the world to talk to Andrew, and he was his trusted old friend. Surely Rasul could help her string together some of the missing pieces from this baffling scenario. She'd already decided that at 9 p.m., she would give up, and catch a late plane back to London. She only had a few more minutes to be patient.

At five minutes until 9, Annie noticed a small blue Fiat slowly pull up in front of Paradigm books. She could make out the faint Uber decal in the window. Through the darkness, she could barely make out a dark figure as he got out of the car and hurried to the front door of the store, just as the car pulled away. The figure appeared to be a large dark-haired man, and Annie sucked in her breath. She gathered her purse and jacket, and downed the last drops of her coffee. Exiting the coffee shop, she hurried across the street, just as the man closed the door to Paradigm books behind him and appeared to be locking the front door. Annie rushed up to the door.

Knocking on the front door as loudly as she could, Annie could see the man through the glass front door disappear into the back room. In a moment, the light overhead above the sign clicked off, and Annie was standing on the Rue de Crimee' alone in the pitch dark. She instantly knew that this was not a safe place for a woman to be standing alone, and certainly not when some strange character had been following her since she got into a cab yesterday afternoon. The hair on the back of her neck stood up as she banged on the door and softly called out the name of the man who she hoped would help her.

"Rasul! Rasul!"

The store remained dark and quiet.

"Rasul Aziz! My name is Annelise Craig! I came all the way from London to speak with you! Please let me in!"

She continued to knock until her knuckles were throbbing, repeating her plea for the man who had disappeared into the back room.

"Rasul! Rasul Aziz! Please, my name is Annelise Craig, I was a friend of Andrew's!"

After what seemed like an eternity, the light above the sign flickered back on, and Annie was once again bathed in light. In a moment, the store lit up, and at the front door a face peered back at her through the glass windowpanes. Annie gasped as the face of a very angry and hostile Middle Eastern man jeered at her through the glass. For a moment, she almost took off running as fast as she could. Surely this man could not be Andrew's friend. One look into his eyes and Annie felt like she was looking into the eyes of a monster.

But then something moved across the man's face, and his entire demeanor changed in an instant. The angry scowl turned into a pleasant smile, and his eyes lit up with a friendly gaze. Annie ignored her inner gut instinct and convinced herself that this man was obviously a friend. Her gut had surely been wrong. Opening the door, Rasul smiled and held the door open, Annie stepped inside with trepidation.

"Come inside, please!" Rasul put on his best friendly face. This woman knew about his existence, and she obviously knew Andrew, which meant she was a potential threat to him. Right now, he needed to convince her that he was a friend, at least until he could figure out what to do with her.

"Thank you so much!" She said as she stepped in from the biting cold wind. Rubbing her hands together, she tried to warm her body and put on a smile at the same time, trying to appear friendly on this cold and bleak night.

"I'm so sorry to appear here so late tonight, but I've actually been waiting for you all day... My name is Annelise Craig. I'm – was – a friend of Andrew's." Annie thrust out her cold right hand, trying to instill a little normality into an otherwise awkward situation.

So, this is the woman Andrew was sleeping with . . . Rasul was thinking to himself, while he stuck out his right hand and shook her hand in return. *What is she doing here?* he wondered with suspicion.

"Oh, yes, Ms. Craig. I received the voice mail from Jeffrey, but unfortunately I lost my phone yesterday and didn't have his number. And I'm sorry, but I've been very busy. I was called away on a family emergency today. I've only just returned. I'm distraught over the terrible tragedy, and of course Andrew's death. He was a very dear friend. He told me that the two of you were close as well."

Tears sprang to Annie's eyes at the mention of Andrew's name. He had talked to Rasul about her after all. Thank goodness. Maybe Rasul would know something about Andrew's life as well. Maybe Andrew had talked to Rasul about the file – about any suspicions or theories he had. And maybe, just maybe, he had talked to Rasul about her. Maybe Rasul could fill in some of the missing parts of Andrew's thinking that he kept hidden away from everyone, including her.

"Yes, we were close. Actually, that's why I'm here. I know this all seems strange right now, me showing up like this out of the blue, but I was very much wondering if we could talk. Could we go for a drink maybe, or coffee, or whatever you want? I just have some questions I'd like to ask you about Andrew. About what you did last weekend when he was here in Paris? What he talked about? I have so many questions about his death, and if he mentioned me at all."

Annie knew she looked and sounded like some half-desperate, half-crazed woman at this point, but she didn't care anymore. It was late, she was distraught and exhausted, and somewhere in Paris, someone was still out there trying to find her, and very likely wanting her dead. Her life was a mess, her job was in jeopardy, and she had lost the only man she truly loved. Right now, she felt like there wasn't anything else left to risk, so the last thing she cared about at this point was what this Middle Eastern stranger thought about her.

At the same time, Rasul was growing more agitated with the situation by the second. Why was this woman here, and what did she know about Andrew's death? Was she suspicious about Rasul's involvement in anything Andrew had uncovered? What exactly had Andrew told her?

Rasul realized in a flash that none of his questions mattered. He had to get rid of this lady. Whatever she knew, it was too much. She was a danger to him. She had to go, and fast. With all that Rasul had already done, getting rid of this over-wrought, emotional woman would be no skin off his back.

Rasul had moved to his usual position behind the counter, and stood facing Annie, who was now standing at the back of the shop. While Annelise rambled on, Rasul began to scan the room, analyzing the situation and trying to figure out what the best method would be. Since they were both here in his bookshop, and he had no idea for sure who might know she was here, he needed to get rid of her and leave no trace. No blood, no hair, no fingerprints. She needed to disappear completely. He had no qualms about the task; he'd done this kind of thing many times before.

"Of course, Ms. Craig. Andrew told me so much about you. Certainly, we can go for a drink, I'll just need to grab a few things in the back and lock the place up. Follow me back to my office and we can leave through the back door."

With that, Rasul moved toward Annie. He reached for his scarf on the counter. He didn't like killing women with his bare hands, a scarf would make it easier on both of them. Rasul was so concentrated on the job in front of him, he did not notice the sound of the bookshop door opening behind him. Only the look on Annie's face alerted him that someone had entered the store. Turning to face the unwanted intruder, Rasul Aziz and Annelise Craig stood face to face with an AK-47 aimed directly at their chests. Instantly, Annelise recognized the man from the cab yesterday, the man who had been following her through the streets of Paris. And now here he was in this bookstore, holding the gun aimed straight at her and Rasul.

Terror raced through Annelise's body at the sight of the man entering the shop with the gun. Her legs were frozen, and she was unable to move a muscle. She couldn't run, and she couldn't scream. Slowly, she backed up against the door to the backroom, and began to cry, her body shaking with desperate fear. She had her back to the storeroom door, but escaping was impossible, he would kill her before she could even get the door open. There was absolutely no way out.

"Please, don't shoot us. I will give you whatever you want. Please!" Annelise's voice screeched out of her throat as if she were being strangled.

"Tawqaf! nhan ealaa nfs aljanib lak ahmq!" Rasul shouted in Arabic, and Annelise could not think fast enough. As Rasul shouted, the man with the gun began shouting back, speaking some dialect of Arabic and Annie had no clue what was being said. Her only thought was that she was going to die, right here in this Muslim bookshop, in a Muslim neighborhood in Paris with two men she did not know. She was petrified with fear.

"Rasul! Tell him we are innocent! He told me his name is Tom Khan in a cab yesterday, and I have no idea why he has been following me, and I don't know anything. I will give him my purse, or whatever else he wants, just please don't kill us!" Annelise was crying and shaking, and begging Rasul to help save them.

At that moment, she had no clue that Rasul was trying to convince Akeem that he and Akeem were on the same side of this fight.

"Kill the bitch!" he yelled in Arabic. "We are brothers!"

Nothing Rasul was saying was having any effect on the man with the gun – that much Annie could plainly see. In a moment, Tom Khan – or whatever his name was – began gesturing wildly for them to move outside, onto the dark street. Annie and Rasul, with the gunman close behind, walked out of the bookshop and onto the sidewalk in front of the store. As they exited the building, a black SUV screeched to a halt right in front of the store, and the man with the gun edged toward the car motioning for them to get in. Rasul kept screeching in Arabic and now the man with the gun began telling him to "Shut Up" in English. That much Annie could understand. Annie realized that Rasul's attempts to save them were having no effect.

Annie and Rasul shuffled into the back seat, and Tom Khan butted Rasul's head with his gun for good measure as he slammed the door. He then climbed into the front seat and pivoted so that he could keep the gun aimed squarely at their heads. The driver was a young man with blondish hair and indecipherable origin who never looked back or said a word. He just drove. Squealing away from the curb in front of the bookshop, the foursome drove into the night, and Annie had no idea where they might be going. She realized that she was probably going to die tonight, and no one could save her now, not Andrew, not Jeffrey, not the British government, and from the looks of it, not Rasul either. She dropped her face to her chest and began to sob.

CHAPTER FORTY

The grinding of the landing gear descending into position awoke Jorge from a deep sleep. He raised his window shade and looked out at the black sky. Down below, the City of Lights was living up to its name, aglow with twinkling lights that were neatly lining out the wide boulevards of Paris. Jorge loved Paris and was happy to be landing there. He had completely blocked the reason for the trip from his mind, at least for a little while. Paris was a glorious city, even in the pitch dark, he thought to himself.

As the plane touched down, Jorge checked his watch: 5:30 p.m. New York time, which meant it was 22:15 French time – 10:15 p.m. After Charlie's threats, he had been lucky enough to make a late morning flight out of New York, and thankfully he'd been able to catch a couple of hours sleep on the plane. Maybe he could check in to a hotel in the city and grab a little more sleep before he thought about how he was going to take care of this nasty assignment. At the moment, his strategy was to delay, delay, delay. Charlie had never asked him to do anything like this before, and he was still in denial about actually completing it.

He was used to being the errand boy, that much was for sure. But his jobs normally entailed much easier tasks like facilitating the transfer of money to and from off-shore accounts, carrying cash and other assets across borders, and the occasional delivery of a message. He knew their group had executed plans that involved the killing of innocent people many times before, but Jorge had never been directly involved in any of that unpleasantness. He had never had any trouble keeping the true nature of their work far from his own mind. But this was different. This was too personal, and Jorge wasn't sure if he could, or would be able to pull it off. To make matters even worse, he completely believed that this was a fool's errand ... he had no idea where Rasul was, or how he would even find him. He wasn't a cold-blooded killer, and Jorge wondered if there was some way he could get out of this horrible assignment.

As the plane touched down at Charles de Gaulle and taxied toward the gate, Jorge pulled out his phone and pressed the power button. After powering up and connecting with the French cell towers, he began to feel the soft vibrations of text messages and emails arriving on his phone. Twelve new text messages lit up on his screen.

Scanning through the usual messages from his sister and mother, he landed on one from Charlie.

"Rasul is in Paris. Take a car to 17 Rue des Carmes when you land. Someone will meet you."

Damn it. I'm not prepared for this. I haven't even thought about what I'm here to do, let alone how to do it. This is crap, and I'm sick and tired of doing Charlie's bidding. Who made him the boss anyway?

With no luggage and the late flight, the airport had a scarce number of travelers and Jorge made it through customs in just a few minutes and was in a cab headed toward Paris within an additional ten minutes. He texted Charlie as he had been instructed and let him know he'd landed early in Paris and was headed to the address he'd been given. He received no response from Charlie which irritated him all over again. Here he was flying across the Atlantic at the drop of a hat, and Charlie couldn't even be bothered to respond to his text. He decided then and there that this was the last errand he was doing for Charlie or anyone else involved in this vile scheme. He was tired of this disgusting business, he was tired of the despicable people he was involved with, and he was sick and tired of taking directions from people who obviously didn't care an iota for him. He wanted out, now. He would take care of this one last errand, and then he was taking his money and getting out.

As he rode in the backseat of the taxi, headed for his assigned destination, he thought about where he would go and what he would do when he got out of this terrible business. Maybe he would return to Texas he thought. He would be loaded with money from his share of their latest little venture. Sure, most of it would be tied up in offshore accounts for years, but he would find a way to launder a sizeable chunk of the money back into the United States through some little business venture in Texas. Something to occupy his time. Maybe he would open a baseball training facility and utilize his natural skills, working with kids. He would love it. And the money would guarantee he could live a cushy life. Most of those businesses dealt a lot in cash. It would be an easy front. Life wouldn't be as stressful, and he could once and for all get off the drugs. Hell, he would even go into rehab if that's what it took. He could have his pick of the best places – maybe some place that resembled a resort spa – and kick the habit once and for all. He would make a vacation of it. He could definitely make it work. Jorge smiled to himself that for the first time in a long time, he actually had a plan for his life that involved doing something good.

But first, he had to take care of this nasty assignment. How in the hell was he supposed to kill Rasul Aziz? If that weirdo old man with the white hair at the Islamic Center in Oxford he'd heard about couldn't do the job, why did they think he could? Jorge assumed that whomever he was being sent to meet up with right now at Rue des Carmes would undoubtedly have more information for him, and hopefully hand off a weapon of some sort. He had shot a gun a few times, but never at a human. This whole assignment was ill-planned and ill-advised. Surely the liaison he was being sent to meet up with would know the best way to go about this. Maybe he would even help execute the plan. Whatever. Jorge just wanted to get it done and get back on a New York-bound plane.

If he played his cards right, he could be back in his office in New York by late tomorrow evening. He just needed to eliminate this guy quick, and get home before anyone even discovered the body. Jorge wondered again how it would feel, killing someone with his own hands. The fact that Rasul was such an evil guy would make the job infinitely easier to execute. And given the fact that Rasul had played such a direct role in the killing of all those innocent people on the train, he realized he wouldn't feel too bad about getting rid of him. Jorge had always consoled himself with the idea that he was simply an indirect participant in all the bloodshed. He didn't really have blood on his hands. But Rasul had always been much more directly involved. He was a cold-blooded killer, and the world would be a better place without him. He would actually be doing a good thing. It shouldn't be too hard, Jorge told himself again. He would be doing a good deed, helping the world get rid of a really evil man. And with that, Jorge relaxed in the backseat of the cab, smiled to himself, and thought about how much fun it would be to be back in Dallas, helping kids learn to throw a fastball.

CHAPTER FORTY-ONE

The dashboard clock read 9:52 p.m., as they sped through the streets of Paris in the black SUV. Annie and Rasul sat in the backseat with an AK-47 still trained on their heads. They were now crossing the Seine, and Annie recognized the ancient bridge they were on as they crossed the river. She had crossed the Pont Notre-Dame many times during her student days in Paris. The bridge, the oldest and she thought most beautiful bridge in Paris stood on the site where people had been crossing the Seine since the beginning of recorded time. This particular bridge had stood here, just as it had since its completion in 1507, providing an entry point to Ile de Cite' and the magnificent Notre Dame Cathedral. And now, Annie thought to herself, it was the route taking her to her death.

Within moments, they were now crossing Petit Pont, onto the Rue Saint-Jacques. Annie knew these streets by heart. Where in hell were they taking her? Looking up, she recognized the magnificent Eglise Saint-Severin, the imposing Gothic Catholic Church that had stood on Paris' left bank since the early thirteenth century. The gargoyles high up on the arches seemed to leer down at her as she was being whisked away to what she believed was certain death. With an AK-47 still positioned now at her chest, there was little hope she would escape from this deadly cab ride.

Beside her in the backseat Rasul Aziz was whimpering. He had been blathering in Arabic or some Middle Eastern language for much of their dizzy trip through Paris, but he was obviously not getting anywhere with his diatribe. The man with the gun and the driver mostly ignored him, but occasionally they told him to "shut up" or sneered something in Arabic at him. Rasul was growing increasingly frantic, and Annie was growing increasingly quiet, except for the occasional sniffle as tears flowed freely down her cheeks. She tried to devise an escape plan, but the long metal barrel aimed at her heart left little room for an escape plan.

Within moments, the car swerved into a hard left onto Rue des Ecoles, and then two quick rights in succession, and then another right onto Rue des Carmes. They were mere blocks from the Sorbonne, and somehow the familiarity of the streets was a strange counterpoint to the terror she felt trapped in the backseat with a gun aimed at her. She kept trying to discern where they must be going, but nothing made any sense. Why did they want her and Rasul both? What in the hell did he have to do with this? She knew that her relationship with Andrew had somehow made her a target, but why Rasul Aziz? Nothing made sense.

In a moment, the car stopped short in the middle of a dark block. Although the Rue des Carmes was usually a busy street, it was almost 10 p.m. now, and except for a couple walking far down the block, it was deserted. The driver said something in Arabic to the gunman, and Annie picked out the gunman's real name – Akeem. So, he wasn't Tom Khan after all, and he obviously wasn't a businessman in Paris for work. In fact, everything about him had been a charade – for her benefit? Had she somehow been a target since arriving in Paris? In shock, it suddenly dawned on Annie that all of this was so much bigger than she had ever imagined. Andrew's death, the terrorist attack, Rasul, the robbery at her house, the man with the gun in London, the stolen folder – it was all part of a much larger puzzle that she was somehow caught up in. But right now, these seemingly disjointed facts were all a jumble in her brain, and all she could focus on was the gun now again aimed directly at her head.

Akeem and the driver motioned wildly for them to get out of the car. For a split-second Annie thought that maybe they were going to leave them there on the sidewalk, alone. She held her breath as she and Rasul sprang out onto the sidewalk, hoping against hope that the car would speed away. But instead, she heard the slam of the SUV front door as Akeem stepped out behind them, the gun tucked discreetly into his jacket, but with his finger still poised securely on the trigger.

They were standing on the street, with large white French Baroque buildings lining the sidewalk in front of them. Akeem motioned for them to walk between two of the large buildings, still mumbling Arabic under his breath. Rasul had largely given up his rant, and was now attempting to talk to Annie, low under his breath. He was obviously devising some new alternative plan, but Annie had the distinct feeling he couldn't really be trusted either. His eyes had returned to the angry menacing look they had the first time she saw him, and his gestures in the car while he was rambling at Akeem in Arabic didn't look too much like he was too worried about Annie's fate at all.

For a moment Annie considered making a wild, last minute attempt at escape – just making a break for it as hard and fast as she could run. What was Akeem going to do? Shoot her here on this Paris street? He couldn't shoot her, and keep the gun trained on Rasul at the same time. In desperation, she thought that at least she would have a fifty percent chance of surviving.

Turning in the direction Akeem was forcing them to walk, Annie noticed a tall wrought iron gate spanning the middle of the three meter fence that bridged the space between the two buildings. The fence loomed ahead as the threesome made their way toward the gate and a courtyard beyond. Akeem motioned for them to proceed through the gate. Rasul pushed the metal door open, and he and Annie walked through, with Akeem close behind. He pushed the gate closed, and motioned for them to proceed.

Despite the dark, after a moment, Annie began to make out the shape and details on the old building in front of them. It was a beautiful old stone church. The exterior façade was one large Corinthian arch, with a small cross positioned directly above it. For a French church, it was very small, and unusually set back from the street in this gated courtyard. For a moment, the site of the cross gave Annie a comforting, sheltered feeling, as if the church walls themselves could protect her somehow.

As they neared the building, Annie saw a small sign with the name Eglise Saint-Ephrim etched on it, and recognized it as the name of an old Syrian Catholic church on the outskirts of the Sorbonne, one she'd visited once while she was a student. She'd had a friend at the Sorbonne who was a music student and Annie remembered that she'd attended her friend's recital here one warm summer night twelve or so years ago. Annie had not wanted to attend the recital but felt obligated for her friend's sake. Annie remembered being mesmerized by the unusual mix of Catholic and Middle Eastern imagery in the church. She remembered hearing that they conducted services in Aramaic and Arabic, which always struck Annie as being so odd. Either way, it was a beautiful church, which made no sense to Annie, but eased her fear a little all the same.

Akeem grumbled something indecipherable to Rasul, and he opened the front door of the church. Completely dark except for the soft yellow flickering of a dozen or so candles burning along the wall, Annie's momentary calm vanished as she realized the church was deserted. The interior, with its gray stone walls and floor was vacant except for some statutes of Catholic Saints positioned along the side corridors. There was no one here to rescue Annie, or help her make her escape. She broke into a cold sweat of terror as she realized once again that she was trapped.

Pushing them forward with the barrel of his AK-47, Annie and Rasul stumbled up the main aisle of the small chapel. Stained glass Saints watched from the windows above as she and Rasul were prodded up the aisle like wayward sheep being led to slaughter. Annie's tears were running down her cheeks by now, and made it all the harder to see where she was being herded. As the threesome neared the altar, Annie turned and made one last plea for her life.

"Please, Akeem, or Tom, or whatever your name is. I don't know what you want from me. I have no idea why I'm here or why you've been following me. I swear to you, I don't know anything about anything that you might be involved with. If it's something to do with Andrew, I swear he never told me anything. I'm a married woman – married to someone else. Andrew was just my ...," and Annie realized she had no idea what to call him. "Lover" sounded so trashy, and "boyfriend" sounded juvenile. She settled on "friend", which was true enough.

"He was just my friend," she said, and realized at that moment how sad and true that statement really was.

"Please, if you let me go, you'll never see or hear from me again. I will tell no one what has happened here tonight. I want nothing to do with any of this. I just want to go home to my husband."

And with that, a wave of sadness swept over her at the thought of poor Richard, how innocent he was in all of this, knowing absolutely nothing. He was probably home right now, discovering the break in, and wondering where she was. Unable to make contact by now, he was no doubt worried sick at this point. When he found out everything that Annie had been involved in, it would devastate him, ruin his life. And for the first time since starting her affair with Andrew, she felt a giant wave of guilt wash over her at the thought of her unsuspecting husband.

But her words fell on deaf ears. Akeem couldn't care less. He pushed the barrel of the gun into her chest and gave her a hard push. With that, Annie stumbled backward against Rasul, who gave her a second shove to return her to her feet. And with that one gesture, Annie knew for certain that Rasul Aziz was no friend of hers either. They were two unwitting victims being led to their death side by side, but neither knowing nor caring about the other.

As they approached the front of the church, Akeem motioned for them to walk through a small door positioned to the far right of the altar. Rasul led the way, and they entered a small room, dark and dank, with the smell of mold emanating from the thick stone walls. Akeem turned the metal lever on a wall sconce, and a small dim flame illuminated the room. The room was empty except for a small wooden prayer altar that looked like it had been a very long time since anyone had offered up any petitions to God from this room.

Without fanfare, Akeem walked over to the wooden altar and kicked it aside. Only then did Annie see the little metal door on the floor. Old and corroded, the door was only about half a meter wide and half a meter long. Akeem grumbled something to Rasul and motioned for him to open the hatch. Rasul launched into a tirade in Arabic, which prompted Akeem to raise the barrel of his gun straight at Rasul's head and deliver a severe blow across his forehead. With that, Rasul dropped to his knees and began pleading for his life. Annie closed her eyes, unable to stand the site of what she thought was about to happen. This was obviously the end for both she and Rasul, and below this metal door obviously laid their graves. She would spend eternity here under the floor of this ancient church, and no one might ever even discover her body. Her short life was ending right here in this chapel, with two men who didn't even bother explaining to her why she was being executed so summarily.

Annie put her hands to her face and braced for the inevitable. Her tears rolled down through her fingers, down her forearms, and onto the front of her blouse. She thought of Richard, she thought of Andrew, and she thought of Jeffrey, her boss and friend, who would be mystified by what had happened to her. She stood there bracing for death, and wondering what she would feel when the end came.

She stood there holding her breath, tears stinging her eyes, until finally she realized she had been standing there for quite a while. Nothing was happening. Slowly, she pulled her hands down, just low enough to peek out above her fingertips. There, flickering in the soft glow of the lamp, she was shocked to see Rasul descending a ladder through the gaping hole in the floor. Akeem was glaring at her, and she realized that she too was expected to descend the little ladder below the floorboards. What was this? A hallucination? Her mind's last ditch effort to soften the reality of death? But as Rasul descended further, she could hear the faint sound of water dripping, and softly splashing as it hit more water.

And in an instant it hit her . . . the Tunnels.

CHAPTER FORTY-TWO

They run all through this part of Paris, deep under the city streets, even far below the Metro lines. Lined with the bones of millions of Parisians from the Eighteenth and Ninetieth centuries, the tunnels became the burial grounds during the Plague when the city's cemeteries were overrun with death. Now, the tunnels and catacombs snake all through the underground city for hundreds of miles, giving rise to an underground labyrinth that has drawn criminals, curiosity-seekers, and even tourists on occasion.

Annie had never descended into their dark caverns herself, but had known many people who had. Some of her student friends during her summer in Paris had even thrown a party somewhere down here once, entering through a little known and long forgotten entrance in the basement of one of the university libraries. She'd heard plenty of stories of the cavernous tunnels. There were even the occasional stories of people getting lost in the dark tunnels for days or even weeks, and some never heard from again. She had never desired to see the ominous warren during her time in Paris, but now she was being forced to at gunpoint.

Descending the long, corroding metal ladder into the tunnel, she could hear Rasul's heavy breathing below her, and the sound of the gun clanking on each rung as the trio descended into the darkness. Annie's blood ran cold with each descending step, knowing that what lay below would no doubt be her grave, hundreds of feet below the streets of Paris.

Each succeeding step took Annie further and further from the surface, and from any available light source. The world below was frigid, dark, and menacing. Other than their heavy breathing, as the sounds of the world above faded further and further in the distance, the only sound she could hear was the steady *drip, drip, drip*, of a trickle of water somewhere far down below. As the source of that sound grew increasingly louder, Annie knew that they were close to the bottom. Peering above her head, she could see the faint rim of light around the trap door that had been pulled closed over their heads. With each step down, the air grew icier, and her panic increased.

Annie heard Rasul's foot hit solid ground, and then a scuffle. She imagined that he was trying to make some sort of last ditch get away in the pitch dark. Given the fact that she could barely see her hands in front of her face at this point, she knew any escape attempt would be futile. You can't flee when you don't even know which way to run. The next sound she heard was a thud, and realized Rasul had already fallen to the ground, bringing his desperate escape attempt to a halt. With her next step, Annie's left foot hit the dirt as well, and she stumbled out of the way to avoid being hit in the head by her captor as he descended the final few rungs.

Annie stood still in the dark, waiting on the inevitable. What would happen next? Would he kill them right here and leave their bodies to rot in this little stream of water running underneath her feet? She waited in the pitch blackness, until she heard the third set of feet hit the ground, and knew that the end was almost here.

In a moment, a light pierced the blackness. Akeem had pulled a large battery operated lantern off of a hook on the wall, and had flicked on the bulb. The light was so bright, Annie winced at the purple spots that clouded her vision. It took a good sixty seconds for Annie's eyes to adjust to the light, and allow her to have a good look at her surroundings. Once her vision cleared, she could make out the muddied walls of the tunnel, but there was little to see otherwise.

The tunnel was only about three meters wide and three meters high. Other than the dark gray mud that lined the walls, and the small stream of water about two centimeters deep running down the middle, there was not much to look at. Clearly there had been no clandestine parties being thrown in this branch of the tunnel maze.

Akeem growled some new command in Arabic and Rasul started walking. Annie followed behind, as her only other option was to run off into the pitch dark like a blind animal. They followed the stream, and the beam of light through the tunnel about two hundred meters, and then then Akeem switched to English.

"Turn right here, through that opening in the wall."

Annie looked to the right, but could see nothing but gray mud. Rasul was obviously in the same boat, as he peered at the wall with the same look of incomprehension.

"There, down low." Akeem said.

And then Annie saw it, a small opening about one-meter square. Akeem shined his light on the hole, and Annie could see that it opened into a much larger space. With no hope left, she dropped to her knees and crawled through the space, Rasul lingering behind.

Behind her, she heard another scuffle, this one much more intense than the last. Rasul had obviously decided to make another last-ditch attempt to wrestle the gun away from Akeem. Annie could hear their gruff voices wailing in Arabic as the sounds of a high stakes fight for the gun was in play. She could hear crashes and blows of the struggle echoing up and down the tunnel. In the half light of the lantern, Annie could make out the feet and legs of the two as they thrashed and flailed in a mortal battle for the gun.

Annie scrambled for a place to hide or escape from her new chamber in the tunnel, but could see nothing more than the mud floor a few meters around her where the light from the tunnel made a small circle and illuminated the floor. She crouched against the wall, watching the struggle underway in the tunnel from her limited vantage point, trying to make out who was winning the scuffle. Suddenly, two shots rang out, reverberating through the tunnel. Annie let out a shriek and thrust her hands to her face, too afraid to see whose body fell to the ground. She held her breath as tears flooded her eyes. She wiped her eyes and strained through the dim light to see who was left standing. For several seconds there was no sound.

And then she heard his body fall. Rasul's head hit the ground, and his face was turned in a grotesque angle straight toward her. She could look directly into his eyes, but knew he wasn't seeing her. Annie sucked in her breathe and cowered into the dark hole even further.

In a moment, the piercing beam from the flashlight turned on her and she recoiled at the glaring light. Akeem's face appeared next to the light, scowling at her through the patches of light and dark.

"Get inside, bitch."

Annie scooted backwards into the hole, and suddenly realized that this was no hole in the wall at all. She was now sitting on the concrete floor of a cavernous room, dimly lit by the light being thrown off by Akeem's lone light source.

Behind her, Akeem scrambled into the room. Once Akeem was in the room, the entire space was ablaze in light. Annie realized this was no abandoned tunnel after all. There were three makeshift tables, haphazardly assembled out of 2x4s and plywood, and a smattering of chairs that had been assembled with the same crude materials. The place was littered with trash – cans, paper plates, empty water jugs, and sacks from a grocery store, where obviously someone had brought in food and had stayed down here for some extended length of time. In the corner, an old cereal box had obviously turned into dinner for some rats. Someone had obviously spent some serious time down here.

On top of the three tables, it looked like an electronics lab of some sort was in full operation. The tables had been pushed together, and on top of the largest were spools of electrical wiring, circuit boards, a mishmash of miscellaneous electronic devices, and three or four laptop computers. Taking it all in, Annie knew instantly what she was looking at.

Annie turned and faced Akeem. For some reason, she felt a surge of strength in what she believed were her final moments, and wanted to look her killer in the eyes before he pulled the trigger.

"I have no idea why you've brought me here to kill me. I told you, I have no knowledge of anything that would make me a risk for someone like you. Please let me go. I swear to you that I will never tell anyone about you or this place." Annie was making her final desperate plea.

"Shut up and sit down on that carpet." Akeem glared at her and kept his gun aimed squarely at her head, with his finger on the trigger. Annie looked around, and saw a small square of old carpet along the wall. Affixed to the tunnel wall next to it was a long metal chain with a small metal bracket on the end. She sat down on the carpet as she was told, and Akeem secured the bracket around her ankle, imprisoning her in the dark alcove, twenty meters below the little Catholic Chapel above.

As soon as the metal clamp was locked around her ankle, from outside the opening and down the tunnel, they heard a distinct *clang*, the sound of metal hitting metal. Akeem jumped and turned around, his gun waving wildly in the air, aimed at everything and nothing. Annie sucked in her breath, and sat motionless, listening for the sound of someone coming. She did not take a breath or utter a sound, waiting for some other sign that someone might be coming to rescue her. But no sound came. Was it someone in the tunnel? Or was it just some innocuous sound from far away echoing through the underground labyrinth? Akeem had obviously heard it too. He kneeled on the ground and tried to peer out of the hole, and down the tunnel, looking for someone to emerge out of the shaft leading down from the surface. The tunnel was too dark, and he could see no one.

Just as Akeem started to stand, the sound rang out again, but much louder this time. *CLANG.*

CHAPTER FORTY-THREE

Jeffrey's plane landed in Paris at 9:20 p.m. at Paris's Orly airport. With the exception of two pilots and a steward, he was the only one on the flight. The military level crew made routine flights like this on a daily basis for members of the British government, so no one asked very many questions. Given the current state of emergency, no one would question a quick visit to Paris anyway.

Other than filing a flight plan, Jeffrey eschewed any formal travel arrangements once he landed in Paris. He wanted this trip to be as low key as possible, so he had reported that beyond the Paris airport, transportation would be provided by private car upon his arrival. Once he landed, he summoned an Uber for the half hour drive into the city. So far his impromptu trip was going according to plan. Within forty-five minutes of landing, Jeffrey's Uber driver already had him entering the streets of Paris's Latin Quarter, cruising along the streets circling the Sorbonne, surrounded by old buildings resplendent in their beautiful classic architecture.

In a few minutes, the Uber driver had found the address Jeffrey had given him. Jeffrey looked down at his watch: 10:00 p.m. sharp. Surely this address wasn't right. Why on earth would Annie want to meet him here on this dark Parisian street in front of an old church? He punched in the tip amount on his phone for the Uber driver, and got out of the car. A light snow was falling, and regardless of the circumstances, Jeffrey could not help but notice how beautiful the little church was in the moonlight.

Jeffrey waited on the pavement outside the church, and after ten minutes, he was growing increasingly impatient and freezing cold. Surely there had been some sort of misunderstanding. He checked his text message again. For the now second time, he hit the icon to reply and hurriedly typed *"I'm here. Where are you?"* Again, there was no response.

About ready to give up and summon his Uber back, Jeffrey pulled on the iron gates of the chapel courtyard and was surprised to find them open. For the first time it dawned on him that maybe Annie had meant to meet him inside the chapel. Why hadn't he thought of that before?

Walking up to the tall front doors, he was surprised again to find them open as well. Who would leave a church open this late on a weeknight? Maybe it was left open for people needing to pray? Jeffrey had no idea if churches really did things like that, but he'd seen it in the movies, so it seemed plausible enough to him.

Pushing open the heavy wooden doors, he could see the soft glow of candlelight emanating from the small alcove off to the right in the entryway. He pulled the door closed softly behind him, feeling a little eerie in a church alone this late at night. This was all starting to feel extremely uncomfortable for Jeffrey and he was ready to turn tail and escape with each passing moment. But his concern for Annie kept him moving forward.

The church was empty, save for the stone Saints scattered around the small chapel. Each of his footsteps echoed in the chamber, and in the absence of any other sound, his own breathing sounded inordinately loud. He thought he could hear the soft creaking of old wood, settling in cold damp air.

And then he saw him.

The man was sitting alone at the front of the church in one of the short pews positioned up near the altar. The little pew the man was sitting on sat at a ninety-degree angle to the regular pews, and was the type usually reserved for the priests and other VIPs. He was dressed in a heavy black coat, but his face was turned away, looking toward the gilded altar. Jeffrey assumed he must be a priest, the caretaker of this ancient chapel. Who else would be in a deserted church this time of night?

Not wanting to interrupt the priest's quiet contemplation, Jeffrey waited a moment, and then softly cleared his throat to alert the man to his presence. The man did not budge or turn his head. For a moment Jeffrey thought he must be asleep.

Moving up the center aisle, Jeffrey tried to walk softly so as not to disturb him. With each step, he could more clearly see the man's profile, and an odd familiarity began to dawn on Jeffrey. In the dimness of the chapel, he knew his eyes must be playing tricks on him.

At the front of the church Jeffrey stopped and bowed his head, like he thought one should probably do at the front of a church. Instead of prayer, however, his thoughts were tied up wondering how to garner the man's attention. He needed to ask him if he might have seen a woman waiting in here, or around the premises.

When he raised his head, Jeffrey recoiled in shock. He sucked in his breath, and almost fell backwards. There, now standing silently just a few feet in front of him, was none other than Fletcher LaForge, Jeffrey's longtime friend and Wellington's respected Deputy National Security Advisor. LaForge's eyebrows were furrowed, and his face looked beleaguered and fraught. His eyes were cold, his jaw set, and his lips curled up in a look of disgust that Jeffrey had never seen before.

"Fletcher, what are you doing here? Why are you here? What in the hell is going on?" Jeffrey was incredulous, trying to wrap his brain around what was happening.

"Sit down, Jeffrey," Fletcher shot back in a menacing tone.

Jeffrey did not sit down. He took two steps toward Fletcher, who stood his ground. As he got closer, Jeffrey could see the man's jaws clenching in a way he had never seen before. Clearly something was horribly wrong.

"Fletch, tell me what's going on."

Only then did Jeffrey notice Fletcher's right arm thrust inside his coat pocket. Inside the coat, Jeffrey recognized the threatening, hard outline of a small hand gun, and the barrel was aimed straight at him.

"What the hell, Fletch?"

"I said sit down, Jeffrey, now."

Jeffrey lowered his body on the front pew, perching on the edge of the hard wooden bench. He stared at Fletcher, his mind unable to make sense of what was happening. As he gripped the front of the wooden seat, he realized his palms were wet with sweat.

"Fletch, I'm here to meet Annie. Hell, I told you what she's going through. She's in danger. She texted me and told me to meet her here, tonight. I'm here to get her and take her back to London. But why are you here?"

And then a light bulb went on in his head, and it suddenly dawned on him that that must be why Fletcher was here too. Annie must have summoned him here as well. But why? And then slowly, the full story started to dawn on him. The ominous realization of the gun trained on him made him realize that Fletch's presence was not some kind of crazy coincidence, and this was not going to end well.

"Jeffrey, you idiot, you've always been such a fool. You're blinded by your friendships and your loyalties, always to the wrong people. You get tied up with losers who are too stupid to take advantage of their opportunities, and they drag you down. But you've been doing that since Oxford, so I guess no one should be surprised. I could've made you a partner too, you would've been filthy rich by now, but instead you tied yourself to losers like Wellington and Andrew Bolling. I could've brought them in on this a long time ago as well. But they were always so busy being do-gooders, that they missed the amazing opportunities right below their noses. Your guy won the election four years ago you idiot, but we're the ones making off with the spoils of victory now."

Jeffrey just stared at him, uncomprehending. What was he talking about? What in the hell did Wellington and Andrew Bolling have to do with this? They had all worked side by side for four years. LaForge was a trusted member of the Prime Minister's inner circle. They had labored in the trenches together and shared in the victories along with Wellington, as well as the challenges inherent in running one of the most important countries in the world. They had shared more than a few victory dinners, strategy meetings, golf games, late nights at the office, and weathered the ups and downs of political life together. Who was this nutcase standing in front of him right now, ranting about money and lost opportunities?

LaForge could see from the look on Jeffrey's face that he still wasn't getting it, and it infuriated him. He walked up to him where Jeffrey still sat on the bench, grabbed his face in his left hand, and shoved him so hard backward that Jeffrey's head snapped back and hit the back of the pew. It happened so hard and fast that for a moment Jeffrey thought his neck might be broken. A walnut sized knot swelled up on the back of his head and immediately began to throb. Only then did the full realization of what was happening completely dawn on Jeffrey Hunter.

Jeffrey's incredulity had now turned to rage. He stood up, ready to charge LaForge. The gun was the last thing on his mind at this point. In that moment, Jeffrey didn't give a damn what happened to him anymore. He'd had enough. The terrorist attack, Andrew's death, Annie's disappearance, he couldn't take any more evil people destroying his life.

"Where is she? Where is Annie? She told me to meet her here...What in the hell have you done with her?"

"You stupid fool, she didn't send you that text. I did. Unfortunately for her, Annelise knew too much. Her illicit relationship with Andrew Bolling sealed her fate. Don't be too worried about it though, mate. She really wasn't very good at her job anyway." Fletcher added the last little phrase with a sarcastic smirk on his face.

Jeffrey dropped back to the hard church bench in shock. What was Fletcher LaForge saying? That Andrew had been murdered? That Annie had been killed too?

"Let me lay it out for you, Jeffrey. While you and your old buddy Wellington have been busy having tea with the queen and passing useless legislation for the past four years, a few of us old friends from Oxford have been busy taking advantage of a handful of opportunities we were in a position to help arrange. While you and Wellington and your cronies thought you were fighting terrorism and protecting the country, all you were really doing was cleaning up after a few 'economic incidents' we were able to help orchestrate. Fortuitously for us, there were extremely lucrative financial rewards for those of us involved in planning and executing the incidents."

LaForge smiled mockingly at Jeffrey, showing his enjoyment at finally getting to tell his story to the one person who had been unwittingly playing a role in the entire scheme.

"But what about the phone call I received that morning after the attack? The one saying it was a terrorist attack?" Jeffrey was still trying to connect the dots.

"We had to throw you a red herring, something to keep you busy and darting off in the wrong direction. We just threw Andrew's name in the mix for fun."

Jeffrey stared in disbelief. "You mean Andrew was involved in this too?"

LaForge laughed out loud. "Andy? Uh, no. In case you haven't noticed, Andy is dead. He didn't volunteer for that job. We had to get rid of old Andy because he was starting to put the pieces together. He was starting to notice the correlation between currency fluctuations and the terror attacks. He had begun to realize that a few investors were making obscene amounts of money on what were otherwise random acts of terrorism. Or at least what everyone thought was terrorism. He was asking too many questions. It was only a matter of time before he started researching who were the biggest beneficiaries of the currency fluctuations, and realize that the same group of people were behind the investments that were realizing incredible profits every time there was an apparent random act of terrorism. Of course, we didn't coordinate every single one of the terrorist hits of the past few years, a lot of what has happened has been real. We just added to the mix, and reaped the financial gains where we could. Let me say, it has been a brilliant and very lucrative operation." LaForge's eyes were shining as he was finally getting the satisfaction of revealing his insidious plan to one of the few people who could appreciate its diabolical brilliance and accomplishment.

"Are you saying you orchestrated the entire EuroStar explosion to kill Andrew?"

"No, of course not. That was already in the works. We just made sure he was on the train. Killing two birds with one stone, so to speak." LaForge smirked again at his own cleverness.

Jeffrey's mind was scrambling to connect the dots.

"Who else is involved? Who else did you convince to help you commit mass murder? Including one of your best friends? What kind of sick maniac are you?" Jeffrey's fury was escalating as the enormity of the pure evil LaForge was revealing began to sink in.

"Oh, a few of your friends, Jeffrey.... Rasul Aziz, Charlie Turner, just to name two. Everyone plays a part. Feeling left out? I could've included you, but I knew that you would never see the beauty of the plan. You and Wellington are such goody-two-shoes. You would've never gone for it."

"Raz? So, he's the reason Andrew was on that train?"

"Now you're getting it Jeffrey boy! Rasul has been very valuable to us. He started out being a true believer... you know, thought he was working for 'the cause,' – whatever that is. But once he saw how much money we could make with so little relative effort, he joined up just for the sheer financial windfall. Of course it's a pity now. Our operations have gotten so big, so complicated, and so successful, too many people know now. The EuroStar job was enormously successful, and will probably be our last for a while, which means we need to whittle our ranks. Unfortunately, we're going to have to get rid of Rasul. He knows far too much, and there were far too many loose ends tying him to Andrew and the explosion. It's only a matter of time before his face is plastered all over the globe as the prime suspect for the Eurostar explosion. If the police don't figure out it was him themselves, then we'll just feed his name to the press as a suspect, and in a few weeks, they'll find his body. Case closed. You would be surprised how easy it is to orchestrate such things. Pity you couldn't have joined us."

"You're insane, LaForge. You'll never get away with this. If Andrew could figure it out, others will. It's only a matter of time. You, Charlie, Rasul, you'll all rot in hell for this."

"I don't think so, Jeffrey. You're right, someone will figure it out. But by then, I'll be safely ensconced in my sweet financial haven, enjoying the fruits of my labor." With that picture in his mind LaForge started laughing again.

At hearing LaForge's words, Jeffrey finally snapped. His mixture of fury, fear, and adrenaline boiled over. Everything and everyone he'd ever known, lived for, and fought for, was being mocked by this lunatic. Without giving another thought, he lunged at LaForge. Grabbing him around the waist, he knocked him to the floor, LaForge pulling him down along with him. LaForge struggled to pull his gun from his coat pocket. In the scuffle, the gun went off, but the bullet went straight for the ceiling and lodged in the rafters near the top of a stained glass window. Jeffrey grabbed at the gun with all of his might, twisting and turning it, trying to wrestle it from LaForge's hand. The two rolled on the floor, first left, and then right, in a mortal struggle to overpower the other and gain control of the gun.

The gun went off again, this time the bullet found a statue of St. Stephen, knocking it off its pedestal, and sending it crashing to the floor below. Jeffrey was finally able to knock the gun from LaForge's hand, but sent it skidding across the floor, five meters from where they were rolling on the floor near the altar.

Jeffrey jumped to his feet, and grabbed the first thing we could see, a large heavy brass chalice sitting on the table at the foot of the altar. Before LaForge could scramble to his feet, Jeffrey crashed the chalice down on this skull with all of his might. LaForge stumbled backward, blood running from beneath his hairline. As he fell, Jeffrey delivered another crashing blow, this time to the side of his head for good measure. LaForge stumbled sideways, crashing into the altar table, sending brass bowls, platters, and holy relics scattering across the floor. He landed face down, blood now running in a steady stream down his face and onto the floor of the chapel. He was unconscious and bleeding out profusely, with a steady red stream across the floor.

For a moment, Jeffrey thought about finishing him off, killing him right then and there. No one would blame him. He could make it look like it happened during the course of the struggle. He deserved to die, that Jeffrey was sure of. But as he stood there contemplating the thought, he realized he could never do it. He couldn't kill someone with his bare hands, or even with the gun. He had spent his life making laws to protect people, to pursue justice, he couldn't bring himself to ignore all of that now, even if a big part of him wanted revenge for Andrew, Annie, and all the other people LaForge had hurt and killed.

Jeffrey looked around for some way to immobilize him, to make sure he couldn't escape. His eyes landed on a stack of priest's robes and vestments neatly lying on a chair in the corner. Coiled carefully on top was a slender white rope, worn as a belt by priests, but perfect to tie up the hands of a killer.

While Jeffrey cinched LaForge's hands behind his back, he started to moan. The trickle of blood hadn't slowed down, and Jeffrey wondered if he might die after all. If that happened, then so be it. He certainly wasn't going to lift a finger to help this guy survive, that much was certain.

Jeffrey still didn't know where Annie was. Was she really dead as LaForge had insinuated? Or was she alive somewhere here in Paris? Could he get to her before she too was murdered? He realized that he'd better get rid of LaForge's body first, and then figure out what to do next. Looking around for a hiding place, he noticed a side door in the chapel, and dragged LaForge's heavy body across the stone floor of the church, and into the small musty room. Without turning on the light, he pulled LaForge to the corner, almost tripping over something in the middle of the room as he went. Depositing the killer's body in a crumpled heap in the corner, Jeffrey found a velvet tablecloth to throw over the body, mostly camouflaging it in the cluttered store room. He was just about to flick on the light to examine his handiwork when he heard the echo of the front doors of the church opening and closing.

Jeffrey realized it must be a Priest entering the building to close up the place for the night. After all, who else would be entering a dark church this late at night?

Straightening his hair and clothes as quickly as possible, and composing his face into a relaxed smile, Jeffrey sauntered out of the small room to face the unwelcome intruder. Reentering the chapel from the side room, he could see the Priest walking casually up the center aisle. Strangely, he noticed that the Priest was wearing black slacks and a white dress shirt, but wrote it off to the late hour or maybe all the changes he'd heard about in the Catholic Church these days.

After almost twenty years, Jeffrey did not recognize his old college buddy Jorge Morales.

"Good Evening Father," Jeffrey said as he stepped into the light. "I hope I'm not intruding. I just stopped in here to pray for a few minutes."

CHAPTER FORTY-FOUR

This new little plot twist was going to dovetail perfectly with the original plan, Charlie thought smugly to himself. Still sitting at his desk, and looking out over Battery Park, Charlie was pleased with his little brainstorm. This new twist would tie up all the loose ends so nicely. Jorge had been a problem now for months. His drug habit made him an unacceptable risk, and he could no longer be trusted. Of course, it made Charlie feel a certain amount of guilt, knowing he was sending Jorge to his death. The guy had been his life-long friend, after all. But it couldn't be helped. Jorge had chosen this path for himself when he refused to kick his drug habit. He had to go, or else risk the entire money-generating strategy that had been so hugely successful for so many years. And without Jorge in the picture, it would have the added advantage of increasing his share of the pie, Charlie was pleased to realize.

In fact, with Jorge taking out Rasul, and then LaForge taking advantage of the opportunity to get rid of both Jeffrey Hunter and Jorge on the same evening in one fell swoop, it would be such a fortuitous turn of events. Charlie's share in the profits had just increased from 25% to 50%, after they paid off the operatives, Akeem and the others, of course. He and LaForge would double their profits, and eliminate the two biggest risks to their scheme at the same time. It was the perfect way to tie up all the loose ends. After these last little tasks were complete, he and LaForge could lay low for a while and figure out how he was going to spend it all. It was the perfect end to a most advantageous conspiracy.

Charlie looked down again as his personal phone buzzed again with Jorge's text, alerting him that he had landed in Paris.

"Goodbye old Pal," Charlie said out loud to himself, "and thanks for your help."

* * *

Jorge stepped into the church, not sure what to expect. The contact person Charlie had promised him must be somewhere around here, someone who could fill him in on the specifics of the plan. Someone was going to have to enlighten him in on details soon, because he sure as hell didn't know where Rasul was, or how to go about finding him. What's more, he was also going to need access to a weapon of some type. Hell, what if they wanted him to figure out all by himself how to kill Rasul? What would he use – a gun? Strangle him? He refused to even consider a knife... far too violent and repulsive for his tastes. With any luck, maybe somebody else will have already taken care of the ghastly deed before he even got here. He could only hope. Jorge was being forced to think about the logistics of this nasty assignment and he didn't like it one bit. He didn't sign up to be a damn assassin.

Jorge wandered into the chapel and looked around. It was dim and quiet in the room, no sign of anyone around. The only light was the illumination of a couple of candles flickering on a side table. Light from the full moon outside flooded through the chapel windows, illuminating the colorful stained-glass windows. Jorge looked around and was struck by the beauty of the chapel. It reminded him of Vespers back at Jesuit High School in Dallas, and for a moment, he was transported back to that simpler and happier time.

"Good Evening, Father ...," Jeffrey addressed Jorge as he reentered the chapel.

Jorge snapped to attention, catching sight of the man who had entered the chapel from a side door.

"I hope I'm not intruding. I just stopped in here to pray for a few minutes." Jeffrey was doing his dead level best not to arouse suspicion.

Jorge stopped dead in his tracks, momentarily confused. Who was this character? He seemed familiar.

The man approached, and Jorge was struggling to recognize the face, but he couldn't place him. He decided for the moment that he was just some guy off the street who had inadvertently wandered into a very dangerous situation.

"Oh, that's no problem, sir. We keep the doors open late just for that purpose," Jorge said with a pastoral smile. He might be a drug-addicted loose cannon, but his years of moving illicit money around the globe had made him an excellent improvisational liar.

The two men shook hands.

"Could I help you with something? Perhaps pray for some need you have?" Jorge was starting to enjoy his little charade.

"Oh no, Father. I was actually on my way out." Jeffrey started to leave, but then noticed the brass relics, still scattered across the front of the church. "I'm sorry but I tripped and knocked over a table near the altar. I was just in that side room looking for more candles since I broke one accidentally."

"That is no problem. I'm glad you came by. Please, go in peace." It suddenly occurred to Jorge that this might be the guy he was supposed to meet, the guy with the details of the plan. Or maybe the guy would be his gun connection. Either way, Jorge needed help. Maybe the guy wasn't recognizing Jorge as his connection either. Perhaps there was a bit of double-confusion going on.

But why was this guy so familiar? Maybe they'd met in some former operation, and that's why he was struggling to recognize him, Jorge thought to himself. So far, this little plan wasn't working out so well, with all the confusion and lack of communication. He was livid again for the lack of organization for this ill-conceived change of plans. Haphazard plans were going to get them all killed, he thought to himself. If this was indeed his contact, Jorge resolved to find a way out. He didn't feel comfortable with the way everything was going down. He decided to go out on a limb.

"You seem so familiar, have we met?"

"I don't think so, Father." Jeffrey was mystified by the question.

Jorge wasn't ready to write it off to coincidence. This guy must be his contact.

"It's just that I was supposed to meet someone here."

For the first time, it occurred to Jeffrey how odd it was that the priest was an American.

Then, as he studied the man in front of him, the recognition hit him like a ton of bricks. He was just about to exclaim the name "Jorge!" but the big picture came crashing down on him just before he opened his mouth. Jorge was involved too! He was part of the conspiracy! This wasn't some random priest; this was Charlie Turner's sidekick! Of course he was involved.

His brain was spinning fast now, connecting the dots. Jorge must be here to meet LaForge, the man he just stuffed under a velvet cover in the side room, the man who might very well already be dead. If Jorge was involved, who else from his past life was involved?

And then he remembered Annie. She was the reason he was here. Where was she in all of this? Dead? Hiding? He had to find out where she was.

"Actually, I think I am the man you are here to meet." Jeffrey was thinking fast now, adlibbing and making it up as he went along. Jorge obviously was not recognizing him at all.

"Oh, really! No wonder you looked so familiar." Jorge was relieved this first little hurdle was over. He just wanted to get the whole nasty business over with and get back on a plane.

"Yes, I was sent to meet you." Jeffrey stalled, waiting for any hint at what exactly he was supposed to be doing at this meeting.

"Good, I'm ready to get this little task over with. What is the plan? Where is Rasul? Have you pinpointed his location? And do you have something for me? A gun, what?" Jorge stared at Jeffrey expectantly, revealing his naiveté and inexperience all in one question.

Jeffrey's brain was in high gear, devising a plan on the fly.

"I actually have him here. In fact, I've already had to deal with him. I'm not sure if he's dead or alive, but he's tied up in that little side storeroom. That's why I was in there."

"Great!" Jorge was relieved at the prospect of getting out of his assignment. "If Rasul is already dead, I'll help you get rid of him, and I'll be back on the next plane to New York."

"Come with me. I'll show you where I stuffed his body." Jeffrey turned toward the sideroom and Jorge followed. Jeffrey was desperately trying to figure out what to do next. As they walked toward the little chapel's side room, he decided his best chance was to lock Jorge in the little room with LaForge, and then figure out what to do next. After that, his best bet would probably be to call the French police. He couldn't keep devising plans on the fly. He needed real help, this situation had gotten way out of control. At this point, there was no way he could find Annie alone, and with their help, and LaForge and Jorge in custody, he might have a chance at finding her.

"He's in here," Jeffrey motioned into the sideroom. Jorge charged in.

And in that moment, the storeroom overhead light flicked on, and there in the glaring light stood Rasul Aziz. They stopped dead in their tracks, as shocked to see him alive, as he was surprised to see them there in the little chapel.

CHAPTER FORTY-FIVE

Jorge blinked in the bright light at Rasul, who had appeared out of nowhere it seemed. He then glanced down at the figure concealed under the velvet cover. Jeffrey stood frozen, immobilized by fear and confusion. Where in the hell did Rasul come from?

Rasul stared at both of them, trying to make sense of why they were here in this dark church, where he'd been taken at gunpoint, ostensibly to be killed.

Rasul, recognizing his co-conspirator, was the first to speak.

"Jorge! What are you doing here?" His face was a mashup of confusion, shock, and panic from the ordeal he'd just survived in the tunnel below.

He then realized that the second man to enter the room was Jeffrey Hunter. For a moment, the three old college friends just stared at each other, trying to make sense of the situation. Rasul defaulted to the only plausible defense he could think of at the moment, playing dumb. But tucked carefully into the back of his pants was the AK-47 he had just wrestled from Akeem, when he ambushed him from behind down in the tunnel.

Akeem had made the rookie and fatal mistake of turning his back on a man he thought was dead down in the tunnel. He'd heard two shots ring out, and in the pitch blackness when he heard Rasul hit the ground, he assumed he had killed him. But Rasul was far smarter and more experienced than Akeem. He took advantage of the darkness to feign his own death, and then ambushed Akeem after luring him back into the tunnel with the metal on metal *clanks.* For Rasul, it was a simple ploy that had worked out beautifully. But unfortunately for Akeem, he had now paid for his mistake with his life. Of course, Rasul had left Annie down there to rot with the rats. He had intended to get rid of her anyway; Akeem had just done the dirty work for him.

"Jeffrey? And what are you doing here too? What the hell is going on here?" Rasul asked, now looking incredulously at Jeffrey as well.

As Rasul called out Jeffrey's name, Jorge spun around and looked at Jeffrey in surprise, for the first time realizing that the man he had been unsuspectingly conversing with was none other than his old college pal Jeffrey Hunter, Assistant to the Prime Minister of Britain.

The three men, who had once been college buddies in Oxford, stood frozen, unsure what to do next. No one was entirely sure who was on which side, and who could be trusted. In the moment, no longer willing to trust anyone, Rasul played his trump card, the only one that mattered at this point.

Pulling the AK-47 from where he'd stowed it in his waistband behind his back, he swung it around and leveled it at both of his former friends.

"So, Jorge, I see how it is now. You and Jeffrey here have come for me too."

Jeffrey quickly gauged that the two accomplices were obviously not on good terms. He decided that his only hope of survival at this point was to lay all of his cards on the table.

"No, Raz, I don't want to be involved in any of this. I'm only here to find Annaliese Craig. I thought she would be here tonight. I have no idea what the two of you have been involved in, and I don't care. I don't know anything about anything else. If either of you know where she is, just tell me and I'll disappear. You two can figure the rest of this out without me. Please, I swear to you, I will forget everything I've seen here tonight. I will never tell a soul about any of this. I just want to find Annie and get out of here."

At that, Raz couldn't help but laugh. The thought of Jeffrey Hunter doing anything at all except exactly what he should do in every situation was humorous.

"Right, Jeffrey. You want me to trust you to keep quiet about the biggest terrorist hit on Britain in history. That sounds exactly like something you would do. There is no way you could ever keep your mouth shut. I can't trust you or that bitch down below either. I've already killed one of my friends this week, I guess I can kill a couple more."

Jeffrey's blood ran cold. He now understood it all. The terrorist attack, his former friends' involvement, the cold-blooded murder of his good friend Andrew, and now the realization that it was all just a part of a much broader conspiracy; A devious plan to kill hundreds of innocent people just to put millions of dollars into the coffers of a handful of evil men. And now, he realized he was on the verge of being the latest victim of the conspiracy to murder for money as well. Terror and panic began to take hold as he realized Rasul had every intention of killing him right here and now.

"Your friend Annie is sitting down in the tunnel right now alone, in the pitch black. She's not alone though. There's our friend Akeem with her, but I'm afraid he probably can't be of much help right now, as he is most assuredly dead. And then of course there are a few thousand hungry rats. They'll find her soon enough. I'm thinking the best way to deal with both of you is to give her a little company down there. So let's move."

With that, Rasul pulled open the heavy metal door on the floor, and for the first time Jorge and Jeffrey realized what he meant. They too were familiar with the tunnels under Paris, as everyone was. But like most Parisians, they thought that random entry points like this had been sealed up and lost track of decades ago. Rasul waved the barrel of the gun, motioning for them to proceed in front of him.

"If you try anything at the bottom of this ladder, the next flash of light you see will be coming from the end of this AK-47. The nice thing about this gun is, you don't have to aim very well to get the job done."

Jorge entered the shaft first, with Jeffrey right behind him, moving rung by rung down the old metal ladder. Jeffrey had already decided that he wasn't going to make this easy for Rasul. He intended to cut and run as soon as they hit the bottom. Rasul would fire on them, but at least they would have a small chance of surviving. At least one of them was bound to be hit, but even if their chances were just 50/50, it was better than facing certain death at the end of the AK-47, or being left as dinner for the legion of rats swarming the tunnels.

As soon as Jeffrey heard Jorge's feet hit the solid floor of the tunnel, he could hear him shuffling in the dirt. Was he running? It didn't sound like it. Jeffrey had already decided that he wasn't going to stand around waiting to see what happened, as soon as he landed, he would move silently away in the dark, hoping he could clear some distance undetected and get his bearings which way he could run, and then he would make a hard break for escape.

As soon as Jeffrey's feet hit dirt, he quietly stepped backward, preparing to make his run in the dark. He was peering into the blackness in every direction, trying to let his eyes gather any available light and get oriented. He watched as Rasul's lower body dropped the last few feet, gun already in position, ready to fire at them both.

Jeffrey stepped quietly back another few steps, three, four, five, six, and in an instant, he pivoted and sprinted wildly into the pitch black of the tunnel. He had no way of knowing where he was running, or even if he was about to slam into a wall. He was just running with all the adrenaline and power he had left in him, running to save his own life.

He ran so fast and furiously, it was at least thirty seconds before it dawned on him that no one was firing at him. In fact, no one even seemed to be chasing him. There was no sound of the AK-47's ricochet of bullets, no flash of light, no yelling, in fact, no sound whatsoever. There was just silence, and the sound of water trickling down the tunnel.

Once he scraped along the wall of the tunnel and realized he'd rounded a bend, Jeffrey stopped running dead in his tracks. He stood stock still, waiting on a noise, any noise. Where was the gun? Where was Rasul? Why wasn't he being pursued?

Peering back around the curve of the tunnel's wall, Jeffrey could make out two figures positioned below the circle of light radiating from the shaft that led up to the church. One figure lay crumpled on the floor of the tunnel, and one stood over him. Staring at the scene, Jeffrey realized that the figure lying prostrate on the floor was Rasul, and the larger man standing over him was Jorge. Trusting his gut, Jeffrey slowly made his way back to the shaft, back to where Jorge stood over Rasul, but ready to cut and run again at any moment.

Approaching the scene, Jeffrey called out to his former friend.

"Jorge? Is he dead? What the hell happened?"

For a moment, Jeffrey thought he was seeing things. Jorge just looked up at him, with a huge grin on his face. He looked like a kid, happy with something he'd just done. Jeffrey moved closer still, until he was standing in the same circle of light with Rasul, still lying motionless on the muddy floor, with blood oozing from a large cut just above his left eye. Jorge, still smiling ear to ear, was standing over him.

"He's out cold. I think his face may be broken too" Jorge said through his grin.

"What? How? What happened to the gun?!"

And then Jeffrey saw it, a solid brass sphere lying next to Rasul's head.

"Yeah, he didn't see it coming. I figured the two of us didn't stand much of a chance against that AK-47, but if you can't see a brass ball coming at you at 94 mph, I figured we might have a chance."

Jeffrey blinked in the half light. So that was it. Jorge took him out with a brass fast ball. Picking up the brass sphere, he recognized it as one of the items that had been lying on the altar in the little chapel above. It looked like it was used for burning incense or something. Jorge must have scooped it up at some point in the chaos upstairs. Jeffrey remembered the stories he'd heard back at Oxford of Jorge's glory days, but he'd never considered the fact that a ball hurtling at 94 mph could literally be a lethal weapon. It turned out Jorge was pretty resourceful after all.

Standing there in disbelief, trying to make sense of what had just happened, he heard Annie yell from several hundred meters down the tunnel in the opposite direction. Without pausing to consider Jorge's involvement, or what might happen next, Jeffrey shot off down the tunnel to find Annie.

CHAPTER FORTY-SIX

Jeffrey folded the newspaper and dropped it on his desktop in his office at #10 Downing, letting the large, bold headline lay face up in the middle of his desk. He stared at the words, and perhaps for the first time in the last dizzying week, took in the immense big picture of what he had helped uncover:

GLOBAL TERROR AND CURRENCY MANIPULATION SCHEME TRACED TO OXFORD CONSPIRACY RING

There, splattered across the top of the page, above the lead story and associated supporting reports, was a horizontal lineup of large, full-color pictures of Jeffrey, and most of his closest college friends: Andrew Bolling, Rasul Aziz, Fletcher LaForge, Charlie Turner, and Jorge Morales. Thankfully, they had not printed a picture of the Prime Minister along with the conspirators. It was bad enough the P.M. was already linked with them by former association, the last thing they needed was pictures to cement his link to the deadly criminal conspiracy.

The newspaper had gotten all the details largely right. The conspiracy was born out of a group of brilliant, yet overly privileged, greedy and ruthless college friends. Led by their former professor, Fletcher LaForge, the group had started out as rookie day traders, earning pocket money to fund their college partying. Turner, Morales, Aziz, and LaForge had initially learned the ropes of making money off of minor blips in the routine currency valuations of the British Pound, the Euro, and even the American Dollar. Over the years, they had done their research and figured out how the largest currency fluctuations were always one of the first and fastest after-shocks of a terrorist attack. Investors who just happened to have their money situated in exactly the right position would recognize enormous profits from these seemingly random acts of terror. They realized that if say, your money was parked in an asset denominated in Euros, and then there was an explosion at a European soccer match, the Euro would nosedive, and then recover a few days or weeks later. There were enormous profits to be made in the fluctuation.

But then they took their investment scheme to the next unimaginably depraved level. The nefarious group realized they could reap huge profits by taking the "random" out of the equation. They began orchestrating these profit opportunities by masterminding and instigating these supposed "random acts of terror." Once they realized how fundamentally simple and uncomplicated their schemes could be, and how relatively easy it was to get away with it, all hell had broken loose. Over the years, untold hundreds of innocent people had lost their lives, all in service to their greedy, wicked and coldblooded profit-generating strategy. They attributed the success of their ruthless plan to their self-supposed brilliance and resourcefulness, and arrogantly began referring to it as The Cornmarket Conspiracy, after the street where their scheme was first launched back in Oxford.

LaForge had always been the ringleader and ultimate insider of the group. He masterminded the hits, and as Assistant National Security Advisor, he knew where and when it would be easiest to strike. He was intimately familiar with the security operations of Britain and where their vulnerabilities could most easily be breached. His access to the vast security operations of the country left ample targets open and unguarded, securing the success of their malicious strategies.

Charlie Turner was the money guy, handling the strategic investments and profits through an intricate network of off-shore accounts and foreign trading companies. Cornmarket Holdings, named after their beloved street in Oxford where they had all been roommates at one time or another, handled most of the trades from its off-shore location in Georgetown, Grand Cayman, and then their individual profits would be distributed to their personal accounts hidden in tax havens all over the globe.

Turner's position on Wall Street gave him the perfect cover and afforded him access to information that made trading in the clandestine network of off-shore accounts easy and accessible. He handled all the money, and utilized his buddy Jorge Morales for most of the legwork and small tasks. Jorge wasn't the smartest of the group, or at least that's what Charlie had thought, but he could be counted on to do as he was told. Or at least that's what Charlie and the group believed. It had turned out to be their biggest miscalculation.

Rasul had started out as the ideal guy for the front lines and the heavy-duty dirty work. Although he was never a true believer in the radicalism that drove most global terror rings, his access to the extremist networks that operated on the fringes of his Muslim neighborhood made him a perfect go-to guy to arrange the actual attacks. He was usually able to recruit volunteers for the actual attacks, promising money, and in some cases Paradise for them, along with a nice lump sum payment for their families. That's where he had found and recruited Akeem, and a dozen more like him. But Rasul had never acted out of radicalism, or some misplaced ideology. Like LaForge, Charlie, and Jorge, he was strictly in it for the money. It had always been all about the money and the access it could buy. His plan had always been to spend a few years and amass a tidy fortune from their little conspiracy ring, and then to buy an elegant estate somewhere in the English countryside, where he would establish a family and buy his way into respectability. That was the endgame: Money, respectability, access – everything he had been eyeing since his days at Oxford.

And in the end, as the newspaper reports explained, money is what brought their downfall. Like most malicious conspirators, they eventually turned on each other. A group who operates on the core operating strategy that they will betray others for money, will eventually betray each other for the same greedy mentality.

Fletcher LaForge was sitting in a three by four-meter cell in central London, awaiting indictment in front of the English Court. He would likely face a life sentence under the British 2006 Terrorism Act. Charlie Turner was being held in Federal Prison in New York. He had been arrested for conspiracy to commit murder, money laundering, and a host of other capital crimes. Unfortunately for him, the United States has capital punishment, which means he would almost certainly face a death gurney in twenty years, after his court-appointed attorney ran out of Hail Marys on his behalf.

Rasul Aziz was being held in a French prison awaiting extradition to the United Kingdom. As the main perpetrator of the Chunnel Train Bombing, he would receive the maximum sentence allowed in the United Kingdom and in France for murder: life imprisonment, with no chance of parole. In the meantime, the stitches across his eye socket would provide a daily and permanent reminder of the brass incense Thurible that came hurtling through the dark at his head at 94 mph. Jorge had been right; Rasul never did see it coming.

Annie had already turned in her resignation. Jeffrey had tried to refuse it, but they both knew that it was what was best for both her and for the administration. No matter how innocent she was in the scandal, no matter how much she had suffered, and no matter how valuable she had been to Jeffrey, the scandal was too great to be linked to the administration. Her role, no matter how unintentional, was still too large to be ignored. Besides that, she realized that if she were to save what was left of her life, she would have to leave and make a fresh start on her marriage. She wanted to move on, and who could blame her.

She and Richard had already taken a cottage in the Cotswolds, far from London and the wreck she had made of her life. She was looking forward to getting away from the city, and the memories and mistakes she had made there. Even after the entire sordid mess had come out during the investigation and was printed in the papers, Richard had loved her, and stuck by her. She was ready to move on, and a new life, and a new baby were perhaps the best way to get started on that.

As for Jorge, he ended up better off than most of his co-conspirators in the whole ordeal. After Jeffrey had found Annie deep in the tunnel that night, and helped free her from the chain, they had returned to the bottom of the tunnel entry shaft to find Jorge long gone. He had escaped up through the ladder shaft, but had left the trap door at the top wide open for him and Annie to escape. It was a sign that let Jeffrey know that Jorge would no longer be a threat to him or anyone else.

Jorge was apprehended soon after, trying to board a plane back to New York that very same night. Leveraging his extensive knowledge of the entire plan along with details about the financial machinations that had fed the greedy motives of the group, Jorge fared better than most. Given his willingness to talk and reveal everything he knew, his lawyers had hammered out a deal to trade his testimony against all of his former accomplices in the conspiracy, for a sentence of life imprisonment. He would be required to serve at least thirty years before there would be any possibility of parole for his part in the scheme.

Jorge would be going away to federal prison for at least three decades, but word was that he was finally happy. As a part of his deal, at his insistence, he had secured an agreement that his incarceration would include ample time working with Juvenile offenders, teaching them baseball skills and managing their prison team. Baseball had given him a shot at life, and he had thrown it away. But maybe he could help others, boys who were like him twenty years ago. He had finally found his life's work, even if it meant fulfilling it behind bars for most of the rest of his life.

* * *

Jeffrey got up from his desk, and checked himself in the mirror that was affixed to the back of the door of his coat closet. It had been five weeks since that night in the Parisian tunnels, and Jeffrey was finally putting his life back in order as well. Now that John O'Leary and MI6 announced this morning that they had completed their work and were closing the investigation, there was one more press conference to be conducted to answer final questions surrounding the case. Jeffrey hated the thought of facing the news cameras again about this personally painful and still raw chapter in his life, but his job required it. What's more, he owed it to Andrew to help clear his name and see justice through to the end.

Wellington would exit his office any moment, ready to face the cameras, and Jeffrey had to be ready to stand with him. No doubt the majority of the questions would be directed at him, given his direct involvement with the arrests in Paris. Jeffrey had steeled himself for the reporter's interrogations to come. He knew some would try and use his connections to the killers against the administration, but he knew that in the end, his only crime had been in trusting the wrong people. And that fact, he would regret for the rest of his life.

As for his job at #10 Downing Street, Jeffrey wasn't sure how much longer he could do this. He and Wellington had accomplished so much, and he was proud of their work. They had helped usher Britain into unprecedented reforms in growing the British economy, guaranteeing the rights and security of British citizens, and helping secure Britain's future in an increasingly dangerous and challenging world. But Wellington had no intention of stepping down now, and he would need Jeffrey there to help guide the administration and its goals into the future.

With one final glance in his mirror, Jeffrey confirmed that his red and blue tie was straight, and his hair was neatly in place. Opening his office door, he met the Prime Minister in the reception area, and together they walked to the front door of #10 Downing.

As the front door opened, the video cameras began to record, cameras flashed, and the two hundred or so members of the global media spun around to face them. The Klieg lights snapped on, and cameras began to click off pictures of their every move. The journalists, reporters, and their crews grew silent and every eye was on Trevor Wellington, Prime Minister of Great Britain. Over his shoulder, Jeffrey Hunter stood ready to face the media.

While Wellington eloquently addressed the crowd, Jeffrey Hunter stood stone faced, ostensibly listening to the press conference. He was standing at Wellington's side, just as he had been since their days in the hallowed halls at Eton. But Hunter's mind was somewhere else.

The world was changing, but so was Jeffrey Hunter. His country would go on, moving determinedly into the future. Politicians would come and go, battles would be won and lost, and evil men would continue to attempt to steal, damage, and destroy. But there were good people who would continue to fight – for the good of themselves, their families, and their country.

Jeffrey wasn't ready to give in. There was still too much to do. This particular threat had been eliminated, but there were others lining up behind them, hell bent on destroying the lives of good people – people who just wanted to work hard and enjoy their families and their lives. Someone had to stand ready, to lead, to protect.

As the red lights on the bank of cameras in front of him burned bright, he could see the earnest look on the faces of the gathered media as they hung on the P.M.'s every word. They were there not simply to record his words, but to offer hope to the people who were desperately looking for leadership. Jeffrey stood unflinching, as the eyes of the world were upon him and the P.M., but his thoughts were firmly fixed elsewhere. In his mind, he was twenty-two years old again, and lying on the breathtaking exquisite grass lawn in All Souls Quadrangle, looking up between the beautiful gothic buildings at the bright blue Oxford sky.

CPSIA information can be obtained
at www.ICGtesting.com
Printed in the USA
JSHW020350250521
15157JS00003B/12

9 781952 439087